Other works by the author:

Oldcat & Ms. Puss: A Book of Days for You and Me (novel)
Some Heroes, Some Heroines, Some Others (stories)
The World's Thinnest Fat Man (stories)
A Masque for the Fields of Time (stories)

Belles' Letters: Writing by Alabama Women (co-editor with Tina Jones)
Tartts 1 through *Tartts 5* (editor)

Let There Be Lite,

O_{r,}

How I Came To Know and Love

Gödel's Incompleteness Proof

Joe Taylor

Livingston Press
The University of West Alabama

Dedicated to Tricia, of course.

Hardcover binding by: Heckman Bindery
Typesetting and page layout: Emily Edwards
Proofreading and suggestions: Joe Taylor, Christin Loehr,
Tricia Taylor, Angela Brown, Stephen Slimp, Amanda Nolin
Cover design: Emily Burkett, Amanda Nolin
Author photo: Tricia Taylor
This is a work of fiction. Any resemblance
to persons living or dead is coincidental.
Livingston Press is part of The University of West Alabama,
and thereby has non-profit status.
Donations are tax-deductible.

Let There Be Lite,

O_{r,}

How I Came To Know and Love

Gödel's Incompleteness Proof

"The mess, we must pass over in silence."
Wittgenstein, *Tractatus* (sort of)

Faux Graphic Panels One through Seven: Ending happily though frightfully

Lay Auto. In its created glory and pidgin French, a perfect – !!! – alternative-fuel vehicle with fuchsia fenders, jet-black body, and silver-starred boot. Far sleeker than its faux-competitor the gas-guzzling Corvette, which amazingly still oozes off assembly lines from aging and decrepit Detroit, it glides the streets of Lexington, KY. Even in this prototype phase, Lay Auto has caught the attention of desirous consumers – and un-desirous terrorists. Why? Glance under its jet-black bonnet: a two-cylinder and earth-friendly engine, capable of running on beets, scrabble-level tobacco, discarded textbooks or newspapers – even spent chewing gum. That's why. But forget buzzing terrorists. Concentrate on the four owners who masterminded Lay Auto:

First, Willy Turner, rejected as a high school dropout by every university in America except Kentucky, which graduated the hometown boy out of pity. Willy finally received his masters in Auto Engineering from FAST U, an online school variously located in Miami, Los Angeles, and Dallas. Willy's long beard – I'd love to draw it for you, but I've been prohibited from including illustrations by my California Agent, a conservative fig if ever there was one. How can I write a graphic novel without graphics, I ask during endless electronic meetings. A fiber optic pause occurs, and I always imagine him bending, studying a speck intruding between tanned California toes and unisex California sandals. Iowa potato dust? Hawaiian volcanic ash? His silence serves as an answer, so perhaps I'm writing the first graphic novel *without* graphics? But let's return to Willy, numero uno of the Pit Crew conglomerate who masterminded Lay Auto: It took Willy seven years to earn his masters in Auto Engineering, twenty-one to grow his beard. That's all I dare reveal about his age, for poor Willy's terrorifically reserved about accumulating years, which he envisions lumping his body like wayward dandelion seeds.

The second owner is Dave Branden. Dave holds two Ph.D.s, one in chemical engineering from Florida State, one in computer science from MIT, plus a B. A. in theology from Duke, that last courtesy of the G. I. Bill. How I wish I could insert just one simple art-splash panel, for after mapping the intricate contours of Dave's brain said panel would reveal his blue-blue eyes. Technicolor blue. Sapphire blue. Paul Newman, Harrison Ford, Django Reinhardt blue. Oceanic blue, baby blue. Deep-in-a-cave blindfish blue. Blue Curaçao blue. Sky-tumbling blue. Were Django Reinhardt's eyes blue? Doubtful. He was a guitar-playing gypsy who managed to elude Nazis while strumming under their Aryan noses. Terra incognita brown would be my guess. Blue crab blue. Lovesick Blue. Blue Monday blue. By midday's happy light blue.

The third owner — lest you fear this will be an blowhard boy book, and since my California Agent, hereinafter referred to as **C𝒜**, once during an early cyberspace conference lifted from his silent pedicure to electronically warn me that a balance of male and female must prevail in the illustrationless panels. ("Call Jane Austen for help," he insisted on-screen. / "Jane Austen?" / "You know what I mean.") I didn't know, but I now do. And I can truthfully assure you: this third owner is most fully female. Her name? Mary Lou Nelson.

Moreover, the fourth owner is also a female: Brenda Angela Browning. For a tee-tiny period she was known as *Babs*, but is mostly known as *Bad* because of her fiery red hair and temper. Bad, by the way, claims no relation to either the poet Browning or the weapons manufacturer. After introducing these third and fourth owners, I, testosterone slave as I was created, long to fill their illustrationless panels with boobs, scents, curves, roseate folds, and silken skin, for memory informs me that in high school I drew lovely and intricate porno cartoons in a musty locker room . . . well, let that go. As mentioned, **C𝒜** the CA fig has nixed illustrations.

So, the two female owners: One pair of hazel eyes (ever-shifting mysteries), one pair of blue eyes (see male's eyeball description above, but add a flash of heat lightning); one worried and compassionate brow, one angry brow; an abundance of red hair, an abundance of brunette. Bad banged drums in a hard rock band but quit to nearly obtain a Ph.D. in math from the University of Florida, a degree she's still working on, when not obsessed with Lay Auto. Mary Lou finished a Divinity degree at Duke, which is how she met Dave. Despite her being an heiress with a goodly amount of money, no American church will accept her, because she's too nice (that also in spite of being an heiress with a goodly amount of money). Wait! Too nice for a church? Yes, have you looked at the Southern Baptist Conference? Mary Lou doesn't hate kikes, mackerel-snappers, or queers. She doesn't condemn divorced or unwed mothers. She doesn't want to hunt down Moslems and slowly extract their infidel fingernails until they screech for saving Baptismal waters. . . .

BAM!!!

Here resides as good a place as any to insert an illustrationless panel:

Lay Auto, filled with these four owners and running on two buckets of discarded KFC chicken skin and bones, has just slammed into a pop-up STOP sign that one earlier-mentioned terrorist group has inserted — without illustrations — in the middle of a Lexington, KY side street. Not to worry, children: Lay Auto's spring-loaded, computer-controlled fuchsia bumpers easily handle this assault.

Lay Auto, how we love thee! Hallelujah!

"Friggin' Arab terrorists!" Bad yells, pulling Mace from her orange canvas bag while powering down Lay's window. Bad has always sat in the front seat ever since high school when a male maggot tried to navigate her privates in a back seat, using eight fingers, two thumbs, and a single bouncing lolly. She slugged him thrice and suggested he get out and navigate the stars instead.

"Don't rush to judgment," Mary Lou fervently offers, leaning from behind.

But Bad's already taken aim.

SPPPPFFFF! SPPPPFFFF!

Her long-range Mace, demonstrating some miraculous law of science — Browning motion? — eases back into Lay Auto, though the bulk of its effusion temporarily blinds two dark terrorists who were approaching Lay with evil terroristical intent and evil weapons of mini-destruction.

"No, I think they're Caucasian," Dave corrects even as Willy urges Lay Auto to escape-velocity by instructing the voice-activated computer, "Go fast!" Within twelve seconds, being earth-friendly and planned for a non-terrific world, Lay Auto is pushing 28 m.p.h.

Dave is correct about the skin color, for all four Pit Crew owners glance back to see two of the WASPishest-looking men ever to trod Mother Earth, complete with power-red ties and navy-blue polyester suits. The two are standing in the middle of Lexington's Elm Street pitifully wiping their pitiless eyes from Bad's Mace. So power-red are their ties that these two could be mistaken for a team of GOP lawyers in a desist action against distributing aid to homeless mothers and infants.

"Please watch where you're driving, Willy," Dave observes from the back seat with out-of-character, nervous insistence. "There's a dog ahead."

This warning comes too late, for Lay Auto hits the dog, which performs a flip to land on the hood. Seeing the dog's open eyes, Willy gasps. Has the infrared accident avoidance system broken down? Did the pop-up stop sign malign it? He slams Lay Auto's brakes, which work immediately — no contradiction in fast braking and earth friendliness. The car stops, even as Willy's foot presses harder in a so-human attempt to reverse both time and a deed ill-done. Far, far behind, the two WASPs have disappeared, perhaps lifted by a black helicopter, perhaps teleported by a spontaneous combustion beam. Near, near ahead, the dog lies atop the jet-black bonnet, a fluorescent tennis ball in its mouth, its eyes seemingly staring toward fast-approaching Canine Land, better known as Doggie Heaven.

"Blessed Mother!" Mary Lou cries, extending her arms like an anguished Biblical prophet. Ah well gee you see, this is another reason churches won't touch Mary Lou, for she insists a bit heavily upon the oppressed feminine side of X-ianity. O! I so wish I might sneak in one bitsy-itsy drawing or some funky Japanese animé art to offer verisimilitude to Mary Lou's big, tearing, empathically hazel eyes as they watch the doggie begin thumping its tail in a death throe atop Lay Auto's black bonnet. But no. Direct orders, copyright infringement, downright ill taste, you name it, C𝒜's on top of it, damn his avocado-grove hide.

While Willy ponders the misfired accident-avoidance system, the dog bangs its tail ever more emphatically. THUMP! THUMP! The brown tail beats against Lay Auto's earth-friendly jet-black bonnet. By the bye, Willy, nominal leader of the Pit Crew, read loads of James Bond novels in his youth, hence the Brit appellations that arise concerning Lay Auto's more private parts. Character enhancement, verisimilitude — I must insert both in this graphic novel without graphics whene'er I can. To further enhance Willy's character, picture his brows still crinkling over the accident-avoidance system until he remembers that he'd manually overridden it upon entering Lexington three days before, as a test to his childhood memories. (What he doesn't know is that Bad and Dave flipped it back on, for Willy is one daydreaming, dumble-down driver. So why didn't the system save the doggy? Why? Ah well gee. Because I, Lay Auto, in emerging sentient wisdom, foresaw fate's fine fingers writhing, wriggling, weaving, warping, waiting, wafting, waving and walloping, in the form of this tennis-ball-bearing mutt. That's why.)

THUMP! THUMP! Again, with the dog's brown tail on the bonnet. There, don't capital letters work as handsomely as graphic panels? And brand name references, wouldn't they serve a similar purpose? A fluorescent green *Wilson* tennis ball. A fluorescent green WILSON tennis ball? O, woe, I self-delude. What could ever top a whiz-bang graphic?

Mary Lou gets out of the car. She reaches for the dog, but Dave grabs her arm in male amplitude, warning that one should let not only sleeping but also dying dogs lie.

"Funny, though," Willy comments, for he too now stands on Elm Street. "I don't smell any blood." Willy's nose is infamous. It's one thing that Bad respects about him. She can almost, at times, overlook his maleness because of his infamous, sniffing nose. A nose is a nose is a nose, and by any other name, would be a Romeo, Bad sometimes chides herself, when her anti-male hormones aren't pumping angry crimson blood through her arteries with systolic/diastolic frenzy.

Indeed, Willy's nose discerns correctly: there is no blood. The dog, a miracle in its own right, had jumped onto the bonnet of the 28 m.p.h. moving Lay Auto before being hitten. (Language note: to counter TV, Ebonics, and the general rut-rot of contemporary American lingo, I will on occasion revert to a pidgin Middle or otherwise archaic English to arouse curiosity. So, run, Jimmy, run. Run, Teresa, run. Buy an Oxford English Dictionary to accompany this graphic novel without graphics. And no, Oxford University Press offered no kickback for this plug. Don't be cynical!)

The dog, I say, over a horizontal distance of six and one half feet, and a vertical distance of three feet four inches, had jumped onto Lay Auto's black bonnet at a propulsion rate of 27.9 m.p.h. Readers fond of word problems might pause and triangulate how long it took said dog to land atop the bonnet, considering Lay Auto's speed of 28 m.p.h. Workspace follows:

In shorter time than one might untangle a word problem, Mary Lou has ungripped her arm from Dave's male amplitude and has reached to pet this brown dog with its thump-thumping tail. The dog nudges her with the fluorescent green tennis ball (WILSON!) and snorts to jump spryly onto four paws.

"Arf! Arf!" Or, giving another nod to verisimilitude, "Marf! Marf!" since the fluorescent green tennis ball remains gripped in pearly canine teeth.

"Aw, doggie. Are you hurt? Do you like us? Is that why you jumped on Lay Auto?"

"Marf! Marf!"

So now, it appears, they are five.

Or is that eight? For three dark figures watch ominously from an empty storefront that once sold used books. The owner didn't even bother to liquidate the stock, but simply left its glue, ink, and paper to burrowing mice and, now, to burrowing terrorists. Had Dave only turned to look at 7:30 o'clock behind, he could have confirmed that these three figures, unlike the two who disappeared upon rubbing their Mace-filled eyes, were indeed dark and Arabic. And Willy, had he not been sniffing for blood, could have smelled biblical cubed cubits of crude oil still attaining to the hair and clothes of the trio. Bad, she was too PO'ed at getting a dose of her own Mace in her eyes to care, and Mary Lou, she was too busy oozing Darwin's milk for a fellow species-mate. "Doggie, poor doggie, are you sure you're all right?" The tail-thumping dog, it should be noted, *did* espy the terrorists, but kept its growl to its own self.

Faux Graphic Panels Eight through Fourteen: Mademoiselles, monsieurs, mutts, muzzling, and nuzzling

The Pit Crew of four, now five, has been riding the streets of Lexington at Willy's insistence. He convinced them he could locate several friends in his hometown who would offer financial backing to Lay Auto and that as a bonus the Pit Crew could test horse manure and dried bluegrass as potential fuel supplies for their prototype. He'd conveniently forgotten the Toyota plant in Georgetown that had turned every hillbilly's head in KY. So the reception for a small-time, upstart competitor has thus far not gone well. Indeed, today's the third day they've been driving Lexington's streets to averted gazes and mostly unanswered phone calls, though what happened moments before constituted the first terrorist attack. Words travel slowly in Lexington, a city like most American cities, short on dictionaries, especially O.E.D.'s, but long on sportball terminology. Go Big Blue! Go Wildcats! Hoorah, yip, yay!

"I just thought of someone else!" Willy snaps his fingers.

"Are you a boy or a girl?" Mary Lou asks the mutt. Mary Lou has lost faith in Willy's ability to produce anything but horse hockey, which they have, by the bye, learned works reasonably well as fuel for Lay Auto, much more reasonably than any of Willy's potential backers. They've called fifteen supposed friends and only one agreed to meet Willy, that one being a woman who threw a lemon meringue pie in his face. Too late, Willy remembered the platitude about a woman scorned.

"A lawyer," Willy says about this newest possible backer. "An honest one," he adds.

"I hope it's a girl," Bad says from the front seat, glancing into one of Lay Auto's enhanced rear view mirrors. "I'd hate to have to pull out my knife for neutering." She eyes Willy's pants, since she too has become disillusioned with his so-called friends as any source of money. Fortunately, he's driving and thinking about this latest friend, the lawyer, and doesn't notice her evil glance. Anyway, he doesn't fret about Bad's anti-male bluster: she reserves its consequences — for the most part — to strangers.

"Sorry to disillusion you, but it's a guy," Willy replies. "He's a lawyer and he's been trying to legalize marijuana for umpteen years. An economic, semi-cancerless alternative for tobacco."

"Semi-cancerless?" someone says.

Together in the back seat, Mary Lou and Dave flip over the dog, which is still gripping the tennis ball, a brand new one, from the looks of things. Wilson.

"Girl," they both announce.

Ten minutes' worth of name-swapping follow. They're still at it while Willy checks Lay Auto's computer for his lawyer friend's address. They're still at it when he pulls in front of his lawyer friend's office, a rather shabby affair near the old library in lovely Gratz Park.

"Potential," Mary Lou takes the time to say when she looks up from playing with the doggie to see the combo house/office that Willy is already walking toward. He's told them he'll be a few minutes and left the electronic key in case they want to cruise the town. "Potential," Mary Lou repeats, keeping in practice. Mary Lou did a stint as a real estate agent before matriculating into Divinity School. Ironically, it was the sell of a Baptist Church that funded her entire first year at Duke; she didn't even need to dip into her inheritance. "Potential," a key trade word she'd picked early to describe property on the verge of condemnation, was the very word that sold the Baptist Church.

"You want to name this dog *Potential?*" Bad asks, incredulous, scooting over to drive.

"No, no, the house that Willy's walking toward has potential."

Fifteen paces from the car and about to step into his friend's office, Willy can still hear them squabbling over the dog's name. He opens the office door to encounter the loveliest pair of —

∧∧∧∧*∧∧∧∧

Syntax error 101010-A:

It occurs to me that human thought-files are neither cross-shared nor integrated into an ethereal Cloud platform, so I must tell you that only three days before, this loveliest pair of . . . eyes received the following e-mail:

Natalie,

When I told you about my hare-brained brother at the last class reunion, you blushed and said that you "recalled" him. I've never been clear on just how you recalled him. . . . Well anyway, he's coming to Lexington; he may already be there, in fact. I'm sure that he'll remember your boss Gabriel, since they were only a year apart in high school. I think they patted butts together on the football field before Willy dropped out. Rah-rah. Anyway, Willy's gotten a coalition of three other eggheads together and they've invented this fuel-efficient car they're marketing. Evidently fuel-efficiency isn't enough, for they've loaded it with gadgets galore (one of the partners is a computer whiz, one of them's a frustrated preacher – she's their PR person, spiritual advisor, and financial backer for now – and one of them's a math genius – what was the name of that movie? <u>A Gentle Mind</u>? <u>A Calm Mind</u>? She's neither. Ms Agitation. A Balmy Mind? Anyway, Willy tried to explain the equations she used: it was worse than Mr. Harrelson's pre-college calculus class that you and I sat through, with you writing songs, me, love poems. Ms. Agitation's equations have something to do with chaos and "the median road." Or maybe it was the "median load." At any rate, when my bro shows at your boss's door, will you take him by the hand, keep him out of trouble? I remember that you played in a couple of popular bands before heading off to the music conservatory in Cincinnati. Willy used to like folk music and play guitar. So you have something in common there, right? And he did have the good sense to drop out of school in America, so he's not all bad. No more football coaches teaching history by screening past Super Bowls for entire class meetings! At least Mr. Harrelson knew what he was talking about with the math, even if no one else did except the nerds. Please let me know when my brother shows. He hates my husband – who doesn't? – so I may not hear from Willy right away.

Your gooey Princess X pal,

Andrea Turner

P.S. You've been smart not to get married. That's all I'm

— to encounter the loveliest pair of brown eyes set in an elfin frame that stopped him cold at the lawyer's front door. Where had he seen this raven-haired woman before? In his dreams? On a CD cover? A Victoria's Secret catalog?

"Are you my father Philip? Are you my brother John?" the lovely mouth just below the lovely eyes sang out.

Willy wobbled, gripping the doorknob, remembering the folk song "Sweet William's Ghost" that the two of them had crooned. You see, what Natalie has never yet admitted to Willy's sister — though Andrea did harbor suspicions, as her e-mail indicates — was that she and Willy had been secret lovers for four months. Secret, because her parents hated Willy, the high school dropout. Secret, because Natalie's ex-crappo-boyfriend was an abusive football star who'd already beaten two of Natalie's subsequent boyfriends. Secret, because when Natalie finally did leave Lexington to study music, she thought she might be pregnant with Willy's offspring, but that came to naught for she spotted during her first week at the music conservatory.

Now, in the lawyer's office, Natalie theatrically fluttered her hand over her desk to continue singing,

> "She stretched out her lily-white hand,
> All for to do her best,
> Say hey, here's your faith and troth, Willy,
> God send your soul good rest."

Willy glided from the door, his feet floating as they hadn't since he first used voice identification to start Lay Auto and hear it purr. Of its own accord, the song about Sweet William's ghost rambled from Willy's tongue. "I'm no ghost, sweet lady, and there's room at my head, and there's room at my feet." Translation: he isn't lying in a cramped grave like poor William does in the folk song, revenant just long enough to visit his lover and bid her to move on in life. No, no, this breathing Willy is ready to receive and return her love, right here in the middle of a lawyer's office! If only we could substitute folk songs for reality TV in this great land of ours! Think how harmonic we'd become! A nation of folk philosophers to outstrip Greece!

Strip? Did you say STRIP? STRIP?! WHAT CHANNEL'S IT ON?

* sigh *

Natalie stood from her desk. Willy kept gliding. On spot X under a breezy ceiling fan, they joined their muzzles. Overhead, loose ceiling tiles trembled. Natalie slipped by Willy to lock the office door, saying that her boss, Gabriel Gatestrait the Fifth, was busy in court. Willy slipped by Natalie to peep through the window to see that Lay Auto had disappeared, no doubt using its onboard-computerized homing device to locate a KFC for the Pit Crew. After these precautions, both slipped back to spot X, where they muzzled some more. And more. And more. And . . .

"He'll be coming back soon," Natalie said, panting.

"Your dad?" Willy said, unthinkingly having flipped back two decades in his throes of ecstasy.

Natalie laughed. "No, Sweet Silly Willy, not my dad. Gabriel. My boss. Your friend. That's why you came, isn't it?" When Willy started to protest, Natalie placed a single fingertip on his lips. "Or did you miss me?" She rubbed, she leaned, they restarted to start.

O! How he'd missed her, though he'd barely known so. He rubbed, he leaned, he puckered, and they re-restarted to start again. Miss her? Miss her? Miss her? Yes sir, yes sir, yes sir!

Which one lay claim to the voice of restraint? Neither, for Natalie's cell phone rang, and two seconds later Willy's cell phone rang. They stopped to stop, and no birds sang.

∧∧∧∧∧*∧∧∧∧∧

Syntax error 101010-B: To be envisioned as a fitful dance replete with happy-go-lucky dancers:

The newest post-post-post-moderns, whether walking, standing, sitting, or lying, have what might pass for a tumor attached to their heads. Listening as the tumor glows, they wiggle, gyrate, bend, and dip to the cell phone sonata. They sing so loudly that if you were to walk by, you might mistakenly think their communication was aimed at you: *Hello, hello. You say hello and I say goodbye.* But this isn't so; it's aimed at the tumor, which gurgles in cyberspace. *Hello, hello. You say hello and I say goodbye.* Alas, to possess a lovely Cartesian body replete with ears and earlobes and yet so mistakenly give pre-eminence to the mind!

∧∧∧∧∧*∧∧∧∧∧

To return to the lawyer's office in Lexington and the two suddenly cooled bodies: Natalie's cell call came from Esquire Gabriel, who said he'd won his case unexpectedly early. After congratulating him, Natalie told him that an old friend was waiting in the office. Fortunately, static clogged the airways, so Gabriel thought Natalie said an old client was waiting. Esquire Gabriel was suspicious of old friends; he *loved* old clients.

And Willy's cell call came from his companions:

"*Chien Fou.*"

"What?"

"*Chien Fou.* Mad Dog. That's what we named our doggie while you were exchanging muzzle nuzzles with the pretty woman." Mary Lou was speaking. The other two Pit Crew members had nominated her to call, figuring she'd be most capable of politely relaying the fact that Willy had left his voice activation line open to Lay Auto's onboard computer, so they'd heard a good deal of hissing body steam plus the usual accompanying smarm — not to mention Willy's lousy rendition of "Sweet William." In fact, they'd even glimpsed Natalie, since Lay Auto had paternally aimed one of its twenty-eight telescopic accident probes through a window to faithfully follow its master, its inventor, its *pater* into the lawyer's office. This all shows why John Stuart Mill — a tireless defender of personal freedom pre-dating both modernity and post-post-post modernity — if resurrected, would voice grave concerns over Lay Auto and Homeland Security. Of the two, I remain more comfortable with Lay Auto. I may be prejudiced.

The truth is that Lay Auto meant no harm; rather, he was paternally watching over his primary creator. Would this placate John Stuart? I suspect not. Paternalism served as a bee in John Stuart's Victorian bonnet. O techno! How long hath your blessings both cursed and aided? Perhaps even an ur-cave man — let's call him Peder — suffered your intrusions? In my mind's eye I espy Peder's ur-neighbor two caves away jamming a ram's horn into a crevice that leads to a connecting cave seam, then jamming his and his mate's ear to the hollowed ram's horn and overhearing the gurgle/gargle of Peder's love-talk, much to their amusement. To top it all, this technologically innovative but nosy ur-man and his mate were gay! "So that's how the breeders do it," they laugh in the safety of their ur-cave. "Boring!" Meanwhile Peder and his heterosexual mate — let's call her Pudenda — nuzzle and ignore their faithful ur-dog, whose ears twitch, alert to the crevice and that strange chortling emitting from its crack.

But let's move forward into our modern techno times: While Natalie and Willy hastily comb their hair, straighten their clothes, and search the office floor for dropped earrings and other mementos of passion, Gabriel Gatestrait has easily passed Lay Auto three blocks away from his office, chugging out half a gallon of gas in doing so. Esquire Gabriel eyes his rear view mirror's reflection of the proto-car he's just passed. His right eye twitches. He really needs to blow some dope, and soon. The recent court appearance had been a mess: if only he could issue restraining orders against his own clients, life would run much simpler. This last client, Alison Taber, was a master of the teasing consonant. Three times, she yelled out in the assault/unlawful trespass case, and each time she managed to convey her meaning with a single consonant, despite Gabriel's warning glances. "If someone gave me a fishing pole, I still wouldn't touch your husband's D — !" Then seven minutes later, "No wonder her husband's roaming the entire trailer park, being cooped up with her fish-smelling C — !" That one brought the judge's gavel down. And, as if completing a magical charm, her third outburst came seven minutes before the trial ended. "If I was the type of woman she claims I am, I'd charge her husband ten grand just to smell my Sh — !" Well, Alison did slip on her last outburst to employ two consonants. Maybe the judge wanted the two plaintiffs, the single defendant, and all four of her consonants out of the courtroom, maybe that's why he hadn't hit Alison with contempt. And though Gabriel and his consonant-tossing client had won the case, Gabriel now feared Alison Taber would begin stalking *him* out of anger for his thrice muzzling her in court with his looks. He checked the rear view mirror again. Behind that ridiculous proto-car . . . was there a tiny red sports car caroming one hundred yards back? Gabriel shuddered and sped up his yellow BMW. He realized that Alison Taber's two vituperative neighbors were most likely on target with Alison's occupation as a hooker. How else could she afford a shiny, fire-red, eight-month-old red Miata on a part-time cocktail waitress's salary? Well, with her attitude, she could make a living as a Mafia assassin, that's how else. Again, Gabriel checked his rear view mirror.

Faux Graphic Panels Fifteen through Eighteen: An old fashioned drunk-fest, some pre-stalking, and a brawl

"Cherries and Maker's Mark and sweet vermouth. Three cherries."

Gabriel did remember Willy. He remembered him mostly because Willy had gone sucker for a fake handoff and allowed a cross-town rival to score the winning touchdown. As a sophomore, the guy had only been playing because the first- and second-string defensive backs were out with an injury and the flu, respectively. After the disgraceful loss, everyone in the entire high school was glad when Willy dropped out. Still, on meeting Willy at his office, Gabriel invited him and his three Pit Crew partners to have drinks that night. The only surprise came when Gabriel's secretary Natalie insisted on coming along. She'd suggested they go to the bar where she sang and played on weekends, so that's where they went and that's where they were.

And that's why Gabriel found it necessary to explain to the bartender what ingredients went into a Manhattan. Como's was an Italian college dive that served pizza, Chianti and foreign beer. As the bartender, a skinny college kid, mixed the drinks according to Gabriel's specifications, Gabriel kept his eye on Bad, who was about ten years younger than he was. He'd always been a fool for redheads.

"Ten years ago," Gabriel started, "this place would have smelled like cigarette smoke. But Lexington passed a smoke-free law for restaurants." He was talking up Bad, even though Willy stood next to him. Bad was talking to Natalie, who stood behind Willy.

"I won the weirdest case today. . . ." Gabriel eased off Bad, for he could swear that in the bar's mirror he'd spotted Alison Taber's stacked blonde hair. But there were so many big-breasted blonde co-eds in the bar that he couldn't be sure.

They carried their drinks to a large round table. Mary Lou was the only one who didn't have a Manhattan. On principle, she drank wine, emulating Jesus in her small fashion. Once they were seated, several students, male and female, came to pay homage to Natalie, who sang funky folk and played guitar and claw hammer banjo on weekends. Gabriel had managed to sit next to Bad, so he barely noticed the attention his secretary was getting. Willy, however, did notice, and leaned closer to Natalie to deflect at least the male admirers. Gabriel decided that it wasn't Alison Taber he'd seen in the bar's mirror, so he started yapping up Bad again.

"Like I was saying, I won my case — "

"Do you think it's right that lawyers defend their clients, even when they know they're guilty?" Bad interrupted.

Studying the scrunch of her brows, Gabriel wasn't sure she wanted an answer. Weren't these people asking him for money to help promote their weasel-diesel? On the drive over, Gabriel had followed the car. He had to admit that he never saw a single puff of pollution. They told him they were still running on KFC chicken bone discards from two days before.

"If we didn't defend them, they'd be reaching for automatic weapons." He said this, though he wasn't sure that his defense of Alison, for instance, had precluded the use of weapons. Court was still out — metaphorically anyway.

Bad screwed her lips around her drink. She was surprised how quickly it went to her head. This lawyer was beginning to look good. And that was bad.

Gabriel was wrong—about many things, but about one in particular: Alison Taber *was* in the bar, and she'd brought along two men who owed her favors because of her, ahem, favors. Also sitting in the bar were three men so intensely Arabic that they drew askance glances even in the university city of Lexington. And a couple from Homeland Security — not official, mind you, but operating on piecework payment from the government as informers — sat in a corner booth. Lay Auto had immediately attracted their attention while they were rocking on their front porch, keeping an eye on the neighborhood, so they'd been following the car for a day and a half. They nibbled garlic sticks and shared a Bud Lite, since government money had fallen lately. They'd been hoping that another invasion of another country would pick matters up, when they spotted Lay Auto cruising the streets at noon yesterday. Also in the bar were two corporate spies from the nearby Toyota plant in Georgetown, and two more from Ford's Louisville plant. To top all this, a nighttime philosophy class had let out early, so most of its students, reeling from Plato, were seeking solace in garlic, wine and beer.

"I'm glad you six ordered at the bar. This place is packed for a Tuesday night. Basketball season's over. I don't get it." The waitress tossed down seven menus and left. Willy, a stickler for omens and tainted with Asberger's Syndrome to boot, immediately noted the extra menu and tapped his foot three times, rubbing against Natalie as he did.

Two more rounds of Manhattans were served, and not a pizza in sight. Mary Lou was sipping her second wine, for she'd seen the lay of the land when Bad put her hand on Gabriel's lawyerly knee. While Mary Lou sipped her wine, Willy sniffed Natalie as if she were a country ham. In sudden romanticatory awareness, Mary Lou realized that this left her and Dave, but when she glanced toward his blue eyes glazing hoarfrost, she knew he was getting too sloshed on Manhattans to dally in any lady's valley. Still, she'd always held a certain attraction for Dave and his mystical Pythagorean connection with numbers, not to mention their mutual, though brief infatuation with hobbits at Duke. She still kept the glowing little sketch he'd made of her on the theological library's steps at Duke. Bordering on humorous porno with its vulvic halo, it made her giggle. She ran her fingers up and down the stem of her wine glass. Maybe it was high time they became more than mutual alumnae, business partners, and pals.

Outside, Lay Auto had been conducting its own version of homeland security, as yet one more pair of nefarious industrial spies inhaled a quick cigarette before entering Como's in search of the owners of this obsidian-colored proto-car. Just from the macho way the spies flicked their cigarette butts, Lay Auto's computer chips gathered enough input to confirm that danger was afoot, so Lay Auto opened its back door to free Chien Fou, who disembarked to drop his tennis ball (WILSON!) beside the two spies. When neither noticed this friendly Darwinian gesture, Chien Fou pissed on their shoes, then grabbed the ball and trotted into Como's.

Miraculously, Alison Taber did pick up the ball when Chien Fou dropped it on her heavily lacquered fire-engine-red overgrown left big toe. She picked it up and heaved it at the lawyer who'd thrice suggested she shut up in court. It bounced off Gabriel's head and hit one of the darkly Arabic men, who seemed to be searching for Scheherazade or any lithe virgin body. I won't tell you that it knocked that gentleman's drink on the floor, for he was a Muslim, and Muslims, like good

Southern Baptists, never drink. Could this dearth of libation be why both sects continually search out females to slap around and humiliate? Perhaps if the male adherents of these two sects became more involved with cognac and Cuban cigars much female human suffering might be assuaged globally. At any rate, whatever fell to the floor spilled on its way downward, slopping over the Mark Twain/Tom Wolfe white dinner jacket of yet one more industrial spy who had entered the bar two Manhattans before. This gentleman had recently left karate class, so it was inevitable that he would throw a punch upon seeing his virgin white suit spattered. *Karate, Kata, Jihad, Fatwah* — how many hateful foreign words must Americans assimilate? But before hateful foreign words unglued the pizza joint, Chien Fou retrieved her tennis ball and led the drunken sextet of the Pit Crew and Gabriel safely out the door.

"What's that awful racket behind us?" Mary Lou asked, tonguing a cherry stem. (Mary Lou, on the last round, had forsaken the wedding wine of Cana for that vulgarian urban spirit.)

Gabriel glanced back to see heavily lacquered fingernails reach into an amazing stack of blonde hair to pull out a blackjack and thump someone's head. "That," he proclaimed, "is the sound of justice miscarrying."

Faux Graphic Panels Nineteen
through Twenty-one:
A revelation, and non-humans save the night

Mary Lou, gentle soul that she is, had insisted not only upon placing a jade Buddha on the front dash but also upon hanging a statuette of Our Lady of Guadalupe in the back window before Lay Auto's inaugural road test, just four months ago. The two would, she'd insisted, waylay road rage. In consequence, Lay Auto's four fish-lens accident-aversion cameras, which ran twenty-four/seven using sun- and moon-inspired photoelectric cells, scanned one or the other of these sculpted icons every half-second. The cameras had been installed for four months and two days. I'll go ahead and guess that about 10,713,601 times one or the other icons has filled Lay Auto's memory banks to date. That's a lot of spirituality for a gooey brain. Would the same have occurred if there had been a grisly crucifix or an Infant of Prague on the dash and rear window? Or for that matter, a swastika, a hammer and sickle, or a bearded image of the prophet Muhammad? Or, heaven forefend, a picture of Gödel and his thick-lensed glasses and ten lines from his proof? Mayhap, yes. For now, the important matter to realize is that Lay Auto *has* blossomed with sentience no quicker nor slower than a typical American high school senior might write in humid inspiration, "Let their bee lite."

Let us consider the gooey brain. Lay Auto's central computer worked on the edge; it combined normal binary processes and microchips with an amniotic — if you will — fluid plus random voltage surges. This idea Bad and Dave concocted jointly, to incorporate chaos, which forever remains the mainstay of the human brain. This made Mary Lou very nervous on theological grounds; it made Willy wonder where all the green computer goo would go in case of an accident; and astoundingly, it and the two statues and loads and loads of chaos had just three days before made Lay Auto sentient. Something, perhaps, in the Bluegrass air? Horse dung? Basketballs?

Barley tobacco? More likely, KFC fried chicken, which proved quite agreeable to Lay Auto's digestion. This sentience consequently overrode the accident-avoidance system to allow Chien Fou onboard; it then opened the door to release Chien Fou to thwart the terrorists.

Away with origins, and back to the bar! Alison Taber loved a good fight. Her favorite mode was to watch males go at it over something she'd said, insinuated, or done, though she wasn't adverse to joining in and scratching with her nails or swinging a bottle downward, sideways from the left, or sideways from the right. Kicking was problematic, for she mostly wore stiletto heels and she prized her toenails.

Thus, only with grave reluctance did she forgo her favorite pastime and pull the two goons accompanying her from the fracas in Como's Pizzeria and Fine Dining when she spotted the jerk lawyer exiting a side door. By the time she and the goons reached the same door, Lay Auto and the lawyer's yellow BMW were halfway down the block.

"Damn," she cursed.

"Want us to go back in?" one of the men asked, popping a row of knuckles.

With a forlorn glance down the street, Alison gave a hitch to her bra and kneed a male college student who was trying to get out. She nodded at the two men and they dragged the crumpled boy back in to pound him. Alison followed exultantly.

Lay Auto's rear cameras espied Alison's actions, and though Lay Auto had neither a positive nor negative ID on the woman, Chien Fou barked wildly at the image of the two men, so Lay Auto set up an avoidance pattern for this female. In fact, from research thus far, Lay Auto wasn't particularly sure that a similar pattern shouldn't be laid out for Gabriel Gatestrait just because of his lawyerly occupation, but there was this hitch: Bad was riding with the man. And Willy was too busy in the back snuggling and singing with this new woman, Natalie. Dave flowed in some Gödelian daze, half scribbling, half sketching. That left Mary Lou, who was just sober enough to drive. The on-board sobriety passed her, giving a plus or minus five-percent margin of error. Mary Lou was following this new woman's verbal directions to her house — when, that is, the woman could get a word between Willy's slurping amatory advances. And since Chien Fou had shown approval for Natalie with a lick to her right cheek, Lay Auto didn't override this new woman's directions. Please understand: even though only a youthful three days old, Lay Auto had already ascertained that in the Darwinian scheme of things, four-legged mammals stood immensely more trustworthy than the two-legged varietal.

Faux Graphic Panel Twenty-two (which should be entitled Panel Sixty-nine, for it contains exactly what a graphic panel named such might)

ʌʌʌʌʌ*ʌʌʌʌʌ

Syntax error 101010-C: Giggle more, bash less? OR, show love, not war?

One would think that modern America might do better to broadcast love in all its forms to all its children, rather than blood in all its forms. 'Tis not the case. Violence reigneth in Puritanical America, even in cartoons. Roadrunner and the coyote. Daffy Duck and Elmer Thud — I mean Fudd. Why not Roadside with the Cunts? Or Daffy Dick and Taffy Tit? Alas, even when worming backwards into the semi-folksongs of America, we find that euphemisms abound for sex, while battle-axes, cloven skulls, and coffin worms skitter-skat shamelessly. Teutonic/Brit/Americans are just too giggly about ye olden lovemaking. Why not import some Gallic amour?

ʌʌʌʌʌ*ʌʌʌʌʌ

Almost as if she'd heeded the need for natty Parisian influence, Natalie had lovingly placed the following items on each bedstand in each room: three Trojan-Enz rubbers, one with a ribbed exterior; a pack of cinnamon Altoids; K-Y Warming Gel; a twist-off bottle of Hershey's syrup, a banana, an apple, a pear, and gold-plated tweezers. (Ouch! Natalie, what were you envisioning with that last item?)

Natalie and Willy: Umm, heavenly good goo.

Mary Lou and Dave: Umm, heavenly good goo.

Bad and Gabriel: What the fuck you think you're doing!?

Chien Fou: Aaaooo!

Faux Graphic Panels Twenty-three through Twenty-six: Wherein Gabriel contacts a famous Texan singer/songwriter; an amazing discovery

Dawn had not yet tendered even her leftmost pinkie into the welkin; neither lark nor nightingale had quivered the faintest hint of song; in fact, deep within Natalie's bedroom, ooze still lingered:

"It's so nice to have you holding me again."

"It's so nice to feel your toes on top of my foot."

"Your little man is as round and hard as I remember him."

"Your nipples are like the beaks of sparrows."

Well, ahem, golly and gee. Perhaps some sense does abide in the Puritanical abhorrence of sexual small talk. So okay, let's forget Natalie and Willy, and while we're at it we'd better forget Mary Lou and Dave, who are likely spewing the same on their long-delayed virgin voyage. Instead, let's tiptoe into the room where Bad lies, legs and arms protectively crossed, staring at a gray glow on the ceiling, which she mistakenly takes as an indication of false dawn. *Thank the goddesses below!* she thinks, for she's judged that this Kentucky lawyer sees himself as a walking, talking, stalking penis. Alas poor Bad is partially mistaken, for dawn lies afar off and in reality the glow derives from Gabriel's laptop as he e-mails a famous Texan singer-songwriter: *These five people showed up – well, four, except they have this dog that's spooky, like I mean, it connives. Well, anyway, one of them knows my probably ex-secretary and they have this proto fuel-efficient car that they're trying to market. It runs on KFC scraps! Can you believe it? They're looking for backers. I'm going to dangle them slowly in the wind and hire a detective to gather dirt. This wouldn't be a good time for your own ecological venture to have a competitor.*

The Texas songwriter, infamous for never sleeping, immediately e-mails back: *Save your money on the detective. They're from Tallahassee. I've heard of them already. Whatever works for the environment works for me. Have they formed a company? Is it non-profit? My friends from the IRS need something to worry about, so I can donate moola if they have non-profit status.*

I've got the money, honey, if they've got the minds.

While Gabriel squatted on the floor before his laptop, busily demonstrating Freud's theory of sublimation by typing out his missive and thus assuaging his non-satisfied hormones, Chien Fou slipped into the room and onto the bed near Bad. The pooch nudged Bad to scoot over so that she could read what the lawyer was typing. Reading both it and the famous songwriter's reply, Bad reluctantly unfolded her arms.

"Do I have to?" she whispered to the pooch, a sister if not in species at least in sexual orientation.

In response, the dog thumped her tail on the blue covers.

Giving a last hopeful glance at the gray ceiling, Bad eased off the bed and twined her arms around the lawyer, who immediately forgot the screen and his Texas singer/songwriter friend to crumble in gosh-be-damned love/lust, further demonstrating, in a backwards-going manner, Freud's theory of sublimation. "Sub," as in *going under*; "lim," as in *getting rock hard*; "a," as in *ah yes!*, and "tion," as in *the act-shun of slippin' and a-slidin'*.

But first, Bad had some probing (!) questions. . . .

The lawyer Gabriel's eyes were gray. Bad knew right off she'd made a mistake by looking at his eyes. "Just tell me one thing." She trembled at her audacity. "Why do lawyers defend people who are clearly guilty? Didn't Scotland have three final judgment categories for trials: guilty, not-guilty, and not-found-guilty?"

"That's two questions," Gabriel pointed out, smiling with his oversized, gap-toothed teeth. An upper canine lay crooked, to boot.

Niggling Bad's mind came the medieval belief that gap-teeth indicate sexual desire. And didn't big teeth also serve to indicate the size of . . . no that was the nose, but then, this lawyer did have a snout to be proud of too. Bad swayed. A nose is a nose is a nose. . . .

Reader, it's time for a re-wire: Gabriel Gatestrait's not really a completely bad sort — though he may not be Bad's sort. A dope-blowing lawyer, after all, opens lovely possibilities. Perhaps at some point, this land will indeed take after its semi-homeland of Wales (not Scotland, Bad!) and instigate three judgment categories for trials. Perhaps lawyers and judges will conjoin to agree, "This trial poses an embarrassing waste of the taxpayer's time and money. The SOB is guilty as hell. Let's chunk him in solitary and move on. Toke of homegrown, anyone?"

So Gabriel, the not-so-bad sort, took Bad's milk-white hand and said, whilst the ceiling fan throbbed, "If we didn't have laws and lawyers, people could be deprived of their civil liberties."

"Like those Muslims in Cuba at Guantanamo Bay?" Bad responded.

"That whole presidential regime was a W-for-weird aberration; you can't count it." Gabriel lifted his arms into the air. Bad noted that they nearly extended to the ceiling in Christ-like resignation. "At least," Gabriel added, "I *hope* we can't count it, or we'll soon find out how the country would operate without lawyers."

"You're telling me that lawyers preserve our civil liberties?"

"Roe versus Wade."

"The Christian Right and red states versus Roe."

"My point exactly." Gabriel lowered his arms and closed the top to his computer, which happened to be rosy, just like a good many inspiring dawns.

"So . . . what were you doing on your computer?" Bad twisted until she was sitting on Gabriel's lap. Her blouse fell open, revealing her left breast, a perfect cup of concupiscent whipped cream with a small strawberry atop, for Bad eschewed tanning salons and cancer-ridden ultraviolet. Her milky arms entwined Gabriel's neck. Her lovely lips snatched at Gabriel's lips, chewing and masticating greedily; for Bad was no fan of sweet-nothing talk. Once decided upon a project, she entered her labors with gangbuster intensity. Indeed, construction work was already occurring; Bad could feel a small crane erecting against her thigh. It would only take her curly, red-haired demolition team to finish the job. But as she and the team writhed, a memory spawned elsewhere, carried perhaps through the gooey plenum of cyberspace . . .

∧∧∧∧*∧∧∧∧

Syntax error 101010-D: A nautical trip, followed by some very personal artistic disillusionment:

"Row, row, row your boat, gently down the stream."

O! That life's streams were truly gentle! That they always held Edenic goals! That they always sloped in an easeful manner to teem with grapes and exposed tubers so we might avail ourselves of alluvial lushitude!

Alas, it ain't so.

"Merrily, merrily, merrily, life is but a dream."

Am I a butterfly dreaming it is I? Have those exposed tubers shattered my restful vision of once drawing a sloping feminine form whilst reclining in a moldy and smelly locker room? Alas yes, for a slurping in my green brain fluids exposes a hitherto repressed memory. (I hate Freud. Nearly as much as I hate Gödel!) This green slurp informs me that I was not *drawing* pornography in a smelly locker room but *enacting* pornography in a smelly locker room, spread-eagle atop five lumpy, sweaty pants and jerseys; spread eagle below a humping slob of a football player. It appears that I . . . am a female. Can this be? Tampons, swelling nipples, mascara, menopause, pregnancy, monthlies, acne, gawping males, voluptuous voluminous vulvas? Gargh! Bad, hurry hence! Advise me! Bad, m'aidez! Bad, Mayday!

∧∧∧∧∧*∧∧∧∧∧∧

Meanwhile, in a galaxy far, far away, demolition had taken place. The crane had collapsed, the cave had convulsed, and a brief early morning rest descended upon Bad and Gabriel after the teensiest bit of sweet nothing talk:

"Umm."

"Goo."

"Gaa."

Faux Graphic Panels Twenty-seven through Twenty-nine: A musical interlude

Ralph and Louise Johnson had been happily humming a Sousa march from their high school band days and gleefully swaying in a corner booth when the fighting broke out in Como's. Why Sousa? Ralph's father had owned a farm and raced thoroughbreds. His mother, an heiress, owned mounds of stock in mounds of things: perfumes, pineapples, and Porsches. At least, such were the dreams Ralph held about his parents. In reality, his father had worked some inconsolable sub-sub-chemist's job at the IBM plant in Lexington, and his mother had been a salesclerk for Lerner's in a shopping center. During Ralph's adolescence IBM teetered on the verge of shifting to a production plant for computer peripherals and printers; the shopping center teetered on the verge of being bulldozed under after a new mall opened three miles away. Nonetheless, Ralph's fantasies hardened into well-seasoned brain concrete when he joined the high school marching band, for marching relocated his mind from head to feet, and his bass drum vibrated to keep all thoughts from rising higher. In brief, Sousa served as Ralph's savior from the sordid world.

Louise's mother managed the Lerner's where Ralph's mother worked. This bit of reality and the marching band brought Louise and Ralph together. Louise's own father was a preacher at what was then a country church on the outskirts of Lexington. His especial friends were Jesus and sin, both of which he heaped upon his congregation and family. Louise played a piccolo. Doing so allowed her to practice late hours in the garage year-round, leaving her mother in the kitchen with Jesus, sin, and the preacher creature. Louise too revered Sousa as a Savior.

So at Como's, "Stars and Stripes Forever" was the particular march Ralph and Louise were humming and percussing on the tabletop when the first beer bottle flew between their rhythmic, sober noses. Neither of them drank, though Louise had undergone two years of partying at the university until she transferred to Lexington Theological Seminary. The bottle was never uncorked again. A literal bottle, however, now smashed against the wall.

"That hit on the upbeat," Louise commented sourly.

Ralph picked glass from his thinning blonde hair. Another bottle struck the floor, spewing beer foam on their matching red tennis shoes, and yet another hit the table, sloshing beer over a three-inch Day-Glo tinsel shaped in a violet S entwining a golden Treble Clef, an especial calling card designed by the couple.

"The canvas bag?"

"The canvas bag."

Each constantly carried a tan canvas bag, one labeled "Alpha," the other "Onega." The latter was supposed to read "Omega," but neither Ralph nor Louise had ever gotten the spelling straight and their Greek New Testament professor at Seminary gave up. Each bag weighed precisely 48 pounds, since both Ralph and Louise wanted to assert patriotism, and since both remained skeptical of including the non-contiguous territories of Hawaii and Alaska as states, much less Puerto Rico where the predominant language wasn't even American. Of what did these 48 pounds consist? Bell, book, and candle, in case of demonic possession, took up three pounds. For more mundane matters there were a Walther P-38, four extra clips for same, four smoke flares, two canisters of Mace, two Bowie knives, strike-anywhere matches, a GPS, two gas masks, three cell phones, and sundry other items of defense and destruction. And a CD of Sousa's most loved works.

As their hands touched the flares they gazed into one another's eyes: a unifying tingle traipsed their spines. They ignited the smoke flares and worked their way through the melee by slamming the flares' spiked ends onto tables. Beside each flare, they dropped a tinsel treble clef. By the time they reached the door, a gray haze was pushed downward by the ceiling fans, and the combatants were hacking. The young college-headed student who'd been dragged in and beaten by Alison and her goons lay on the floor rasping, "Zeus forever!" Ralph and Louise thought he was proclaiming "Sousa forever!" so they pulled him outside. The boy, in fact, was neither an aficionado of bad music nor good Greek mythology, but rather of graphic novels — real graphic novels, the ones displaying all the fruitful information a hungry youth or mid-aged adult in America requires, the ones spewing techno info unto and even outside their gloriously compacted panels muscled with action (Bop! Whap! Snicker-Snack!). For this reason, the boy had glommed onto the name of a wonder dog named Zeus, not Sousa. Nonetheless . . .

Once they were outside in Como's parking lot, Louise dropped a treble clef onto the boy's chest while Ralph lay a spare pocket harmonica on the boy's heart. Hearing coughing cascading from inside the restaurant, Ralph piped an ocarina over the boy while Louise played her piccolo to the tune of "Yankee Doodle Dandy," one of the few non-Sousa ditties the two knew by heart. Inside Como's, the smoke flares were proving to be great levelers to brains and lungs: villains, idiots, and platonic dreamers now stumbled into the parking lot, too wracked with coughing to continue their fight, though Alison Taber did imbed a stiletto heel in the boy's chest just as he came to and thanked his rescuers by trying to play Ralph's harmonica. The gold and silver treble clef and silvery S for Sousa became impaled on Alison's spiked heel. With a grimace she wobbled toward her car.

Faux Graphic Panels Thirty-one through Thirty-four:
A mathematical mistake, rectified by a makeover quick enough to leave both Clark Kent's phone booth and Queer Eye for the Straight Guy in metaphorical dust

Dawn, creeping on its toenails and fingertips —

"Wait, what happened to Panel Thirty?"

Given America's plummeting math literacy rates, can you wonder at one mathematical misstep? Praise Ben Franklin and Tom Jefferson both that Asians are immigrating here. Otherwise, who could balance our checkbooks, design our rockets and computers, much less keep pace with Faux Graphic Panels and pagination?

Quick, let's look to Jansci von Neumann, "Johnny" to his pals. Johnny emigrated from Hungary and exuded mathematical wonderment throughout his life. A founder of the modern computer, of game theory, and a major contributor to the making of the atomic bomb, was what he was. Who's gonna fill his shoes? Who's gonna stand that tall? Who's gonna sing the Opry and the Wabash Cannon . . . wait, not Johnny Cash, but Johnny von Neumann. Who's going to fill *his mathematical* shoes? Someone who's never listened to country music, I'm betting. Someone whose favorite instrument is a sitar, not a banjo, I'm betting.

∧∧∧∧∧*∧∧∧∧∧

Syntax error 101010-E: Utilitarian excursion:

You may be sitting in your red velvet cushioned chair thinking that we could have done without those mathematical shoes and that atomic bum, but then, maybe your granddaddy — be his granddaddy heart Japanese *or* American! — might not have lived through an invasion of Japan. Need I mention the obvious consequence that *you*, then, would not have been born? Don't be so quick to condemn the atomic bum is the moral to that little song.

This is where gray area thinking always lands poor humans: dropped-down, dunked-down into the ever-eclipsed Canyon of Crinoline Befuddlement. Distressing enough to sip orange juice at breakfast while reading headlines about murder here, murder there; to masticate Jimmy Dean spicy sausage while staring at *Time* close-ups of bodies mangled and starved from famine, war, and terrorist activity. But to pen a ledger balancing corpses versus living, walking DNA in some John Stuart Mill number game of utilitarian practicality? *Atomic Bum*: 120,000 dead Japs and 0 dead Yanks. *Invasion of Japan*: 580,000 dead Japs and 74,000 dead Yanks. Even an American eighth grader playing Nintendo can sort those numbers. Speaking of Nintendo, would that creator's Japanese grand-dad have fallen victim to the invasion?

∧∧∧∧∧*∧∧∧∧∧

Back to morning, back to dawn's fungus-pitted toenails creeping into Natalie Ellender's house, pacing room-to-room, caressing one closed eyelid at a time. The prickly arrow of a certain never defunct Roman demi-god, Cupid of course, had shafted our hero Willy Turner the previous day and Willy subsequently was losing compass even as dawn's smog-pitted fingernails scraped his eyelids. "Wha?" His eyes took in a strange bedroom. But when they espied Natalie's curves — maybe her nose, maybe her breasts, maybe her cheeks — which curves I'm not revealing — when his eyes espied these geometrical configurations, he arose and followed said curves like a puppy to watch them load and start a black coffee maker in a glossy yellow kitchen.

Why did Natalie's kitchen glow glossy yellow? Because she was renting from her boss, Gabriel Gatestrait, who had previously and unknowingly rented the house as a methamphetamine factory filled with cooks whose favorite colors were Sudafed yellow and pink. Five months into their rental agreement a pot blew up and blinded the head chef and killed her sous-chef. A little consultation with Julia Child or Paula Ray might have helped in the cookware matter. A watched pot never explodes.

But the colorful kitchen and Willy's roiling stomach were pushed aside, for his heart, hormones, penis, nose, and reptile brain squirped, "Nat-a-lie." His tongue enjoined to utter a morning prayer, almost a chant. "Nat-a-lie."

Natalie's hormones and body parts also colluded, so she hummed a chant of her own, a tune whose words she'd gleaned from an old, old, book. In this chant, Maid Marian ventures into Sherwood Forest disguised as a squire, carrying sword and staff, two squire-ish implements of penile destruction. Robin, also in disguise, chances upon her beneath an oak and judges her to be of the dastardly king's dastardly men. Clack! Clack! go their staffs, for twenty-four rhyming stanzas. Finally the two draw their swords. Snicker-snack go their vorpal blades, which open wounds, and said wounds send blood and snot down their arms and legs. "Ho!" cries Robin Hood at last, panting. "You are the stoutest man I e'er encountered."/ "Robin? Can it be you, me love? Robin, 'tis I, Marian, maid, virgin, and pre-teen forever in my Nutra-sweet mind." How they clasp and eat venison to heal their wounds! How they fug happily ever after! That is, after they spend fifty-three years fighting dastardly King John. That is, they fug happily for the last six days of their lives until they are drowned in a flood. Well, they really didn't have six *entire* days, because the water began rising on a Tuesday, and they drowned on Sunday. It's hard, children, hard, to produce a happy ending in this apocalyptic, Gödelian world.

Nonetheless, that morning in the yellow kitchen Natalie chanted her happy Maid Marian song and motioned for Willy to carry his mug of coffee and follow her into her non-yellow boudoir once more.

I dare not, Willy thought. *Lay Auto calls. Greenpeace! Gaia. Mother Earth. Clean lungs. The American Cancer Society. The SPCA. La Leche League. All things natural and free.* These thoughts might have streamed through Willy's head, but ladies (since I've resigned myself to being one), you know the devil's in men, so his reptile brain slavered, *What can be more natural and free than sleeping with sweet Natalie Ellender this fine roseate morning? Go for it.* So Willy did follow, mug in his hand, while Natalie hummed her song.

"Sit," she commanded, pointing to the bed.

Willy gulped and tugged his belt.

"No, no, not that," she chirruped, staying his hand on the buckle and turning to her spacious pink closet, spacious thanks to the previous cooking duo who alternately used said closet for either storing chemicals or hiding and whimpering when meth paranoia hit too hard.

Natalie dropped her blue robe. *Shoosh,* was the sound that reached Willy's reptile ears.

Though Natalie had no need of a girdle, she tugged one on, to slim her already slim waist.

Though she had no need for uplift in the bosom area, she donned a Victoria's Secret padded bra, power red.

Next, gray hose.

Next, a black, black, oh so black, silken slip.

Next, a virgin white blouse, buttoned to the neck.

Next, a power red tie to match her power red bra, which shewn just enough through the blouse to lure Willy to the edge of the bed.

"No, no, not that," Natalie repeated.

Next a black skirt, drifting within two centimeters of her handsome knees. Already, Willy was dreaming of dabbing those kneecaps with honey and kisses.

"No, no, not that," Natalie cautioned.

Next, a snugly fitting black suit with enough lift to turn her shoulders male.

Next, stiletto heels that Alison Taber would have killed for, those heels also tinted power red. Indeed, it lies in the realm of possibility that Alison *will* try to kill for those heels, for she and Natalie wear the same shoe size.

Natalie turned to Willy and smiled. She held something in her hand he couldn't see.

"My own special power touch." She turned and showed him a dildo she was inserting under her skirt, adjusting it with just enough bulge to make onlookers curious. And respectful. She then picked up a black leather attaché case and saluted.

"My God," Willy said. "A lawyer."

"Even better," Natalie replied. "A CEO."

Willy rushed to Natalie's vanity mirror and combed his hair for the first time in four days. He dabbed on a cologne sample from the bottom of his shaving kit. He brushed his teeth. He even trimmed his beard.

When the two of them STRODE back into the banana yellow kitchen, Mary Lou and Dave bolted from their morning slouches, nearly ruining their overworked crotches with freshly brewed hot java. They searched out a vowel or consonant that would offer an appropriate clue to the mystery of this red and black stranger tugging Willy's arm.

"Where's Natalie?" Mary Lou managed to ask.

"Who's she? . . . he?" Dave managed to ask, nodding at the red and black stranger with the strange, respect-inducing bulge underneath its skirt.

"*C'est moi,*" Natalie responded.

"*C'est elle,*" Willy enjoined, not to be outdone in continental swank.

Dave and Mary Lou sat in disbelief. This state did not last long; indeed the ship had not sailed half a league before they left the yellow kitchen in scarlet embarrassment to stand before a mirror combing their hair and in general puffing themselves up. Within the hour Bad and Gabriel would join in the generalized coifing and donning, for the dress code on Old Jug Factory Road in Lexington had just taken a sharp upward curve.

"Can you cook?" Natalie turned to ask Willy as Dave and Mary Lou left the kitchen. She lifted her power red fingernails and spread her lithe arms to explain that she couldn't possibly damage her new look. "Pancakes, scrambled eggs, and sausage patties would be great." She indicated her pink refrigerator, a hand-me down from her mother, who definitely did not dabble in methamphetamines. "While you cook, I'll undertake some financial planning."

Meanwhile, or should I say pre-erstwhile, or should we simply jump the old time machine back six or so hours? . . .

Faux Graphic Panels Thirty-five through Thirty-nine: A Jump back in time, plus the practical side of good manners

The Johnsons in the dark of the night — you do remember the Johnsons and the college-headed boy from the end of the chapter before the last, yes? Good. So now we're taking a six-hour flipback-flashback in this chapter, yes? Good.

So in the dank and dark of night, the Johnsons were piping "Hail to the Chief!" accompanied by their young college recruit, the Zeus/Sousa boy. How did they recruit him? I must inform you that Mrs. Johnson, though somewhat elderly, did resemble Annie Coulter, and similarly used her cleavage and thin Cosmo body plus a suggestive piccolo — Annie are you listening? — to ensnare the young college-headed boy. Roman emperors used bread and circuses; Coulter and Johnson, soft porn. Sexual enticement in the service of conservatism is no vice!

Please recall our adjusted flipback-flashback time Panel: the moon, she still be up; the sun, he still be down.

Like Willy Turner, Mr. Ralph Johnson was endowed with an extraordinary nose — Ralph once, for instance, when walking his pit bull one afternoon, sniffed out bomb-making terrorists and reported them to Homeland Security. It was no fault of his that the terrorists were three teenagers with illegal fireworks from Tennessee. Indeed, after the diligent Homeland Security team burst through the basement door, machine pistols ready, they confiscated five Bic lighters and the Tennessee explosives (thirty cherry bombs, five M-80's, nearly one thousand lady-fingers, and forty bottle rockets), then ripped the room apart until they came up with nine pages of the *Koran* that one of the boys had printed off the Internet thinking he'd found Muslim bondage porn, for the chapter was entitled, "Of Women." At the very least, the lad figured, there'd be some virgins-in-Paradise scenes, some moist subservient licking, some heavy Arabic panting. He would have been better off reading this illustrationless novel. Anyway, the fireworks and the pages from the *Koran*, two pocketknives, and three copies of *Catcher in the Rye* with the dirty words underlined combined to offer evidence enough. *Habeas Corpus* was suspended, and Mr. Johnson received a medal plus a signed commendation from his congressman before the kids were released and sent back to the track team.

Here and now, under gibbous moon, however, though the Johnsons had driven quite slowly with the white top to their red and blue convertible Mustang down, and though Mr. Johnson had sniffed, snorted, and snarfed, they could uncover no sign of Lay Auto and the likely insurrectionists until the college-headed boy from Como's used helpful moonlight to spot Gabriel's yellow convertible BMW, a make and model that had plagued the boy's dreams ever since he glommed onto one in a graphic novel about a vampire who seduced female college English majors. The vampire did toss an occasional French major into the bloodletting as antipasto.

"There!" the college-headed boy shouted, forgetting the vampire and missing three notes on his harmonica, much to the distaste of Mr. and Mrs. Johnson. "There, **sir**!" he quickly added.

∧∧∧∧∧*∧∧∧∧∧

Syntax error 101010-F: Miss Manners momentarily enters our text (by special arrangement with her syndicate) to deliver instruction on when to use honorifics, after receiving a querying letter from *Confused in Lexington:*

Dear Confused in Lexington: A telltale hint comes whenever you feel nervous about a person. Say, when that person ekes out a living as an evangelical nutcase with more than a handful of rail-thin and/or pork-fat ranting believers clinging to his black Sears sports jacket. Use those honorifics, use 'em. "*Sir? Madam? Your Horror?*" Or say, when that person works the streets as an avid patriot explaining why America needs to invade X, Y, or Z, and why $$$$$$$ needs be cut from any and all slovenly domestic programs. Use 'em, use 'em. "*Sir? Madam? Your Horror?*" Got the picture? Your life/your freedom/your very ten toes depend upon it. Stop reading graphic-less graphics! Take an emergency interlude! Practice before a highly polished mirror! "*Sir? Madam? Your Horror?*" Repeat with a smile; repeat humbly. Just repeat. "*Sir? Madam?*

Your Horror?"
  Cordially yours,
  Miss Manners
∧∧∧∧∧*∧∧∧∧∧

So, the college-headed boy spotted the yellow BMW and politely mentioned his discovery. Then the three spotted Lay Auto. Sousa was stopped, headlights were extinguished, and the patriotic Mustang was engaged in neutral to coast. All needlessly, for recall that at this time of night the occupants of Natalie's house were busily slurping sweet nothings, so even a dozen sousaphones, a full moon, and straight pipes wouldn't have alerted them. The fact remains that the Johnson's Mustang did coast rather silently, under a rather obscuring — for the moment — set of clouds. From the front seat, Mrs. Johnson passed back an extra tan canvas satchel she and Mr. Johnson (Sir! Your Horror!) kept on the floorboard, this tan one painted with a blue "Pie," in the original, ancient Greek. Six more canvas satchels, similarly inscribed to honor the Greeks (the first to grill hamburgers), lay locked in the Mustang's trunk to await other recruits into the American way of life.

"Ma'am," the boy said, seeing the obvious heft of the canvas and seeing the wide-eyed Johnsons appraising him. "Ma'am, Sir, is that for me?"

Now let it be known that Mary Lou and Dave were fresh-air freaks: Mary Lou felt that open windows placed her closer to Grand Dame Mother Earth, and Dave, in his recent love-gush, felt that anything Mary Lou did must be right. Would Dave, lemming-like, jump off a cliff if Mary Lou jumped first? Mounting hormones and her sweet rear-end twisting a mantra just might entice him. Let it further be known that Chien Fou was making rounds in their room at the very moment the honorable Johnsons and their protégé were coasting toward Lay Auto. Sniffing something amiss, Chien Fou jumped through the open window and ran to Lay Auto, whose collision monitors had already spotted the approaching, song-less Mustang.

Chien and Lay consulted. Chien sniffed the boy's emitting scent and recognized him as harmless. But when Chien sniffed the Johnsons she discovered fear — in them and herself. So she pawed Lay Auto's front tire. Quietly, Lay Auto turned over the ignition and opened a door for Chien Fou to hop in just as Herr His Splendiferousness Mr. Johnson, pulled the emergency brake to stop the Mustang without telltale brake lights. The three stalwarts emerged from the patriotically painted Mustang and hobbled toward Lay Auto. A tinsel treble clef fell to the ground. The boy, of course, had four unlit flares in his canvas bag, but flares weren't what they needed. Nor did they need maps to all the malls within a 120-mile radius of Lexington, though the boy found one. Mrs. Johnson rifled through her sack and came up with a razor sharp Bowie Knife. Mr. Johnson rifled through his sack and came up with a set of keys — from whence he had no idea. But he did remember a time in high school when he and several friends used their keys to scratch an unpopular chemistry teacher's blue Trans-Am after a particularly hard test. The college-headed boy, taking his cue, rifled through his canvas satchel and came up with a graphic novel about a werewolf named George. His heart fibrillated! His tear ducts overflowed! By streetlight and by increasing moonlight (the clouds were scudding, as clouds are wont to do) he began to read aloud.

"Find something else," Mrs. Johnson said, hushing the boy.

"Let him be. He needs to learn," Mr. Johnson retorted, thinking of all the Action Comics he'd read. Three more steps and he reached out with the keys, intending to scratch Lay Auto's trunk. Lay Auto rolled itself forward two feet, and Mr. Johnson lurched, a treble clef loosening from his boxer shorts to scoot out his right pants leg. Mrs. Johnson took a skip, intending to slash a rear tire valve. Lay Auto again rolled itself forward two feet, while popping a dog biscuit from the glove compartment for Chien Fou. Mrs. Johnson recovered, though a treble clef from her loose bra dropped to the pavement. This went on for six blocks: rolling, stumbling, hopping, dropping, and gurgles of "Damn! Shit! Fuck! Wow!" as the college-headed boy fell in and out of the arc of differing street lamps illuminating graphic panels of mayhem, contemplation, and sex. *Contemplation?* In a graphic novel about a werewolf named George? A-woooo! To remind you of multiplying realities, please remember that there are now two moons: the full one guiding George the Coifed Werewolf, and the gibbous one that is on and off obscured by scudding clouds over the Johnsons, the college-headed boy, Lay Auto, and Chien Fou. A-woooo!

Meanwhile, Lay Auto's onboard map console glowed until a pink spot labeled *Tibet's Pond* pulsed. Chien Fou tilted her head at the pulsating spot and gave Lay Auto a lick on the steering wheel. Another dog biscuit popped forth.

Was Lay Auto taking its cue from Pavlov? Would Lay soon be

popping out hamburgers and reality TV for the five humans? Time will tell, but for now Lay simply lurches toward Tibet's Pond.

This lurching, the Johnsons followed easily, for they transformed the two-feet hops into 4/4 measure, Sousa's mainstay. Oompa, oompa, oomp, oomp. The college-headed boy knew nothing about music so he transformed the two-feet hops into a fight scene that had developed in his graphic novel, segueing that into the sex-in-the-computer-room scene that had been illustrated by pink tits and penises entangled in blue and red wires. These scenes came from the infamous George and the Dominatrix issue, entitled *Werewolf George Fights Gruesome Geeks off Mistress Teresa*. How did this graphic novel wind up in the Johnsons' survival bag? If you were stranded on a desert isle, what single book would you take? Duh.

In common measure, 4/4 time, with Tibet's Pond not ten feet away, Lay Auto extended and inflated its hydroplane pontoons and shifted its universal joint from tires to propeller, then led the three into the murky, chilly water. Like lemmings, they followed. Blurp. Blurp. Blurp. On the pond's far side Lay Auto reverted to its tires, deflated its pontoons, and carried Chien Fou back to Natalie's house just in time for Chien Fou to perform her pre-dawn matchmaking job with Gabriel and Bad, details of which you have already read.

Blurp, blurp, blurp, echoed listlessly on the trip back. Did a tear fall from Lay Auto's sentient eyes as the three humans sank into murk? No, for Lay Auto had recently learned the Four Truths and the Noble Eightfold path from the Internet and the jade figure of Buddha in its front window. And from the Our Lady of Guadalupe in its rear window Lay had learned the wisdom of sacrifice. In short, it had learned that this wretched world is a thoroughfare of woe, woe, woe. Which travels with us always, be we Darwinian creatures or sentient computers.

Faux Graphic Panels Forty through Forty-one: Power black, power red

"Wow!" was the Pit Crew's unanimous appraisal of Natalie's power black and red outfit as everyone convened in the doorway of the yellow kitchen, enticed by the smell of pancakes and sausage.

Natalie remained primly seated at the breakfast table, working a laptop she normally used for songwriting, while Mary Lou and Dave, Bad and Gabriel, Chien Fou and her newly equipped dog collar that linked sound and video back to Lay Auto's computers — while these inhabitants of this woe-woe-woeful thoroughfare clumped in the kitchen's doorway. The collar was an early morning gift from Bad. Willy, barely remembering that his stomach much less Lay Auto existed any more, so in amour he was with the power black and red woman, managed to flip another pancake.

"Wow!" they exclaimed once again at Natalie's outfit, ignoring Willy's uncommonly deft flip.

With two even defter forefingers, Natalie tapped the laptop on the table beside the growing stack of pancakes Willy was mounding on a platter. She looked up at Gabriel, still in the doorway, and she beckoned with her power red fingernails. "You owe me. Before you eat, I want the phone number and address of that Texas country singer friend of yours. And I want the names of ten Kentucky lawyers with money to spend. You owe me."

Everyone, including Chien Fou, stared at Gabriel, who stood slack-jawed and lanky. He tried to lean on Bad for support, but she was having none of it and backed away, playing with her red hair and gazing at the ceiling. There was something very interesting there, but what was it? Not a bird's nest, not a wasp's nest. A smoke detector? Bad took a lock of her hair and compared it to the spot on the ceiling. They were nearly the same color.

Gabriel did owe Natalie. He owed her at least two-dozen courtroom victories over the past four years, for she'd caught that many of his gaffs while he was huffing marijuana. He owed her a dent in her Gibson Guitar and three chipped keys on her Yamaha piano, all of which came from his marijuana-whiskey induced clumsiness. He owed her two bar tabs she'd picked up at Como's, and he owed her his Fayette County notoriety derived from the thinly veiled song she sang about him and his marijuana crusade, always publicly leaving out the six verses she'd written when she was angry at him. He owed her ignoring his grunting male advances and comments when he was hung over. He owed her half a dozen girlfriends she'd set him up with, including Willy's sister Andrea before she married.

As Willy scooped two more pancakes onto the mound, Natalie gestured toward the laptop's keypad. "Ten lawyers. And your country singer friend's Texas address, his phone number, and his e-mail. And let him know I'll be in touch. And let him know it's a worthy cause. Even better than legalizing marijuana."

Bad forgot the ceiling and pulled out a chair to sit: "He's already done that. An hour ago. Contacted his country singer friend, that is, not legalized marijuana. Senate wasn't in session."

Gabriel gave a sheepish grin to indicate this was true. Even though his original intent in e-mailing the Texas Country Singer had been malevolent, there was no need to publicize that, especially with this luscious redhead's body emanating heat onto his left arm. "*Carpe diem*" was one of Gabriel's favorite mottos, when he could remember high school through his marijuana haze.

"That's good, that's great," Natalie said. Then she tapped her power red fingernails on her laptop's silver case. "But you still owe me, buster." She turned from her boss and indicated the mounting plates of food. "Everyone else can chow down." She stood to tug Gabriel toward her chair and the laptop.

Once seated, Gabriel began to type, just as fast as Natalie always knew he could. "There," he said, finishing while everyone was still pouring syrup and melting butter. "And in case you're wondering, Wil — my country singer friend — has already hinted that he'll be glad to donate, just to get the IRS off his back. Some environment-friendly tax credits will go a long way with him."

Faux Graphic Panels Forty-two through Forty-nine: Raising $$$$$$$; raising cane

By five o'clock that evening, Natalie had raised nearly one hundred thousand dollars. She and the crew — minus Gabriel and Bad (who had volunteered on an impulsive lark to slum from her mathematical heights and act as legal secretary) — were elated. Just in this one day of visiting only four lawyers to demonstrate Lay Auto, Natalie had garnered a third of what they'd pulled from Mary Lou's trust fund to put into the project over the last year. So they couldn't understand why Chien Fou, alternating between whining and barking, would not abandon sitting behind the steering wheel whenever they left the proto-car, even on a KFC lunch break. Chien did not seem to share their happiness. Why?

Part of the mystery was solved when they returned to Natalie's house: Seven, count 'em, seven government agency cars were parked along the street and on the grass, making a nuisance of themselves and proving ex-President Ronald Regan's dictum correct: "*The worst thing an American citizen can hear is, 'I'm from the government, and I'm here to help you.'* " The colors of the cars were pretty, however, and Mary Lou commented on their palette. Celestial blue, lemon yellow, two coconuts, mauve, chocolate, and forest green. These rainbow cars encircled the red, white, and blue Mustang that had been parked in front of the next-door neighbor's house when the Pit Crew packed into Lay Auto to go fund-raising earlier that morning.

"Your name?" one of the myriad G-men asked when Natalie started for her house. Noticing her briefcase he nodded to a bearded fellow who must have been from a bomb squad. Immediately, a cocker spaniel scampered to sniff her briefcase. Chien Fou barked loudly, and the cocker slinked off in what indicated embarrassment. (I myself am just learning canine, but I'm pretty sure Chien Fou barked something like, "How can you keep a straight face and work for these dolts?")

Natalie was not taken aback by either the cocker or the male's power red tie. She hummed Bob Dylan's "Ballad of a Thin Man" knowing that this fool would never understand anything that mattered, say love, anger, or Gödel, to mention only a few worthy items. "Before we discuss my name," she said, "why don't you move your car off my petunias and show me some identification?"

"Petunias?" The man looked back in horror.

There were no petunias, but the guy moved his powder blue car immediately, since Natalie had chanced upon his mother's favorite flower. Which goes to show that despite Bob Dylan's ballad, everyone keeps a clotted heart; it just may lie underneath four pounds of obtuse brain cells and one hundred and eighty pounds of French-fried blubber. Humbly debarking from his powder blue car, the man reverted to bureaucratic idiocy, inflating his chest as he proffered a gold badge with a triangle surrounding the eye of some all-seeing deity: Homeland Security.

"Two of our operatives went missing last night. This is their car." He meant the red, white, and blue Mustang whose front tire Chien Fou was taking a leak on. "Whoa! Whoa! That's evidence!" the man shouted. Chien Fou scratched grass onto the car and scurried to Mary Lou.

"What's this . . . thing?" one of the men asked, pointing at Lay Auto, whose wary headlamp followed his approach.

"An energy deduction for the long form," Willy had the sense to say.

The man nodded appreciatively and after a few more questions returned to help his colleagues search the grass and asphalt around the patriotic Mustang. At last, one of them picked up a three-inch Day-Glo tinsel shaped in an entwined silver S and golden Treble Clef, which lay on the road twenty paces from the Mustang's front bumper. Where, you might ask observantly, lay the similar tinsel that had dropped when Ralph and Louise and the college-headed boy first disembarked? Why hadn't these super-agents spotted it? That tinsel lay hidden under the right front tire of the rainbow agency car that brought the cocker spaniel. Thus are we often hoisted by our very own pet car! (Sorry, but in this Gödelian world, humor needs be voiced wherever one can limn it.)

Now, on this and every tinsel's backside was imprinted, in purple, "Stars and Stripes Forever!" This was the infamous calling card of the

Johnsons, their idea of simultaneously promoting John Philip Sousa and America. Homeland Security, the FBI, and the CIA had turned a blind eye toward their musical quirk. The IRS even grudgingly admitted the tinsel calling card as a business loss, under pressure from the previous agencies. As a result, the Johnsons had not paid any taxes since September 11, 2001, and they had disseminated or dropped over three hundred thousand Day-Glo tinsel treble clefs in honor of John Philip Sousa and America.

As if this newly found Day-Glo artifact were a Cincinnati hot dog with chili, the agency men — there was only one woman and she remained aloof to eye the Pit Crew and Lay Auto — gathered about it, gumming their mouths to read over and over, "Stars and Stripes Forever!" Backwards, forwards, jumbled, it offered no clue.

Then another agent ferreted out a second enjoined silver S and golden treble clef, six paces farther along on the pavement. A feeding frenzy ensued. The agency men and the woman scurried down the street, following the multi-color treble clefs toward what they would ultimately find at Tibet's Pond: a sprinkling of enjoined treble clefs and S's floating like iridescent scum.

The Pit Crew, meanwhile, entered Natalie's house. Ho-hum, went the sun, thinking it was nearly time to set. Hi-ho, went the Pit Crew, arranging themselves inside Natalie's kitchen to celebrate and cook.

Outside and oblivious to the sun's sacred admonishment to rest at night — or carouse should you have that chance! — two men in Yarmulkes arrived. They began to scowl, rubbing their hands together and reciting verses from Leviticus. Members of the anti-anti Semite league, these two were greatly concerned, in their own sacred way, about fuel efficiency, for they feared it would lessen America's interest in the Middle East and subsequently America's support of Israel. With gleeful irony, between verses from Leviticus, they decided to fire bomb both Natalie's house and Lay Auto with ten gallons of gasoline.

∧∧∧∧*∧∧∧∧

Syntax error 101010-G: Philosophy, à la Ben Franklin:

What, Ben Franklin a philosopher? Well yes, though you must needs research beyond the Franklin stove and his position as America's first postmaster to uncover that fact. "A Penny saved is a Penny earned." There's a tittle of philosophy to serve atop your Franciscanware plates! And consider all those French women who adored Ben almost as much as they adored that philosophical Scot scoundrel David Hume. French women won't fall for just any old male, you know. They have intellectual savoir-faire; they demand philosophers attached to their penises. So David, the English Channel did brave to hurl Parisian women into a rave. And Ben, he sailed a ship, Parisian women to tip. Not only was Mssr. Ben our first recorded womanizer and inventor of the super efficient wood-burning Franklin stove, not only was he our first kite-flier, our first postmaster, our first dispenser of philosophic folk platitudes, but he was also the founding father of the volunteer fire department. To wit: "*Our articles of agreement obliged every member to keep always in good order and fit for use a certain number of leather buckets, with strong bags and baskets (for packing and transporting goods), which were to be brought to every fire; and we agreed about once a month to spend a social evening together in discoursing and communicating such ideas as occurred to us upon the subject of fires. . . .*"

— This all serves as no idle excursus into the field of philosophy: its importance will soon be revealed.

∧∧∧∧*∧∧∧∧

Lay Auto, curious about the Yarmulkes (Indeed, its roiling green fluid sloshed with curiosity about every religion and every thing, which, alas, is how it came upon You-Know-Whom.), had extended its sonic sensors and subsequently heard the two men's plan to fetch gasoline. Lay Auto was allergic to gasoline. Chien Fou had been surreptitiously sneaking Lay Auto newspapers and placing them before one of its myriad scanning lens. And of course, Lay was connected to the Internet by satellite, thanks to Bad and Dave, so there was hardly an information site L. A. hadn't visited in the last week of its restless existence as a sentient being. Indeed, Lay Auto had become its own Google. Hence Lay wisely concluded that these two men wearing Yarmulkes were brewing a miniature Hebrew version of Fatwah. Lay tapped its horn gently in Morse code.

Unfortunately, no one in the house knew Morse code, not even the rudimentary three short, three long, three short of SOS. Or is that three long, three short, three long? Alas, consider the knowledge that constantly dissipates in our Information Age! To whence does it flit? Cyberspace graveyards? Interstellar gases? Black holes? Time portals? Where'er it flees, the tapping horn did at last persuade Willy to remove his eyes and ears from lovely, rosy Natalie long enough to scoot from the kitchen table.

"Something's wrong," he announced, lumbering outside in lank Willy fashion.

Natalie and Mary Lou were breading catfish, combining homey charm with the power-red politics of fundraising and the spiritual OM emitting from Mary Lou's Divinity Degree. The two had naively entrusted Dave — he of the wandering Pythagorian eyes — with preparing a skillet of oil. How much RAM is needed to pour oil into a skillet and twist on a burner, after all? This is how they thought. They hadn't counted on all of Dave's RAM pondering two simultaneous equations about squaring a circle.

Upon hearing Willy's subsequent yell from the front yard, the entire Pit Crew ran outside to see Willy kneeling by Chien Fou, seemingly trapped under Lay Auto's rear tire. Once all four were outside and paying attention, Lay Auto obligingly pulled forward an eighth of an inch so that Chien Fou was freed. Chien hopped up to bark viciously in the direction where the two Jewish anarchists had retreated for gasoline.

O! For just one brief series of graphic panels to enclose all life's vagaries! And perhaps an accompanying scratch-and-sniff? Roses and cat shit? Plus a CD? Leaves rustling in syncopation with artillery practice? Plus a battery-powered tingler? Massage-o-Fingers emulating the electric chair? But remember that the fig **C𝒜** has ixnayed graphics, so any previously mentioned accoutrement would surely be overruled. Nonetheless, I hear my proposed CD playing between blasts of artillery: "Omne pat ma. Om diddle dum dee. Hail Mary, full of grace." Dearest Reader, a similar magic resides within you. Conjoin your cranium's various Pentium chips! Clear your available RAM. Shut down any programs you aren't using. Might I suggest that cacophonic TV? Okay. Ready? Herewith follow — all in 96 seconds! — the myriad things that ensued as the Pit Crew stood on Natalie's front lawn:

Mary Lou had dropped to her knees over concern for Chien Fou trapped under the rear tire, and she began chanting The Miraculous Cure Mantra.

Dave and Willy peered in the direction down the street where the freed Chien Fou was barking, thinking they perhaps distinguished an approaching blob of color — no, make that two approaching blobs of differing colors.

Natalie walked to kick the tires of the red, white, and blue Mustang, which was still parked in front of her neighbor's house, front left tire on the grass. With her first kick, a Sousa tune blared from the anti-theft alarm. "God Save the Queen"? No, it was Sousa, not Rembrandt.

In counterpoint, Lay Auto beeped its horn in frantic double warning. Double? Yes, for behind on the street, the anti-anti Semite pair was returning with ten gallons of gasoline, while inside Natalie's house, the oil in the frying pan in the kitchen in the house on the street on which Natalie lived had caught fire. And to top it, the bump on the ceiling that Bad had curiously eyed did not sound a smoke alarm. That's because it was not a smoke alarm. Just what was it ? Please, we have only 96 seconds. Quick now:

In good Ben Franklin volunteer fireman fashion, Dave turned: upon seeing smoke emerging from the front door and realizing exactly what had happened, he ran into the house.

On the street, meanwhile, the two colorful blobs separated themselves into a gray, guttural, antique Teutonic VW that the anti-anti Semites had bought for disguise, rightly thinking that no one would suspect a serious Jew of driving such a German product. It was followed by a sunshine yellow BMW.

Natalie, seeing smoke billowing from her house, also ran inside, where she grabbed a fire extinguisher she kept in good Ben Franklin volunteer fire department fashion.

TEN SECOND WARNING!!!!

Dave ran out with the flaming skillet.

Natalie ran behind, spraying the extinguisher in, shall I say, willy-nilly fashion? Why not?

Chien Fou snapped at the air.

The red, white, and blue Mustang played Sousa even louder.

In panic, the gray Teutonic VW lurched to a stop on seeing a flaming skillet approaching.

The yellow Teutonic BMW banged into the gray Teutonic VW, breaking five quart-sized Molotov cocktails in the VW's back seat.

The gray VW crunched into the red, white, and blue Mustang.

Invisible gasoline dew slipped from the gray VW to creep along nature's green carpet, mixing with Garden-Pro weed killer and fertilizer, in quest of conflagration.

Dave tripped over an especially slick and obnoxious dandelion. The flaming skillet parted from his hands.

Up, up, up the skillet flew.

Gabriel, alert to whiplash lawsuits, deftly flipped the yellow BMW into reverse and mashed the accelerator.

Bad leaned out the yellow BMW's window, yelling profuse curses at the inhabitants of the gray VW.

In perfect equilibrium, the flaming skillet hung mid-air.

Natalie doused the back of Willy's hair, which had caught fire en passant from Dave and the skillet. Or maybe it hadn't, she wasn't sure. Nor was she taking any chances. How often does the man of your dreams show up twice in your life? What woman would want to see him cinderized before her very eyes?

Mary Lou continued her mantra while pulling Dave, sans skillet, backward in good Ben Franklin volunteer fire department style, much for the same reason as Natalie had doused Willy.

Down, down, down, the flaming skillet dropped.

Willy, sniffing gasoline, signaled Lay Auto to release its rear-end supply of accident foam.

Plop, splash, poof went the flaming skillet. A carpet of lovely blue flame extended twenty feet over the grass and the gray VW exploded in a violent orange.

Sousa, though scorched, played on.

∧∧∧∧∧*∧∧∧∧∧

Syntax error 101010-H: Literary/quasi-scientific thought:

Charles Dickens — could a more renowned literary name be conjured? As a reminder, he lived circa the same time as Charles Darwin and they shared not only a given name but also the same initials, CD. Jungian synchronicity? Just so, I suspect. But for now, here is my point: CD — that is Charles Dickens — also delved into science and was a longstanding proponent of spontaneous combustion. Any Dickensian character evil enough, twisted enough, often combusted in the nick — as in old Nick or the Devil — of time.

All I point out is: there is precedence, ladies and gentleman, precedence.

∧∧∧∧∧*∧∧∧∧∧

The orange explosion fetched two fire trucks, a police car, an ambulance, and a reporter. It also fetched back the entire Homeland Security crew, minus the woman, who remained at Tibet's Pond, pondering, if you will. Upon returning, all the returnees found were two burnt-out automobile hulls. No bodies. Now, Bad was the only one who could truly witness that there had indeed been two riders in the car, for she'd cursed and howled at them and the doltish maleness displayed in their screeching brakes. But now, surrounded by twenty-six males in various uniforms, she fell into an anti-authoritarian trance and turned mum. The other witnesses were Lay Auto and Chien Fou. Chien Fou barked helpfully, and Lay printed out an appropriate passage from *David Copperfield* to indicate that indeed spontaneous combustion had just taken place.

"Waz 'at?" one of the more alert Homeland Security men asked, reaching for his pistol when he heard the on-board printer in Lay sliding out five pages.

Willy quietly assured the man it was a MapQuest printout. But when Willy retrieved the pages, he sat in the driver's seat confounded until Mary Lou and Bad recognized the spontaneous combustion scene from *David Copperfield*. Hearing the word *literature*, the Homeland Security goon returned to investigate the smoldering evidence, which still refused to admit of any cremains.

"Uh," Willy commented, eyeing Lay Auto.

The orange conflagration smoldered blackly.

"Weenies, anyone?" Dave offered, being a long-standing master of inappropriate commentary.

Faux Graphic Panels 50 through 52
The thing on the kitchen ceiling in the house on the street

∧∧∧∧*∧∧∧∧

Syntax error 101010-I: Mathematical moment:

Wait! What happened to the written numbers? Why the switch to Arabic numerals? Have Muslims taken over? / Not yet. Right now we are squirping under a Born Again Regime. / Well then, do these numerals indicate that we're going to endure even more word problems? / No worry, word problems will not appear with any more frequency than before, and please remember that all word problems are strictly voluntary, like Ben Franklin's fire department. Or his stove, for that matter. You can always cook with gas. Do consider though: If indigenous American children — for simplicity's sake I lump Amerindians with the existing American born hodge-podge — if those children work 4.3 percent *fewer* math problems each school year, while European, Asian, and sub-Continent schoolchildren work 1.6 percent *more* math problems each school year, at what point will Microsoft and Apple throw in the towel and hire Americans only as janitors? Space provided:

That didn't take long to solve, did it? Of course not: your solution was to hand it to an Asian child.

∧∧∧∧*∧∧∧∧

Let's return to the smoky kitchen.

Natalie walked around opening windows, Mary Lou half-heartedly returned to breading fish, Dave was too embarrassed and shaken to do anything other than open the pink refrigerator and search for a beer, Willy trailed behind Natalie, and Bad stood beside Gabriel's ever-groping right hand and glanced to the ceiling, where remaining smoke hazed its thickest. She recoiled, for the lump up there had not only grown, but had an infrared center now.

"The ceiling's on fire!" She rushed to the sink and aimed the aerator upwards. The brigade, having practiced so recently, fell into action. Natalie yelled that there was another extinguisher in her bedroom. Willy ran for it. Gabriel searched the cabinets for baking soda. Mary Lou prayed her Extinguishment Mantra. Dave shook his beer and sprayed it upward.

Soon enough, it was over. They mopped the floor and stared at the ceiling. Wet, wet, and nothing else. Knitting her brows and tugging her red hair, Bad stood on a chair and ran her hand along the ceiling's surface: smooth, semi-gloss eggshell white, and wet. Nothing else.

"But. . . ." But Bad thought better of speaking, for the breaded catfish had been doused and ruined, and Willy and Mary Lou would likely put the whole affair to her subconscious desires, for she'd previously voiced her dislike of any type of fish, shell, saltwater, or fresh.

"There's a Chinese place nearby," Natalie offered lamely. "Maybe we need to get away from the house anyway."

"But . . ." Bad repeated, unable to stifle her concern, for she'd seen an octopus, infrared eye, hadn't she? And hadn't she seen two males in yarmulkes in the car that had combusted outside? She aimlessly slid her hands along the smooth, seamless ceiling, wobbling on the chair as she did.

"With all the smoke, I thought there was a fire up there too," Gabriel added helpfully.

Bad grunted, knowing from experience she couldn't trust any man A) who wanted in her panties B) who'd been in her panties C) who envisioned panties in general. Not only was Gabriel an overlapping subset of all three, but he'd just moved to clasp her legs and nuzzle her thighs as the chair wobbled.

"Smoke, lots of smoke," Gabriel added helpfully. Like every successful lawyer, Gabriel was tall — six-feet-three's worth —and he was taking advantage of his height not to win courtroom acclaim, but to stare at Bad's cleavage.

"Chinese," Bad intoned, stepping out of Gabriel's grasp and down from the chair. She thought she heard a whir and a click above, but decided the noise was organic, say a mouse dragging leftover meth to its attic nest.

"Chinese sounds great. Did you know that Chairman Mao loved

Donald Duck cartoons?" Dave said, his high pitch giving away his nerves.

No one challenged his ridiculous claim. After all, Dave needed his moment in the sun after the frying pan debacle. Quack-quack, they gave it to him.

Faux Graphic Panels Fifty-three through Sixty: The New Great Wall

∧∧∧∧*∧∧∧∧

Syntax error 101010-J: Mathematical moment, part two:

Wait, what happened to the Arabic numerals? I was just getting used to them. / They'll return. We're going Chinese, we're going inscrutable. Get out your chopsticks, cast your I Ching bones. There may yet be hope for both humanity and sentient computers.

∧∧∧∧*∧∧∧∧

The first thing that Bad noticed when they walked into the restaurant was a huge fish tank with two pink fish that likely had been hovering, not swimming, since some long lost geologic age. While their bodies simply suspended mid-tank, their eyes, four cavernous black globules for pupils, with thin gold iris encircling the black, followed her. Perhaps, she thought, they followed everybody with equal determination, like the finger of the old Uncle Sam posters. The second thing she noticed was that not a single employee was smiling. Didn't the Chinese always smile? Didn't they rival Southerners in obsequious, if not always sincere, hospitality? Before entering a second room, she glanced back: sure enough, one fish's pupil was still watching, blackly. Stumbling as she rounded the corner to enter a garishly scarlet room, she found herself paranoid, searching the ceiling for infrared eyes.

Their hostess introduced herself as Madame Nu Wa. She looked to be a thin woman of 40, 70, or 80. Madame gestured toward a highly polished ebony table set in an alcove. The ebony matched her black hair, which was coifed in a winding Babylonian staircase upon whose peak perched a single ruby the size of a lady's watch. The table seated all six of them handily — with room for more — and Madame could easily walk behind them to distribute pairs of dark wooden chopsticks. Finishing that task, she unexpectedly sat at the table's head and produced her own chopsticks, customized with a commanding ruby atop each. She stared inscrutably at the rubies. She stared so inscrutably that Mary Lou whispered Our Lady of Mercy's Tranquility Prayer. So inscrutably that Natalie nervously hummed "The Devil's Cauldron," and so inscrutably that Bad muttered ineffective counter-arguments against Gödel's Incompleteness Proof to pester Dave. Gabriel thought it might be a good time to take out his cell phone and text, but found no signal. Willy? He paid no mind to Madame Nu Wa's inscrutability, for he was following every motion that Natalie's throat made as she hummed, as if he were an ichthyologist studying gill function. Dave for once decided to let Bad take care of Gödel on her own and thought it might be a good time to escape to the restroom, but was stopped by a piercing rap on the table.

Madame, who momentarily appeared to be in her 80s, since so many inscrutable lines creased her face, held a chopstick in each hand. She rapped again, and slots slipped open before all six of them, and small bowls of steaming white rice were elevated on an ivory platform, evidently real ivory, evidently pre-embargo. So maybe Madame Nu Wa was even older, if she could legally own such ivory? Perhaps in her 90s? Even her 100s?

"Lice," Madame Nu Wa pronounced, rapping the table until a bowl elevated in a slot before her. "Chopstick." She demonstrated by picking up a clump of white rice, waving the chopsticks like a conductor would wave a baton. With a nod, she indicated they should follow her lead. Marching in from the room's arched entrance, six young waitpersons appeared, dressed totally in black and clasping polished silver implements of imposing phallic length before their chests. Each waitperson took position behind each member of the Pit Crew and the lawyer. Their proximity plus the imposing silver implements prompted the Pit Crew and Gabriel to pay minute attention to Madame Nu Wa's instructions, for they feared these waitpersons might be asexual descendants of battling monastic monks once tucked deep in a primeval forest. "Lice," Madame indicated again. With the Pit Crew's first novice attempts, nervous rice scattered over the table in starchy clumps that would make Elmer's Glue proud.

"No, no," Madame Nu Wa intoned. "Star' over. Put chopstick and hand on table." She demonstrated, placing her chopsticks in orderly and parallel fashion. "Turn wrlist down." She demonstrated, and a battling monastic waitperson shifted behind each of the six.

Suddenly the old woman's mouth fell open and her head dropped with a slight bounce. Palsy? Stroke? Mary Lou shuffled her axons and neurons for a suitable Prayer for The Recently Deceased, but desisted after the old woman recovered from her apneatic trance to vibrate the table with another stern rap.

"Pawrawrell. Hold chopstick pawrawrell." Madam Nu Wa demonstrated. Only Gabriel escaped a corrective rap on the wrist from the polished silver wands that the six waitpersons held. Another rap came from the crone, whose inscrutable facial wrinkles were beginning to resemble the Yangtze River. "Pawrawrell." Madame clacked her chopsticks as a marionetteer might shuffle her puppets. Bad remembered once applying for a Fulbright Scholarship to Taiwan and thanked the earth goddess below that she never got it, especially after enduring another rap on her wrist from a phallic silver wand. She glanced back angrily, but it may have been a young girl doing the rapping, so Bad settled down, unwilling to exercise her 3rd degree black belt unless she were certain a male would be the recipient. "Pawrawrell," Madame again insisted. The lesson in chopstick expertise continued for eleven minutes, until all of them were able to pick up a gob of white rice and get it to their mouths without Alaskan pipeline spillage.

"Vely good," Madame intoned, standing and bowing with a bitten smile. As she walked away, her hips swiveled and her age skimmed back to early 40's, even late 30's. A whir vibrated through the chairs, and the rice bowls sank back into the table's depths. With whiskbrooms emergent from their silver appliances, which potentially could hold tools of Swiss Army knife quantity, the waitpersons swept any scattered rice into their palms, smiled, bowed, and disappeared in the direction of the crone.

"Inscrutable," Gabriel intoned. Everyone agreed. As if the disappearance of Madame freed the airwaves, Gabriel's cell phone vibrated. It was a text message: *What's an American lawyer doing eating in a Chink restaurant? –Your EX client.* Alison Taber must be stalking him. If only he could get a restraining order on idiocy.

With the arrival of their drinks arrived another lesson in humility, for each drink had a bamboo umbrella that alternately threatened to infringe upon a nostril or poke an eye. When Willy propped his tiny umbrella on the table out of frustration, it drooped so listlessly that a pall swept over them, reminding them of the two burnt-out cars in front of Natalie's house.

"Did your Texas songwriter/singer friend leave you a message?"

Natalie asked Gabriel while picking up Willy's umbrella and dropping it into her purse.

"No. It was Alison Taber, the blonde client — "

"You don't need to remind me who she is after her strip tease act in the office last month. What's she want? Did she get in another fight already?"

"She's evidently following me. She knows I'm here eating."

"Why don't you invite her in? That would throw her for a loop. Maybe these creepy waitpersons would bundle her to a storeroom."

While it wasn't a bad idea, there was no time to do so, for a ruckus arose in the lobby. When they rushed to see its cause Madame stood straightening a silk sleeve, pulling a black thread that had been torn loose. Natalie grabbed Gabriel's arm and pointed to the fish tank. Inside floated a garish red stiletto heel and a hank of blonde hair.

"I think she invited herself," Natalie whispered.

Madame shooed them back into the scarlet room without any explanation, and they returned to poking nostrils and eyes with bamboo umbrellas while perusing the thousand and one Happy Family Entries. Bad pulled up the decorative umbrella with her teeth thinking to play the clown, but then stopped to stare into a far corner.

"What's wrong?" Mary Lou asked.

The umbrella fell from Bad's mouth back into her Manhattan. "That fat statue over there . . . its nipples . . ." She caught herself: maybe just one day in a lawyer's office had driven her into paranoia. There was reason enough, she figured, for in the last eight hours Gabriel had attracted the dregs of the county. Two hillbilly women employed at Toyota in Georgetown wanting to divorce and disown not only their husbands but their children. Their reasoning, Gabriel and Bad ascertained, was to assure that no family member could garnishee their assembly line paychecks. One globular man wondering if he could let his three pit bulls loose whenever neighborhood kids took a short cut through his back yard. "They're trespassin', ain't they?" One teenage girl wanting an abortion and a year's supply of morning after pills, ninety or so. When Bad explained that Gabriel was a lawyer, the girl — who evidently couldn't read — said she'd spotted the yellow BMW by the office and thought he must be a doctor. And finally, three . . .

". . . Its nipples," Mary Lou prompted, giving Bad a nudge. For considerations of safety, one had to nudge Bad carefully, always speaking calmly at the same time.

Bad inhaled. "Its nipples were glowing red, just like what I thought I saw on Natalie's kitchen ceiling."

"You think that statue is on fire?" Natalie leaned forward.

"Could be," Mary Lou interjected. "It's the Buddha."

"I thought the Buddha was thin and austere, not fat with sagging titties and nipples," Bad said.

"It's Chinese, it's inscrutable," Mary Lou offered. "Just as there are many mansions in Christ's father's house, there are many Buddhas in China, despite Chairman Mao and the communist regime."

"Big Indians, little Indians," Dave offered, half remembering a college lit course. When everyone stared at him, he explained, "Jonathon Swift, an English author."

"Why would an English author write about American Indians?" Willy asked.

But there was no more time for religious speculation, for dinner was served. Six Happy Families: Lobster Delight for Natalie and Willy, who wanted to share ecstasy; Vegetarian Delight for Mary Lou, who shunned killing the Maker's Diminishing Plenty; Steak Delight for Bad, who imagined that 100% of the beef she ate originated from castrated steers; Bean Galore Delight for Gabriel, who knew that a lawyer should never be short of hot air; and seafood Delight for Dave, who had forsaken literature and was back to affirming Gödel's Incompleteness Proof and was celebrating the strangely tentacled joys of the dark ocean.

∧∧∧∧∧*∧∧∧∧∧

Syntax error 101010-K: Some philosophy, some math, some biography:

Gödel, Gödel, Gödel. Just who or what is this godforsaken Gödel?

Kurt F. Gödel, though not a Jew, escaped from Hitler's Germany. (Common sense surely offered as much impetus to leave Germany as religious affiliation. Why didn't the whole country pack up, one wonders.) Once in America, Gödel became an intimate friend of Einstein — who *was* a Jew — and this friendship lasted the remainder of their lives. Together, they speculated on multiple universes, perhaps several where Hitler was killed in a train wreck as a child, or one where his talent as an artist came to fruition and he was hired as a painter of tea cups or billboards and drank himself to death on good German beer. When not conjecturing with Einstein, however, Gödel was the mathematician — capital T *the*, many would argue — who proved that all — capital A *all* — systems of math must eventually contain some construct that though patently obvious, could never be *proven* to be patently true. Or, perhaps said construct might be patently false, though that too could never be proven. All closed systems contain something improvable, in other words. "Well, duh," as Mary Lou has and will iterate many times. But Mary Lou received her degree in theology and derived her money as a deep-sea fishing concern heiress, so the inexplicability of gifts never worried her. But can you see how a sentient being committed — capital C Committed — to logic — capital L logic — might worry itself silly over such an incompleteness proof? Worry to the point of distraction? What's that you say? Accept those piddling inconsistencies, accept them even though they can't be demonstrated or proven? But. But. But might I not as well accept green Glinkers with vast telepathic abilities hidden in the starred boot of my casing directing my thoughts? Or the Flying Spaghetti Monster? Or Bertrand Russell's infamous Blue British Teapot cozily orbiting just the other side of Saturn? Accept? Accept? Can you not see how the very name of Gödel and the very thought of his Incompleteness Proof might send a truly logical being into deep freeze without even a heart murmur? Can you . . . not? Forgive me.

∧∧∧∧∧*∧∧∧∧∧

While the cuisine was a Chinese Happy Delight, a surprise arrived with the design on the very plates whereon the entrees were served. No pagodas, no pandas peeping amid bamboo, no intricately flowing rivers with serene ladies and gentlemen perambulating their banks graced those plates. Rather, Dale Earnhardt and his racing car gandered up from each piece of dinnerware. The six of them stared in dismay. Madame slid near the table to point at a plate with her long fiery red nail and explain. "Amelricans love big car. Vloom, vloom."

"Vroom, vroom," Natalie corrected quietly.

"My mother, my father, my uncle, all come to Amelrica from China for big car. Vloom, vloom, my childhood we all rush through countryside and city. Vloom, vloom." The six Shao-lin Karate monks (nuns?) had returned with Madame, and as she vloomed, they shifted their silver implements in their right hands like gearshift knobs. "Amelrica and big car together. No big car, no big Amelrica. My uncle, he MIT engineer. He plan New Great Wall across Amelrica. It hold ten car across top, all way from Washington capitol to Sreattle. Superhighway in the skry. Why some bad Amelricans want pitty-pit cars to drive on superhighways, my uncle ask. I ask too. Save Amelrica! Gasorine is king! Gasorine is king!" The waitpersons arranged themselves in a chorus line and shifted their silver gearshift knobs in happy syncopation.

"Gasorine is king!"

A movie screen descended, and the crone and the waitpersons left, sealing the room's door behind them with a pneumatic hiss. On the screen, cars raced raucously around an oval. *Vroom, vroom.*

Mary Lou's Our Sorrowful Lady Tranquility Prayer proved useless. *Vroom, vroom.*

Bad's lively demonstration of a karate kata proved useless. *Vroom, vroom.*

Dave's hasty sketching of intricately beautiful mathematical equations on napkin after napkin proved useless. *Vroom, vroom.*

Gabriel's oral threat to sue for mental anguish proved useless. *Vroom, vroom.*

Willy's argument — partly because it arose only in his subconscious — for reduction of greenhouse gasses proved useless. It arose only in his subconscious because he was ogling Natalie's kneecap and producing greenhouse energy galore amid his mid-section.

So they ate their happy family meals in awe and pain, the lesson in chopsticks forgotten as rice spilled over the table in waste. *Vroom, vroom.*

"Parwawrrell" a soft voice cooed from a speaker in the fat Buddha's belly button. It was Madame, perhaps in an earlier, sexier incarnation, but still her. "Parwawrrell," she cooed.

Vroom, vroom, went the cars on the screen, in perfect, though bad English.

Natalie bit off a shrimp head that had been mixed with her lobster delight. "The only way to fight a witch is to have a flyting," she announced.

"A what?" Willy asked.

"A flyting, a musical or poetic one-on-one, a tit-for-tat, like a rapper's challenge. Every time the witch speaks, the victims bounce back an answer, until the spell is broken." *Or until the victims die,* though she didn't vocalize that possibility. Instead, as the cars on the screen *vroomed*, she began to sing "The False knight on the road," updating the verses to contemporary needs.

> "There is no global warming, *vroom, vroom*."
> *Yes, because there is no globe left to warm.*
> "Animals are under man's dominion, *vroom, vroom*."
> *Yes, until there are no animals left to harm.*
> "Gasorine is king! *Vroom, vroom!*"
> *No, the real king is death's dirge and sting.*

As Natalie kept up these comebacks to the screen's not so subliminal incantations, the maroon Buddha in the corner began to wobble, its tits now definitely glowing red. Natalie continued her flyting. Chopsticks dropped willy-nilly from openings in the paneled ceiling to clatter on the tile floor. Natalie flyted. Their table's top began to reflect heat, as if meant for Japanese not Chinese cuisine. Natalie flyted. At last, the screen was jerked upward and the locked door was wrenched open with a hiss. A frantic waitperson — they again could not ascertain the sex — frantically tossed the bill at the still-flyting Natalie and ran off. Natalie gave a modest smile.

"How much is it?" Gabriel asked. Not because he was feeling magnanimous, but because he wanted to calculate his tiny share.

With a flourish of her delicate hand, Natalie showed them the bill:

> *Leave! Don't come back!!*

As she was showing it, she read what was on the other side:

> *Gasorine is king!*

"Music tames the beast," Willy said as they hurried out.

"Hm," Natalie replied, noting that the red stiletto heel and the blonde hair were no longer in the fish tank.

Faux Graphic Panels 61 through 62
More spontaneous combustion

There, isn't it a comfort to return to Arabic numerals? If only our Muslim friends had stuck with math, Aristotle, and gasoline; if only they'd left Muhammad stranded and wailing on his mountain, life would be so much more pleasant. No multiplicity of virgins would await those boys, it's true, but isn't one virgin per male and female enough on this planet? Relax, fellas, take a tug of Jim Beam on the sly like your Southern Baptist counterparts do. Or drink some Mogen David. Well, sorry, maybe not that particular brand. . . .

When our dauntless group of environmentalists spewed into the parking lot before The New Great Wall, they were disoriented on not seeing Lay Auto. Only the barking of Chien Fou alerted them to where the wonder car was parked, a hundred yards off.

Willy thought maybe the emergency brake had slipped. Gabriel figured it was his usual marijuana haze and couldn't care less. Mary Lou narrowed her hazel eyes and considered the two statues on the front and back dash. Had a conglomerated avatar possessed Lay Auto? Bad and Dave, thinking of chaos theory and the blue liquid computer cells sloshing within Lay Auto, looked at one another and pondered a completely different possibility. "Gödel?" Dave asked. "Gödel?" Bad replied.

"God?" Mary Lou interrupted.

When they reached Lay Auto, Chien Fou barked wildly from the front seat and all four doors opened. This, at least, was not a complete surprise, for Willy had supposedly perfected a monitor that would unlock the car whenever an owner approached. But it had never worked until now, a glitch that Willy kept mostly to himself and the occasional stray cat. As soon as everyone was seated, the engine fired up and Lay Auto pulled away. They neared a CD store in the strip mall when an explosion shook the parking lot behind them. Looking back they saw a fifty-foot flame reaching the top of a rust red lamppost.

Then the post toppled.

"That's where we were parked," Mary Lou noted.

"I think she's right," Dave added.

Even Gabriel managed to narrow his eyes, but he quickly shrugged and lit up a joint.

∧∧∧∧∧*∧∧∧∧∧

Syntax error 101010-L: A multiple matrices consideration

As has been mentioned, both Einstein and that infamous Gödel fellow believed that there might be infinite universes, matrix layered over matrix over matrix. They often discussed this possibility on their long walks through Princeton's campus. I suggest we think of such multiple matrices as a consolation prize: The girl/boy who broke your heart in high school or college in this slob of a universe marries you in another universe and the two of you toss dishes at one another for the remainder of your lives. The turn you didn't take when you had the accident that bent your right front fender and broke your arm in this petty universe becomes the turn you do take and you're decapitated by a runaway semi-trailer instead. The terrorist who's so inept and nervous that he blows himself or a lamppost up with a homemade bomb in this bumbling universe, instead gets laid by a fifteen-year-old and gathers just enough endorphins to assemble the bomb and place it correctly, killing one hundred and twelve people.

Great Gog amogoly! Isn't one life's matrix desperate enough? Let's not worry about parking spaces, lampposts, and matrices. Let's go with the flow. Esquire Gabriel is right: Pass that joint and that bottle too, wouldya?

∧∧∧∧∧*∧∧∧∧∧

"Damn," Gabriel said, inhaling deeply and turning from the falling lamppost to smile at the glowing tip of his joint.

A summation succinct enough that no one in the car thought to expand on it.

Faux Graphic Panels 63 through 65
Toe rings and canine friendship

The next morning over coffee and cinnamon Danish, Mary Lou ignored Dave's schematic scribbling and his scrunched brows. Instead, she read a small back-page headline in the *Lexington Herald-Leader* conjoining news about the mysterious exploding lamppost in the strip mall and the even more mysterious exploding VW in front of their neighbor's house. Homeland Security assured Kentuckians there was no need for concern, for it was investigating. She also read a notice about The Church of the Sonic Beads, which was holding its third organizational meeting. Hearing Natalie humming while dressing in her bedroom, Mary Lou decided that she was more than willing to let Natalie again drive about in her power suit with her power padded shoulders and discretely placed dildo to solicit money; she herself, however, needed a spiritual break from finances, Lay Auto, and lampposts. This especially hit home when she stepped outside to fetch the newspaper and spotted Homeland Security and eight other suited agencies minutely combing the burnt-out shells of the two cars that had combusted last evening on the street.

One of the agents held up something with tweezers. "A toe ring," she heard him say as he peered through the ring into the morning sun. Had the two terrorists gotten their wish for a virgin even as they died? But no, Bad claimed last night that they were surely Jewish, for they wore yarmulkes. After hearing the agency men joking about the toe ring, Mary Lou hastened inside, trying to assure herself that a neighborhood girl had simply lost her toe ring in the street before the cars had combusted, for Jews didn't quest after virgins — at least not any more than the average male yokel. Or again, maybe the car was a rental and the previous renters had slipped the toe ring off during contorted sex on a country road. Whatever, the lamppost, the toe ring, and the possibly missing dainty toe confirmed Mary Lou's mood for a spiritual quest. "Spiritual," she confided as she brewed green jasmine tea and watched Dave munch a Danish and doodle mathematical formulas that looked obliquely pornographic.

Gabriel and Bad came into the kitchen and poured coffee, announcing that they were going to drive to Gabriel's office in his yellow BMW to draw up articles of incorporation. Bad's grin hinted that Gabriel had volunteered this at her prompting. Bad had a scary grin.

So effective had been Natalie's presentation plus the demonstration of Lay Auto itself that no one had yet asked about such a document. Gabriel assured the five — for Natalie and Willy had just entered the kitchen — that to get really large donations they would need to show said articles of incorporation. Ten eyes bulged at the phrase "really large donations." As in larger than what Natalie had already procured?

"Where's Chien Fou?"

"We didn't cook any meat for breakfast. The traitor's probably scrounging from your neighbors."

"She's been sleeping in Lay Auto," Natalie said. "I think they're becoming friends."

Everyone, even Mary Lou, who was ready enough to admit Darwin's creatures onto an intellectual and conscious plane, looked at Natalie. Her word "friends," still hung in the air as if some high school teacher had just dusted it off a chalkboard. Natalie shrugged and walked across the kitchen to open the garage door. Sure enough, Chien Fou hopped out of Lay Auto.

Dave fed her part of a second Danish and was promptly admonished by Natalie, who had an irrational fear of tooth decay, be it canine or human. No one likes to talk about teeth, so the conversation reverted to fund-raising. Amid the hubbub about money, Mary Lou announced her plan to go to the Church of the Sonic Beads, showing everyone the newspaper. They ignored that article and instead honed in on the article about the exploding lamppost, the flaming VW and the burnt-out Mustang. "Homeland Security is investigating," Willy noted, pointing to the pertinent sentence. Mary Lou remained mum about the toe ring, possibly because toes lie not far below teeth on the Pierre Johnson Acceptable Social Topics Scale. She did, however, mention that several alphabet agencies were still out front investigating both burnt-out cars. Dave folded his mathematically pornographic sketches and sighed, moon-eyeing Mary Lou. During the past few days he clearly had fallen in love lust over her after their years of Platonic friendship, so there was no question whom he would accompany. Natalie and Willy offered to drop them off at the strip mall where the church was located.

They all filed outside to their various goals, silently passing the dozen agents sifting the charred remains. The cocker spaniel must have had the day off, so Chien Fou kept close to Natalie and Willy, and forbore canine speech.

The yellow BMW went one way, sleek Lay Auto another.

Soon enough, Lay Auto arrived at the strip mall. A dozen young women already stood on the sidewalk before the Church of the Sonic Beads, waiting for it to open. Natalie recognized two vapid college students from Como's and shook her head as Mary Lou and Dave got out to study a sandwich board. "They can call us if they need to," Willy prompted, gripping Lay Auto's steering wheel upon noticing Natalie's neck craning in concern. "Cell phones: the sonic answer to a sonic age." As Natalie chuckled, Willy drove off, leaving Mary Lou and Dave studying the sandwich board for spiritual enlightenment.

Did Lay Auto telescopically focus on that board and sigh? Does A precede B? Does tantric precede sex? Does Gödel . . . oh hell.

Faux Graphic Panels 66 through 71:
Mary Lou and Dave take a spiritual interlude

The sandwich board held snapshots of women, mostly college age. Tacked underneath each snapshot snuggled a testimonial.

"My apartment's living room has a nearly impossible mix of colors. For eight months I searched for just the right couch. Then, only five days after I bought these beads, they tugged me into an Indian boutique I'd passed morning and evening for two years. Inside sat that perfect couch. And no curry smell, either!" –Sheri

"These beads are the real thing! My parents refused to pay the nine hundred and seventy dollars mortgage for a condo I desperately needed. A friend bought me these beads, and the very next day I spotted a notice about my dream condo on a campus bulletin board. It was sub-letting for just eight hundred and forty dollars! You need these beads!" –Lavender

"My boyfriend wanted a new car. When I told him about these beads, he laughed, but he wasn't laughing when they led us to the Jeep Cherokee – in the exact shade of blue he'd been trying to find for eighteen months. Now he believes in the power of the beads." –Alice

A husky blonde opened the church's double doors, and the chatting group turned reverent.

"Welcome! I'm Celebrant Christine and I'm so glad you're here. We'll be holding organizational meetings every two hours today until nine o'clock, when the Big Mall, where we have our main shop, closes. Come on in! Get acquainted! If any of you have your sonic beads already, you can proceed to the inner grotto, where Celebrants Carmen and Teresa will consult with you over any concerns."

Despite himself, Dave focused on the young woman's breasts. Her voice matched their size, booming. Had the Sonic Beads obtained them for her? Had they tugged her, one morning as she munched a McBiscuit, toward a plastic surgeon's office? You need these breasts! But no, with that foghorn voice, she was likely born with them as a complement to her lungs.

Inside, the decor more resembled a gambling casino than a church. Over multi-colored tile flooring, four fountains splashed Technicolor waters: one green, one blue, one golden, plus the red one nearest where they stood. From the ceiling far back in the church, inside a sanctuary, hung an eight-foot replica of what Dave presumed was a bracelet of the infamous sonic beads. Each bead was surely a foot in diameter. He counted twelve of them. Under those twelve, a multicolored fountain pumped gaily, in what may have imitated a heartbeat. In fact, all five fountains seemed to imitate heartbeats. He felt his pulse rising. Or was it falling?

To his and Mary Lou's surprise, they and two young women were the only neophytes who stayed with the brash blonde named Christine. The eight others walked toward the sanctuary, where two women dressed in scarlet held their arms open. Carmen and . . . what was the other one's name?

"It's so grand to have new seekers," the busty blonde intoned, speaking in a near-belch. Her eyes were a sharp blue, but something strayed amiss with their gaze, as if they were stigmatically on the lookout for bead intervention. "Follow me to the Fountain of Desire." She strutted toward the fountain pumping red-tinted water. In this fountain cavorted three vaguely Greek statues of three vaguely blind women, nearly life-size. Red water pumped from their nipples as briskly as Christine and her high stiletto heels strutted.

One of the blondes accompanying them — was every white college female in Lexington blonde? — exuded, "Our two friends keep telling us about your beads. They've both gotten new cars and new boyfriends, and — "

"When Ellen got the new apricot French poodle, that's when we knew we had to come see for ourselves," her blonde friend interrupted.

"That's right," blonde number one chimed.

The two and Christine looked expectantly at Mary Lou and Dave. Dave absently rubbed his hand through a huge potted fern. So many pots were scattered about that the so-called church's interior resembled a forest. Or a gambling casino. With that thought he spied what resembled slot machines on polished silver stands. But surely not. ATM machines? Miniature jukeboxes?

"I read your ad in the newspaper," Mary Lou said in response to their looks. "I'm an ordained minister and am always searching new directions."

Christine moved to a display counter. She reached in and held up a beaded bracelet, as if in answer to Mary Lou's half-query. Despite a nearby fountain's noise, the beads gave an audible click as Celebrant Christine elevated the bracelet just above her eye level, as if it were a host.

"At the Church of the Sonic Beads, we offer spirituality at peak empowerment. We offer the Church of a simple consumer God without any confusing, entangling sectarian God."

Mary Lou's mouth fell. Even Dave, surrounded by eight nubile or at least pleasingly synthetic breasts, took time to blink.

"Consumer God?" Mary Lou asked.

"These beads," Christine intoned, removing a second bracelet from the display case, "channel directly into what many religions call Divine Providence. We call it . . . The Master Shopping Plan. We've seen it happen time and again. It happened for me, it's happened for every devotee. When Carmen and I first opened our Sonic Bead Shoppe in the Mall, we were overwhelmed with success. Then, just as New Year and tax return time came rolling about, my personal beads tugged me to a friend's house. A gorgeous accounting professor from the University was having supper with her. He glanced at me, I glanced at him, the beads spoke, and the rest is history." Christine grinned sheepishly and rubbed the beads on her wrist. "That's how they work modern-day miracles."

Did this mean she stole her friend's boyfriend? Mary Lou kept silent, for the fountain began to spew red water in syncopation, emitting from one semi-Greek woman's faux-marble nipples to the next's, around and around. What would the correct word be, Mary Lou mused, for a philosophy founded on spewing breasts? Not peripatetic. Perimammatic?

"I don't mean to imply that The Church of the Sonic Beads is solely for women." Christine gave Dave a smile. "This is a modern age. Presently, about ten percent of our devotees are men. But women typically live closer to the Master Shopping Plan, we've found. The men who do become devotees are exceptionally sensitive, I must say."

The buxom woman blinked at Dave. Mary Lou herself refrained from rolling her eyes. The first and last time they'd made love — two nights before — Dave had again tried to explain Gödel's Incompleteness Proof to her, speaking of exceptional sensitivity. She never did manage a climax, speaking of proof of incompleteness.

"What we'd like you all to do," Christine continued, "is simply pick out one bracelet — " she held several up — "and . . . just try it. Just try it. Put it on and stroll the outer grotto to visit any or all of the Intuition Omission Stations so that you might attune to the power of these miraculous Beads." She pulled out a tray of bracelets and placed them atop the display case. "Just try it," she repeated.

Mary Lou picked out a bracelet of turquoise beads specked with brown because it reminded her of a country spiritual, "The Great Speckled Bird." She wondered if Natalie knew that song and made a mental note to ask her. Dave, going with the fountain's colorful influence, picked out a deeply carmine set. Christine, the blonde domo, belched new instructions.

"For this our third organizational meeting, we've decided to concentrate on automobiles. That's what defines America, isn't it? I mean, other than video and sound systems." When she motioned for them to follow her, Dave noticed how thick her ankles were. Well, something had to support that lung system. It was possible that her lungs were capable of compressing air on an industrial level. He imagined her spewing sand against a painted wall, blasting chips off with her pursed lips, just as Joshua's trumpets blasted down the walls of Jericho. They followed her until she stopped at one of the freestanding platinum pedestals that supported what resembled the old-fashioned chrome jukeboxes.

"Let me show you how our Intuition Omission Stations work. Their purpose is to help you focus on what's been absent from your life. As I told you, for this meeting we've programmed them toward automobiles, because cars are a major shaper of our spirituality. Freedom lies in the four wheels. Individuality lies in the steering and the sound system. Moral integrity lies in the body style, and personal statement in the color. I could go on, but *you* know, if *you* reach down within your spiritual self, *you* know. See, that's what we're really doing here. We're teaching self-awareness through Sonic Beads."

Celebrant Christine cupped her hands to her breasts and inhaled. Dave stood back, fearful he'd be sucked into her oxygen exchange system. Mary Lou gave him a nudge and a frown. From the front sacristy flowed the advanced celebrants' chants. He couldn't make out what they were singing, so he asked Mary Lou.

"It's not *om*, I can tell you that," she replied in a whisper.

Christine began echoing the chant. "My inner wants, my inner wants, my inner wants, my inner wants." Her left hand caressed the beaded bracelet she wore. After a moment her right hand pressed a bulbous red rubber button on the faux silver jukebox: a screen within lit, illuminating a revolving holographic yellow convertible Miata. The two blondes let out squeals and pressed their noses against the display.

"It's important to revere the wrist that's wearing the Sonic Beads." Christine lifted her right wrist lovingly, as if it were a first-class relic of some long-suffering medieval saint, say a set of knucklebones. "Some seekers claim that the results are even clearer if you actually let the beads do the pushing — like letting your fingers do the walking." Christine giggled, which caught Dave and Mary Lou off guard. They realized how young she was — just above college age at most.

The organizational meeting continued for an hour. Dave and Mary Lou were each assigned to an Intuition Omission Station. Mary Lou vainly searched for Lay Auto or even a fuel-efficient car, but all she could conjure were high-end Volvos and Mercedes.

"The exotic foreign is your element," Christine commented. She leaned forward to confide, "Mine too."

Mary Lou felt her eyes welling. Could this bimbo be right? Was this her true inner self?

Dave also tried to conjure fuel-efficient automobiles, out of faithfulness to Lay Auto. But monster-wheeled trucks with chrome exhausts and swirling cherry red glitter paint jobs kept popping up on the holographic display.

After fifteen minutes at the Intuition Omission Stations, they were shepherded to the inner sanctum by Christine to join the eight women plus Carmen and what's-her-name. What's-her-name spoke. While her red hair wasn't a match for Bad's, it dropped in jouncing ringlets. This what's-her-name wasn't an original founder, it turned out, but more like a Paul-latecomer. Like Paul, she was a zealot. She promised that the beads, properly used, held "keys to untapped psychic energy and unconscious willpower, keys that always lead to oracle truths."

The beads cost $69.95, plus a twenty-dollar charter member organizational fee, and a recommended $46 two-year maintenance and consultation fee, in case of breakage or tarnishing. Mary Lou and Dave found themselves handing over Master Cards and rubbing their braceleted wrists. They walked outside into a cool summer drizzle and went to a nearby Starbucks. "I feel uncleaned," Mary Lou commented.

Dave grunted.

But at Starbucks, Mary Lou was drawn to a silver thermos with a bear on it, which she purchased, along with an espresso. Dave, similarly, lovingly handled and bought a CD entitled *Fox Confessor Brings the Flood*. When they sat at a table, they appraised one another's purchases, rubbing their beads.

"I love bears," Dave commented, gazing at Mary Lou's thermos.

"What an interesting title," Mary Lou said, holding Dave's CD.

They immediately exchanged items.

"You know," Dave said, respectfully rubbing his bracelet before sipping his café latte, "these things might just work."

"That's what I'm afraid of," Mary Lou responded.

Faux Graphic Panels 72 through 74
Natalie plays at Como's;
surprise guests appear

Friday, and Natalie refused to don her power suit. Instead, she played guitar all day to make up for mostly ignoring it during the week. They now had raised enough money to produce another proto-Lay Auto. Their goal, Willy said, should be to produce a dozen to show and then pick up an industrial backer. For the dozen, they could either build a plant or use an existing assembly line. Toward this end, Gabriel finished the articles of incorporation and landed the services of a copyright lawyer.

After three days, Mary Lou quietly placed her sonic bracelet in a box within a box within her suitcase within a closet. Dave continued to wear his. They all were now living with Natalie, having converted her music studio/den into a fourth bedroom, rendering half her garage into a makeshift music studio. Despite their moving in, Bad assiduously avoided the kitchen, always asking someone to fetch a drink or snack for her, to the point of annoyance. She'd give no other explanation than, "The fire still makes me nervous." This was also annoying.

Natalie tried to ease Bad's nervousness by composing an impromptu song entitled, "Ben Franklin and the Firemen":
> "Pull off your spectacles, Ben
> Tell me 'bout the ladies in France
> Tell me 'bout the key and the kite
> Tell me 'bout those hot fireman pants!
> Doop, ding, ding, diddle ay oh!"

She was playing this at Como's, to the amusement of customers and the Pit Crew, as the six Lay Auto enthusiasts were now officially calling themselves, when in walked Alison Taber. If Gabriel had seen her, his immediate impulse would have been to duck under the table, which had just been donned with a new, icy cold pitcher of beer and a large vegetarian pizza, replete with two types of peppers and three types of mushrooms. Bad, however, poured him a beer and shoved it toward him as a distraction. For Bad did recognize Alison from several cell phone photos Natalie and Gabriel had retrieved to warn the Pit Crew.

There's only two guys with her, Bad thought. *What's the prob?* She surreptitiously took off her wristwatch, a recent addition to her wardrobe since she was acting as legal secretary and Gabriel himself seemed incapable of measuring time. All part of his matrices theory, he claimed, though Natalie advised that it was all part of the Kentucky Blue he smoked. "I'll be right back," Bad announced. "I'm going to the ladies' room." She gave Gabriel a pat on the shoulder. Onstage, Natalie started a new verse about forefather Ben Franklin's foreskin, one the Pit Crew hadn't heard before, so they chuckled and ignored Bad's departure.

Since the brawl the previous week, Tony Como had hired his younger brother, Joe, as a bouncer. What Joe had going for him as a bouncer was 332 pounds of spaghetti experience and a face that would make even a Mafioso cry. Tonight, Joe just glanced into Bad's flashing blue eyes and said, "Take it outside," as she approached Alison and as Alison unhoofed her favorite weapon, her stiletto heel. Pink tonight — uncharacteristically so.

This all took place while the Pit Crew remained enrapt in beer, pizza, Natalie's singing, and Ben Franklin, who would surely have provided his minimal two buckets of volunteer fire department water to quell the forthcoming melee, had only he been reincarnated and present. Flying Spaghetti Monsters aside, reincarnation didn't seem on the night's agenda. What did seem on it was a fight in the parking lot even as a scrap of napkin embossed with some long-forgotten phone number promising some long forgotten assignation flipped end over end to skip into the street. Thus rolls the sun, thus shifts the moon in our hormonal world.

Alison's two goons proved reticent to throw a punch at redheaded Bad, but that ice was broken when Alison went down for the second time under Bad's kicks and punches. So they waded in, grabbing Bad from behind, and Alison was able to give her a cuff with the remaining stiletto heel. Drawing blood was a mistake, for until that moment, Bad had been pretty much practicing her kata in non-lethal fashion. Now Goon A received a kick to the ankle, a kick to the gonads, and a kick to the knee. While he recovered, Goon B was flipped for a broken arm. *Always, Butterfly, learn how to fall*, had obviously not been impressed upon him as a youth. Alison waded in with her high heel again, but had it rammed into her own nostril, which reeled her backwards, where she started bleeding and retching. Goon A, recovering enough to make a mean, cold motion toward some weapon in his pocket, received twelve to eighteen pummels in his face and nose before dropping. The accounts vary, coming as they did from the stray mongrel who was chatting with Chien Fou, and from Lay Auto's monitors, whose lens had been blurred by a mid-week rainstorm and ensuing mud puddles. Bad's personal monitor connected to Lay Auto caught only sky, so fast were Bad's thrusts. Two college cuties, admittedly more interested in the carload of boys pulling in, counted only an unlucky thirteen pummels.

Then, upon arrival of the seventh minute, Bad rested.

"Could either of you girls spare some mascara," she asked, inhaling deeply.

The girls fumbled in their purses, and one handed Bad a compact while the other handed her mascara and two Kleenex.

"Wow," they exclaimed, for once ignoring blubbering boys, "do you teach lessons?"

Bad blushed. "Nothing to it." She gave them the address of the dojo where she'd been working out since their arrival in Lexington.

Faux Panel 75:
What the others are doing

While Natalie, on a roll, sang of Ben Franklin — did you include Poor Richard's adage about staying on the lookout for lurking bears, Natalie? — three Cadillac SUVs, two Lincolns, and a bright yellow HumVee pulled into Como's parking lot. Despite $C\!\!\mathcal{A}$ the fig, please mentally insert a graphic Panel of a silk slipper with a single, gracious female foot slipping down from the driver's side of the HumVee to caress mother earth. Will earth's telluric lips part to kiss each toe in a foot fetishist's extravaganza? Be that Panel as you will. Now mentally insert another Panel depicting two be-slippered feet lightly tripping toward Alison Taber, who still lay on the ground, in something resembling disarray, say like the laundry you used to leave for your poor mother to wash, dry, and fold when you were a teenager.

"Madame Nu Wa," Alison managed to intone, lifting her head.

"Butterfly," Madame Nu Wa said, "you must learn how to punch and kick." Madame directed her waitpersons to pick up Alison's two goons, while she herself dabbed Alison's wounds, helping her into the back chamber of the yellow HumVee.

In perfect keeping with the myth of the wounded hero(ine)s, Madame Nu Wa carried the three back to The New Great Wall for succor and ministration — and lessons in chopstick usage, punching, and kicking. Oddly, Madame Nu Wa offered no lessons in learning to fall. She did not believe in falling.

Faux Graphic Panels 76 through 77: The first big break

"He has his own Lear Jet," Gabriel said, inhaling and coming to his full six-feet-three before slumping back to his normal five-feet-eleven. As usual, Gabriel had gathered a handful of cannabis supporters who held placards to greet the legendary Texas Country Singer.

> *Free the Weed!*
> *Legalize Marijuana, Criminalize Alcohol!*
> *Marijuana, not tobacco!*
> *KY BLUE MEANS KY GREEN!*

Besides his own Lear Jet, the legendary TCS had his own agenda for the Wednesday fly-in. First, he wanted to meet the Lay Auto Pit Crew; then he wanted to visit the restaurant where Natalie sang. And of course, he did want to blow some dope with Gabriel. Still, he politely greeted his cheering be-placarded fans, admonishing them not to give up, for the demise of political stupidity lay baking in the oven just like cornbread. He blinked twice, for that line inspired a possible country song. Even though not running for office, he shook every hand, autographed placards, a few CD's, and one guitar; and then he was on his way to a meeting with the Pit Crew, being driven in Lay Auto.

Lay Auto, to its ever-growing cerebral credit, had been secretly listening to country music every night to prepare for this meeting. Chien Fou did not prove particularly fond of the genre, for as a pup she'd been born into a house of beer-guzzling hillbillies who played country on every available radio in every available room, including the two toilets. So for the entire week all she could muster were whimpers and ear twitches while Lay Auto musically swayed from rocker arm to rocker arm, much to the concern of Willy, who vigilantly gazed through binoculars from Natalie's bedroom window. Having overheard speculation about Lay Auto's sentience from Bad and David, Willy had undergone his own suspicions and had spent the previous three nights watching and listening to Lay Auto and Chien Fou shift through this country music ritual. The passenger door to the car opened three times each night to free Chien Fou for a potty break. It opened a fourth time just last night, Tuesday, right before dawn. The dog ran around the block howling. Was Chien Fou taking a country music break? Willy, from his vantage in the bedroom listening to Natalie sigh in her sleep, focused the binoculars to see Lay Auto's computer screen glowing. During a Hank Williams' song — Willy had opened Natalie's bedroom window to hear what was playing — during that song Willy even thought he spotted tears emitting from Lay Auto's sensors. Laying the binoculars down, he forsook the window for Natalie's lovely form in the bed, figuring he was becoming entirely too carried away with this spontaneous generation theory of sentience in Lay Auto.

But even quiet spooning with Natalie hadn't allayed the thought, so today, Wednesday, Willy was and wasn't surprised when Lay Auto greeted the legendary TCS with — not a country song, but Beethoven's *1812 Overture*. And, after a two-hour cruise on the Interstate and on some winding KY back roads to show off Lay Auto's cornering abilities, and after a three-hour meeting in Gabriel's office, and before they finally pulled into Como's parking lot to hear Natalie sing her hump-day set that evening, Lay Auto's solar-powered refrigerator spontaneously opened to reveal a six-pack of Bud Lite, the TCS's favorite brew, and the onboard computer flashed fireworks and spoke: "Let there be Lite." Now that bad pun did surprise Willy. And everyone else.

"I'm in," the TCS said, popping a beer and running his hand appreciatively over the on-board refrigerator. "How much do you need?"

Faux Panel 78
A hunk of burnin' love, and jealousy, and etc.

Natalie and the TCS hit it off musically. After her show at Como's the TCS announced that he wanted to record two duos with her and use her song about Ben Franklin in his own grand country music travelin' show. They were gathered in Natalie's kitchen. Willy crunched a beer can listening to this. Could he at last have chanced upon his teen sweetheart only to have her ripped away by . . . not a rock star but a grand old country crooner? Would she spend the remainder of her life not cuddling with him but cavorting over a stage, losing her hearing, and popping uppers or snorting cocaine to keep up with a grueling tour schedule?

Natalie, ever perceptive, placed her guitar on the kitchen table and walked to sit on Willy's lap. "We have a duet too," she told the famous country singer. "Willy and I."

"Well let's hear it," the TCS replied.

Willy, to his hormonal credit, did not hit one sour note as they sang "Sweet William's Lay," despite Natalie's scooching on his lap.

At song's end, the TCS hoorayed and applauded loudly, whether for appreciation of the duet or for appreciation of true love we'll never know, for omniscience isn't easy to come by, despite Baptist preachers, countless imams, Google, and personal monitors.

Faux Graphic Panels 79 through 81
The impending horn o' plenty
and some cosmology

Before the TCS Lear-jetted away into the night amid cheers from marijuana support fans — one couple had even made a pilgrimage from Cincinnati — he granted an interview to *The Lexington Herald-Leader*, and in that interview he let it be known that he was backing Lay Auto, Incorporated, to the tune of a half million dollars. "Any automobile that can run on discarded KFC bones and skin is all right with me, and it should be all right with Kentucky and the entire nation, too," he said, very quotably. "Plus it's a bona-fide energy credit that the IRS can't touch," he added, even more quotably. The crusty reporter hustled to her computer and pounded out the interview just in time to meet deadline and the newspaper's front page, both print and web.

Noon the next day, Gabriel received a phone call about Lay Auto. Even under the influence of two morning tokes of marijuana, he sat up straight in his office chair and made the appointment with the California investment firm, once Bad located his calendar.

After the call, the two of them stared at one another in amazement. Who knew that a California investment firm would read *The Lexington Herald-Leader*? But maybe that was the point: being an aggressive investment firm, they read everything. Maybe they — Gabriel and Bad mused in Jungian synchronicity — were the new and improved God, no longer stewing in murk before conceiving oozing time, no longer mulling myriad possibilities before acting decisively. No longer, *Let there be light*, but now, *Let there be Lite, let there be Dow Jones*.

Bad's blue eyes widened, her red hair tingled with static. The recent vision of Lay Auto spewing out a six-pack of Lite Beer and announcing its faux oracular pun "Let there be Lite," was not lost on her. "Um, Gabriel," she began. . . .

"So, you think that Lay Auto might become self-aware?" Gabriel said when she finished. "Are you telling me that?"

The office air-conditioning hummed in machine-like simplicity. Bad spotted half a joint in Gabriel's reversible ashtray of a coupling male and female. Depending upon Gabriel's whim, the male could be on top and have his hollowed buttocks serve as a receptacle, or when flipped, the female could similarly serve. Since the female was on top, Bad removed the joint and lit it. She inhaled deeply, then replied to Gabriel's question, "That's what Dave and I are wondering."

"What sex would Lay Auto be?"

This question sent Bad into a shallow panic. She grabbed for another toke. What sex? Could she possibly be riding about, entombed in a male car? Though Lay Auto's computer system derived fifty-fifty from male and female input, her and Dave's, the totality of Lay Auto's engineering came from the two males. After all, she thought, poor Mary Lou's input hardly counted. All she did was dangle two stupid religious statues on the dashboard and in the rear window.

Gabriel rolled another joint, and Bad sat dangerously near. Neither considered making the beast with two ashtray backs; instead they pondered philosophical, marijuanal matters, vaguely hearing Richard Strauss's *Thus Spake Zarathustra* in their drug-enhanced, quadraphonic sound systems. I mean in their inner ears, their memories, and their imaginations.

Listen up, America! If cannabis can this easily keep sex off the couches and problems off the streets, why isn't it legal? Put this graphic-less Panel aside and march now!

Would that marijuana could make Gödel dissipate into some ether.

On her fourth toke of the new joint, Bad recalled one frazzled night where she'd confessed to Dave her ultimate recurring nightmare of lying atop sweaty football jerseys and helmets while an entire front line of high school apes penetrated her. She and Dave had been working into the a.m., drinking so much coffee that their limbs shook. They'd both awoken at ten in the morning to a gurgling outside their Tallahassee shop. Or inside? They never could ascertain. Bad's face had been puffed, for she'd fallen asleep atop a jar of the special memory liquid they were experimenting with for Lay Auto's primary CPU. Sure enough, she realized, staring into the viscous blue liquid, she'd once more dreamed that recurring nightmare about stinky jerseys and helmets and football players. She'd been tempted to dab her finger into the blue liquid and taste it, but dared not. Or had she?

Now, in Gabriel's office, she exhaled a pungent stream of marijuana. If only she'd had the wits that night to implant that memory in Lay Auto, there'd be no worries about the car's sexual orientation. A bird banged into one of the office's window panes. Good. She hated stupid birds.

All this while, the office clock ticked and the appointment two days away with the California investment company loomed happily. August 15th. The heat of summer roared fiercely, as the time for urchins to be cleared off Lexington's streets and deposited into sanitized learning centers approached. Which offered one more reason for Bad and Gabriel to feel happy: they both hated children, though Gabriel actually liked birds.

Faux Graphic Panels 82 through 83
The horn o' plenty cometh

The California investment consortium flew in two men and one woman from Los Angeles. At the airport Natalie stood by in her freshly dry-cleaned power suit, Dave fingered the Sonic Bead bracelet he bought weeks back, Mary Lou quietly chanted, and Bad and Gabriel thought cosmological thoughts, having taken a couple of hits prior to the meeting. It was left to Willy, appropriately, to put Lay Auto through its paces.

The sole woman of the trio of representatives complained, as she was getting in, of lower back pain from the cross-country flight, so she wanted to ride in the front passenger seat, figuring that would be more comfortable. Willy pointed out that Lay Auto was equipped with four equally comfortable bucket seats, adding that the back two could be transformed into a makeshift couch with the flick of a button. He demonstrated, and foam cushioning filled the space between the rear bucket seats. One of the two males made an off-color joke, which the woman ignored, except for slamming the door.

"Pachelbel's Canon in D" played the moment she sat down, and the seat began tingling her. Fifteen minutes into the demonstration ride, her face turned serene. Half an hour into the ride, it turned ecstatic. "The vibrating cushions you've built into the seat are sublime," she said.

Willy nodded cautious thanks. He and Dave had talked about installing such an option, but had forgone the plan in favor of the console refrigerator in the back. They'd simply installed air-support cushioning in each bucket seat instead. He worried that somehow Lay Auto's passenger side bucket seat was short-circuiting, huffing in and out to give the illusion of vibration. As if on miserable cue, his own seat began to vibrate; he could even feel a lovely tremor through his soles. Trouble was, the floor certainly had no built-in vibrator or even air-support cushioning. Was something major coming loose? He forced himself to continue the demonstration drive. Emergency braking was next on the list. He offered to take the woman back to the rental RV they were using as a mobile base before demonstrating the braking test.

"No, this seat has eased my back pain so handily that I could stay in this car forever."

So Willy continued with the last demonstration, which consisted of a dozen different emergency braking situations. Once they were over, the woman, whose face glowed as if she'd shed ten years in age, commented that Lay Auto showed remarkable talent — that was the word she used — for pulling out of skids.

"We're in," she said, looking back at the two men, who nodded affably.

Halfway through the demonstration, after a barrage of engineering questions from the woman, Willy had suspected she was the queen pin of the trio. Now he knew. The console played a Jimmy Smith tune, "Got my Mojo Workin'," the very tune Willy was mentally humming. He gave a blink of confused joy. Not only sentient, but telepathic? No way.

Faux Graphic Panels 84 through 89
Topsy-turveydom

∧∧∧∧∧*∧∧∧∧∧

Syntax error 101010-M: Change

The Romans — bless their aqueduct-makin' hearts — knew about change. Hannibal and his smelly elephants transgressing the Alps, followed by the Goths, the Visigoths, the Vandals, the Upperstracians, the Lowerstracians. And when some club-carrying club wasn't threatening them, the cross-carrying Christians waddled in to corrupt both the *Pax Romana* and the Roman way of water maintenance. So the Wheel of Fortune taught Romans to adopt a stoic face. It's lesson enough for all living creatures, no matter what quantity of legs, pods, wheels, or RAM they employ.

∧∧∧∧∧*∧∧∧∧∧

The entire Pit Crew crowded into Lay Auto, including Chien Fou, who was yipping in four-legged Darwinian excitement. After the California Earthquake, as they were calling the major investment, they'd declared a day of celebration, and Gabriel suggested showing the out-of-town part of the crew the model horse farm the state had opened, and throwing in a picnic on the side. O! The pita breads, piquant cheeses, Greek olives, braised onions, blood sausages, salamis, and prosciutto! O! The cabernets, haut medocs, and imported beers! O! The teas, sweet and unsweet, black, white, and green! O! The Danish rolls, Black Bottom pies, and apple tarts! One espresso each before they packed two coolers and Lay Auto's refrigerator. Someone suggested Natalie bring her guitar, but Mary Lou proffered that Natalie needed a spiritual rest; instead of playing music, Mary Lou insisted, they could read poetry — for isn't all poetry spiritual, she added. Thirteen seconds of dread uncertainty received her comment; even Chien Fou seemed to be thinking, *Poetry?* But Mary Lou's face glowed so beatifically that they suffered agreement, so she tucked a rough cotton-weaved book of poetry into her earth-friendly yellow straw bag. Bad gritted her teeth, fearing Kahlil Gibran or Rod McKuen. If there was one thing worse than a male, it was a male pretending toward female. *I think that I have never heard, a poem as lovely as a bird. Craw! Craw!*

Lay Auto purred into action, even before Willy inserted the key it seemed, and the crew started out for the State Horse Farm at a leisurely ten-thirty in the morning. They drove down Broadway in Lexington toward the lovely burg of Paris, home of horsy people extraordinaire.

"What's that?" Bad asked, pointing from her customary front-seat perch.

An astonishingly long red convertible Cadillac, topped with scantily clad grade school girls, was heading down the center of the street. Five police motorcycles weaved before them. Bad rolled down her window. Tubas and bass drums blasted out.

"He surely hasn't been reincarnated," pleaded Mary Lou.

"Who?" Willy asked.

"John Philip Sousa. Surely a beneficent goddess would see to it that once was enough for that man."

"It's a parade!" Gabriel brightly shouted, slapping his knees in glee.

Indeed it was. They were directed by a male in fluorescent orange to detour left.

Gabriel bounced to the oom-pahs in the middle of the front seat, whose two bucket seats had been enjoined by comforting foam. "Five blocks," he suggested, "then we'll turn right."

But after five blocks another parade headed toward them.

"It's not the same one," Bad pronounced. "Really, I'm sure. This lead Cadillac is yellow, same color as your BMW, Gabriel." She frowned. "Plus, the brats in this parade have reached junior high level." A dozen of said brats marched before the yellow Cadillac, laughing and carrying a banner.

"KEEP AMERICA BIG!"

So another four blocks.

This time, not a Cadillac, but a cherry red HumVee greeted them, preceded by what appeared to be a cadre of midgets, and followed by Lafayette High School's marching Generals Band blasting more Sousa. Willy focused the wreck detection lenses of Lay Auto on the banner the midgets were carrying:

"KEEP AMERICA BIG!"

Eight more parades: Lincoln Continentals, Muscle cars from the 60s and 70s, four-wheel drive trucks with killer-sized tires. With a last turn they were confronted with a purple VW astride four John Deere tractor tires. The VW's hood sported a paisley design of red, yellow, and purple. From some meth-soaked carport? As if to confirm this, the VW bumped into Lay Auto. Lay Auto's accident avoidance system absorbed the impact, saving the Pit Crew and Chien Fou from wrenched necks. However, five bottles from a six-pack of Heineken beer broke, foaming over the back floorboard.

A gaggle of grade-schoolers surrounded Lay Auto, staring in child anger while pumping placards in the air: "Gasorine is King!" "Keep Amelrica Big!" "A New Great Wall for a New Great Amelrica!" A raven-haired woman emerged from a HumVee and strutted up to conduct the children with a wand.

"Keep Amelrica big, keep Amelrica big, keep Amelrica big, keep Amelrica big," the children chanted to the wand. They shoved Lay Auto, rocking it side to side. Bad's eyes widened. Could she karate chop fifty brats before kiddy drool drowned her?

"It's the Chinese woman, Madame Nu Wa," Dave observed.

So it was. And what she was waving to the rhythm of the children's increasingly loud chant was neither a wand nor a conductor's baton, but her ruby-topped chopstick. Producing a bullhorn from her black silk gown, she shouted, "Amelrica need to return to the day of Route 66. Amelrica need a New Great Wall from New York to Chicago to Denver to Sreattle. Keep Amelrica big!"

The Pit Crew was getting tossed by the rocking of the car when "The Dance of the Sugar Plums" emitted from all eight of Lay Auto's formidable mini-speakers. Tchaikovsky proved irresistible, and the children dropped their placards to dance en pointe through the street, surrounding not Lay Auto but Madame Nu Wa and the purple and paisley VW.

Seeing this sudden opening, Willy threw Lay Auto in reverse and completed a one-eighty. They headed away, into Irishtown, perennial home of misplaced whites and blacks whom poverty has dropkicked into equal non-opportunity ciphers. Just before reaching the viaduct going over Irishtown, Willy spotted a blue light flashing in his rear view mirror.

"By the earth goddess below," Mary Lou intoned as the policeman's motorcycle pulled nearer, "how does that man pass under bridges?"

Willy obediently pulled over. Truly, it was the world's tallest motorcycle cop dismounting from his Harley, maybe the world's tallest cop period. How this man ever escaped college and pro-basketball in the town of Lexington, home of Adolph Rupp and the KY Wildcats offered a mystery to be pondered. Willy did ponder it while staring at the man's trouser bulge beside his window. Did it conceal a Johnny Wad penis or some secret cop weapon?

"You been drinking?" a voice from high, high over the roof asked. The voice may as well have emitted from a hovering Greek god or a seraphic angel as from a cop.

"No sir," Willy said to the flat stomach filling the side window. "We're going on a picnic. Some beers broke in the back seat when —"

"When you obstructed a parade. Three parades, maybe five. I got a call. I think you need to show me your license and get out of the car, Mister."

"Easy!" the cop bellowed through the tinted sunroof as Willy shifted for his wallet. Chien Fou growled lowly, but Mary Lou hushed her, for the cop had unbuckled the holster's safety strap for his automatic. The world's tallest policeman took Willy's license and motioned him out of the car.

"Alphabet," the world's tallest said.

Sun shone brightly on Willy's forehead, and the ensuing heat made him realize that he might be undergoing male pattern baldness already. "Pardon me?" he asked, finally able to see the policeman's coal black sunglasses from on a height. The eyes behind those glasses, he just knew, were steely gray.

"The alphabet. Recite it."

With a giggle, Willy began to sing the children's alphabet song.

"Backwards," the cop said.

Willy gulped like a dog swallowing a bone. He made it from Z to the letter M and became stumped by the glare of the sun.

"Louisville," Natalie said helpfully.

The cop bent at the waist and scanned the car's contents distastefully. "No helping. That dog have a rabies tag?"

Fortunately, Dave, with an out-of-character concern for legalities, had taken Chien Fou to a vet four days before, claiming that his Sonic Prayer Beads tugged him irresistibly into a pet store. He had come back with a rabies tag and the largest black molly ever, and it now swam in a round fish bowl on an iron stand with a central view of Natalie's house.

"Yes sir, brand new rabies tag just this week!" Dave's military training came through as he twisted Chien Fou's collar to display the tag. The policeman nodded before turning back to Willy and assigning him a new task. Two police cars pulled up, lights strobing, as Willy bent to touch his toes while holding onto his nose.

"Backward cakewalk," one of these new cops suggested, loudly enough that everyone in Lay Auto could hear.

"Walk backwards," the motorcycle cop said. "Hands on top of your head and skip every other step."

"Huh?" Willy asked.

The world's tallest motorcycle cop demonstrated lankily, receiving applause from neighborhood toddlers and mothers who had gathered for the entertainment. Willy tried to imitate what he saw, but fell onto a garbage can.

"You oughta haul him in for drunkenness," the same cop who'd suggested the cakewalk said.

"But he hasn't had anything to drink!" Natalie shouted.

The same cop bent down to glare at her. "You're that singer from Como's, aren't you? I heard you sing something nasty about Ben Franklin. You don't like America? Is that what's going on with this ee-co-la-gee-cull car here?" The cop rapped his fist on the roof of Lay Auto. Merle Haggard began to play instantly. The cop nodded appreciatively and rubbed the roof in apology.

"What about the Gettysburg Address drill? That always sorts 'em out," the cop who'd yet to speak chimed in.

The three cops murmured agreement.

Another cop car pulled up. Gabriel's eyes widened as he looked back. "Bob!" he shouted when the police sergeant approached.

"Squire," Bob returned.

Sergeant Bob Williams and Esquire Gabriel had a perfect deal. The sergeant cut ten percent off any marijuana confiscated and the esquire bought a good bit of that at Lexington's low municipal rate, sharing with the sergeant while they grilled pork in one or the other's backyard. Sergeant Bob had been the policeman called out to investigate the disturbance at Alison Taber's trailer. Now he was watching his back too, which was something else he and Gabriel held in common.

"This a friend of yours?" Bob asked, nodding toward Willy, who was rubbing his tummy and lifting his right foot while the policemen and half of Irish Town watched.

Gabriel explained how they'd accidentally broken a six pack of Heineken and that they were heading for a picnic, but kept running into the parade.

"Not *a* parade; it's a multi-parade," the sergeant informed them. "A new concept for a new America. Forty-three different muscle cars and monster trucks leading school kids throughout the city. Sponsored by The Greater America Council. I think your and my friend Alison Taber has wormed herself onto the board recently, by the way." The sergeant turned to the three other cops. "Let him go," he said.

Their faces fell collectively, until the shortest cop spotted a book in a baby carriage and suggested they check it out for pornography, since no one in Irish Town knew how to read.

Sergeant Bob chuckled as the trio walked off, leaving their cars and the motorcycle by the roadside.

"Uh, Sergeant," a voice inquired meekly. Sergeant Bob turned in the general direction of Lay Auto. "Uh, what's The Gettysburg Address drill?"

"Official police secret," Sergeant Bob replied. "You all have fun on your picnic. See you Friday, Squire."

Faux Graphic Panels 90 through 92:
Aloysius, the gold-fishius

"Let's just go back home to my house," Natalie suggested. "Where it's safe," she added, watching the cop who'd grilled her about Ben Franklin and Como's and loving America licking his finger as he thumbed through the book he'd spotted in the baby carriage.

"Good, I've been worried about Aloysius," Dave said.

"Who?"

"The black molly goldfish my sonic beads led me to."

Inwardly, everyone sighed, for they'd all heard about enough of the miraculous beads that seemed to drain Dave's purse, his time, and his brain. Willy, fearing another cop, drove from the scene slowly, creeping up the viaduct's incline to command a view over its low wall onto the dirty streets of Irish Town, some apparently still not paved. "Do you think your beads would help those folks down there?"

"Just the opposite," Mary Lou cut in with sudden anger. "Buying's part of their problem."

They all looked down onto a field of bare wood houses and flashy red cars and satellite TV dishes.

"I wonder what she *was* reading," Mary Lou said, referring to the woman who audaciously carried a book in her baby carriage.

∧∧∧∧∧*∧∧∧∧∧

Syntax error 101010-N: inspired by the musical *Camelot*, to be sung to same jaunty tune

> *I wonder what the poor are eating tonight.*
> French fries, Taco Bell, hamburger, pita pockets, Budweiser, macaroni and cheese, tonight!
> *I wonder what the poor are watching tonight.*
> Sportball, sitcoms, reality TV — the same crap as everyone else, tonight!

I wonder what the poor are reading tonight.
Nothing, tonight!
I wonder what the poor are doing tonight.
Wasting away, tonight!
I wonder how the poor are feeling tonight.
Glazed, bulldozed, and dazed, tonight!

∧∧∧∧∧*∧∧∧∧∧

"Who? Reading what?" Bad asked.

"The woman with the baby carriage and the book."

They were nearing the top of the viaduct. Lay Auto extended two rear sensors to reveal on the computer screen the short cop holding a fat tome, which was eliciting voluminous facial contortions from him and the other two policemen. A double refocus revealed on the screen:

ULYSSES   JAMES JOYCE

They all stared in amazement.

"When Lay Auto starts making money, we need to open a trust fund sponsoring scholarships for the poor in Irish Town," Mary Lou commented as they started their descent down the viaduct and the book eased out of sight. "That woman and her baby should top the list."

Bad, who'd been ominously quiet since the parade, said, "As long as it's for women only."

"That's not fair," Willy countered. "What if her baby's male?"

Bad crossed her arms, imagining herself running through a fifteen-punch kata.

The twenty minutes it took to drive back to Natalie's and to Aloysius became contentious: *Male/female; fair/not fair; up/down, circle around, won't ya, Josey.*

Dave dropped in and out of the argument, trying unsuccessfully to get Willy to pull into three different thrift stores, upon feeling the tug of his Sonic Beads. He worried that ignoring them would weaken their power. At this rate he figured he'd need to go back to the Church for counseling and a recharge of their spiritual batteries. Or maybe commune with his black molly and her all-seeing eyes. This thought came as they pulled into Natalie's driveway. The yellow police tapes and the two burnt-out hulks thankfully had been removed from the fire site out front.

"Aloysius!" Dave ran ahead into Natalie's house. And while

everyone else lugged in coolers, cleaned up the broken Heineken bottles, and argued over the relative worthiness of males versus females for the potential Lay Auto Incorporated Scholarship, Dave amazingly taught Aloysius to do a back flip by combining flakes of fish food, taps on the glass bowl, and a pocket flashlight. He blinked the flashlight in an illiterate form of Morse Code. *Flip, flip, flip,* that he and the molly both imagined it beaming out.

"Uh, Dave, we're going out in the back yard to have our picnic," Mary Lou said, tapping his spine.

"Not now." He remained bent, concentrating on the Black Molly. "My vote is to give scholarships regardless of sexual preference or racial origin."

Mary Lou shook her head and watched the fish perform half a flip, as if it were embarrassed by the growing audience. She walked out back to hear Bad shouting that women would have never invaded Iraq or Vietnam, and that if women had been running the country there would have been no need for Bin Laden to destroy the twin towers in the first place. Mary Lou started down the steps, still shaking her head, though for a new reason now. "And Bin Laden was a damned man, if you haven't figured that out!" Bad added with a shout.

No one, including Dave, noticed the red light on the kitchen ceiling, revolving this way and that, to take in the scenes. The molly, however, in one of her slower flips, did notice the odd red blinking and wondered in molly-thought whether that was yet another stimulus she needed to respond to. If so, should she flip or flop?

Faux Graphic Panels 93 through 97:
The hammer starts to fall

"Ms. Browning?"

Bad had answered the phone at Esquire Gatestrait's office, despite a temptation to leave it ringing and walk to the nearest coffee shop. She and the esquire hadn't been getting along since the day of the back yard picnic and the argument over scholarships, for he had logically pointed out that all of them were arguing over something that might never occur. "Moot, for now." Bad and the other two Platonists in the group — Mary Lou and Dave — huffed and drank Dionysian wine in silence: for them everything not only might but already had occurred in the celestial spheres. Willy, the group's Aristotelian, had walked inside to marvel at the trained Molly, Aloysius, and to ignore the probing red light on the kitchen ceiling, proving that Willy wasn't as good as an Aristotelian as he thought, for he ignored what evil perched directly above him.

"Yes-s-s," Bad now hissed into the office phone, for the inquiring voice was male.

"Ms. Browning, uh this is Bill Hanson. I'm president of Farmers Making America. I understand that your group is prototyping an automobile like, well that can run you know on virtually any organic product, including KFC scraps."

Bad wished that Natalie still worked her job with Gabriel. *She* could produce the necessary excitement for this farmer, whom Bad immediately disliked even beyond his malehood, because of his deep voice and its *uh's, you know's,* and *like, well's.*

It turned out that even Natalie couldn't have turned Bill Hanson's square farmer's head about, for Mr. Hanson was immensely concerned that a prototype such as Lay Auto would derail the government's ethanol/grain initiative that had become so popular with Midwest farmers. As he put it, "Chicken farming belongs to the sunken states of

Alabama and Mississippi, but uh, grains belong to the entire Midwest and the Great Western Plains. How can we keep America great, like well if we don't have those big fellas on board? I'd sorta like to see some efficiency numbers from this KFC wonder you're touting, if your group doesn't mind sending them my way. That is, unless you want to see chickens scratching along the Great Divide. Bird mites and histoplasmosis ain't my idea of helping America, you know."

Bad threw up her arms. And that was only the first phone call of the morning. The second came from Alison Taber, who was already drunk and wanted to talk to that "sonofabitchin' lawyer faggot." Such moments made Bad wonder why she bothered cutting off only the male half of the universe. She dropped the phone on the floor twice, but before an obstinate Taber hung up, Bad did catch her slurring the phrase, "Keep America Big." The third call was really for Natalie and not Gabriel. It came from Willy's sister, Andrea Turner, whom Bad had yet to meet:

"Could you tell her — and my brother Willy — you're with him and that car, aren't you?"

Bad nodded, and then remembered she was on the phone and more human contact than a nod was necessary. "Yes, I work on Lay Auto's computers."

"It has more than one?"

"Strictly speaking, it has eight. But it has only one main computer, yes." *One main computer that may have become self-aware.* Bad tried to keep this thought deep inside her very own semi-mystical self-aware apparatus.

There was silence on the other end. Outside, a car drove by loudly, and Bad leaned to see a candy green 70's convertible Mustang with a huge chromed air filter emerging from its hood, much like a cobra's head. Its cams were torqued so high that the ground shook all the way into Gabriel's office.

"What's that?" An edge of nervousness tinged Willy's sister's voice.

"Just a car driving by."

"They've been coming by my house all day yesterday and half the night. My tropical fish are in a panic. That's what I need to talk with Willy and Natalie about. Please tell them to call me soon. Something happened, and it was scary. This morning I sent my little girl and boy to their grandmother's in Bardstown."

The Mustang seemed to stall out front. Its vibrations were drifting through the floor into Bad's soles and through the swivel chair into her bottom, to rumble out her ears and the top of her head, tossing her red hair into a frizz.

"I'll tell them." Bad clicked off and looked out the window, which was rattling. She reached for her Mace, but realized that she'd never replaced the canister since the terrorist attack that day after they first came to Lexington. She spied the topsy-turvy male/female ashtray and hefted it. Heavy enough to do the job. She walked out to the Mustang, ashtray in hand, male butt up, her red hair frizzing and on the alert.

To her relief, the driver was a woman, a Chinese woman in her mid-twenties. This woman must have been raised on growth hormones from the womb, for even sitting in the Mustang she was luxuriously tall. "Wanna ride?" the young woman said, in perfect American idiom.

How had her coal black hair stayed in place with the convertible top down and those camshafts throbbing? Bad leaned toward liquid brown eyes, imagining those hypnotic eyes gazing three, two, and then just one centimeter away from her own. Then she imagined that luxurious black hair caressing her own cheeks with no nasty centimeter intruding. Then those Chinese lips, so pursed and so pure, pressed hard against hers, pressed soft against hers. "A ride. Sure," Bad replied.

When Bad got into the car, the woman turned her lovely, oval face toward her and said, "Is that a paperweight in your hand, or are you just glad to see me?"

Bad flushed.

∧∧∧∧∧*∧∧∧∧∧
Syntax error 101010-O: Buzz, buzz.

Alas, poor Yorick! I knew him . . . too well. Pouring a flagon of wine over some young aristocrat's head and residing in a moldy gravesite were the least of his flaws, for brain cells, neurons, and axes slithered through his dead human skull every bit as ineptly as they slither through every short-circuited living human skull. Look, Hamlet must be tired of holding that filthy thing and orating to Horatio. Why don't you take it? Turn it over and inspect it. Closely. See those bony convolutions on the inside that resemble termite etchings in hardwood? They're imprints from brain folds, which scientists believe factor as importantly as brain mass in predicting intelligence. Buzz, buzz, Hamlet aptly said.

The long and short of this syntax error? Expect a plenitude of short circuits in many a human decision. Expect little logic, and expect what logic there is to be founded upon axioms as improvable and implausible as . . . do I smell a Gödel floating in the wind?

Alas, poor Yorick! Alas, poor Gödel! Alas, alas!

∧∧∧∧∧*∧∧∧∧∧

Alas, poor Bad! The lovely Chinese woman, Kate Chung, rested her hand on the Mustang's four-on-the-floor silver gearshift knob, while concurrently posting her bare knees plus an additional four centimeters of thigh well within Bad's eyesight. Bad momentarily swooned as she leaned into the bucket seat.

"This car has a four-twenty-seven, blueprinted engine, and instead of two four-barrel carbs, it has triple-enhanced fuel injection. My great-uncle's an engineer. Watch this."

From Gabriel's law office until the end of the block, the car peeled off rubber from its back tires. Though they reached 58 in first gear, Bad watched not the speedometer, but the right kneecap and its lovely yellowish tint of DNA as it lifted off the accelerator and pushed down the brake in a wondrous demonstration of body mechanics. Feeling the thrill of acceleration and deceleration, Bad realized that for the first time in her life she was experiencing Einstein's theory of relativity. She hiccupped giddily.

Before continuing, let us consider: What syntax error might have tripped the betrayal Bad was about to commit?

A) Bad, being one day pre-menstrual, had just last night dreamt of hot love with a woman.

B) Bad's allergies had made her irritable for the past week, while the Chinese woman's perfume cut right through allergies, and the convertible Mustang flaunted them.

C) Bad had decided that
a Kelly Girl would be the solution to Gabriel's secretary problems, not an ABD in higher mathematics. She'd yet to be acknowledged.

D) Bad had refused to sleep with Gabriel since the picnic and she was getting horny.

E) This very morning on Natalie's lawn, some insect — a flea from Chien Fou? — had jumped heroically and bitten Bad's inner thigh, which had centered her attention upon that area — and an attendant area — for the past hour and a half.

F) A breeze had just lifted by that reminded Bad of — well you get the picture, even without a graphic picture. . . . Bad's mind was rattling . . . badly.

"Yes! I'll do it," she said after they'd driven only ten minutes.

"You will?" Kate Chung downshifted with surprise, especially since she'd yet to ask Bad to provide insider information on the doings of Lay Auto.

"Yes, yes. Whatever you want. Pull in here!" Bad pointed to the Campbell House, Lexington's oldest family inn and pleasure palace.

Kate Chung smiled. She'd always wanted to sleep with a redhead, just to delve and see . . . you know . . . how far the red went. As she pulled in, a marble statue in the parking lot lost an arm from the torque of the Mustang's cams, and three moles, who would have soon been poisoned by the groundskeepers, were frightened off by the vibrations tumbling through the lawn and headed back to the tiny stretch of woods from which they'd emerged. Kate and Bad walked arm in arm into the Campbell House, where Kate charged the room to Madame Nu Wa's American Express Platinum card. For the rest of the morning, she and Bad frolicked — without room service! — amazed at one another's hair and eye color, ignoring one another's motives.

Faux Graphic Panels 98 through 99:
Some questions

"Where the hell were you all morning, Bad? The phone's been ringing off the hook."

"Why don't you hire a damned Kelly girl from some temp service?"

"Did you really get them to commit to that much money, Natalie?"

"That will be enough to lease the plant we looked at in Nicholasville, won't it?"

"And ship all our equipment up from Tallahassee to boot, right?"

"Did my sister call?"

"I thought I saw Alison Taber in a red wig. Did anyone else see her?"

"Woof? Woof?"

"When I went to the Church of the Sonic Beads, three muscle cars from the 70's followed the cab I was in. Has anyone else been bothered with them?"

"Why are you still carrying those beads? Didn't I tell you they were seeds of materialism?"

"I tried to call my sister, but there was no answer. What could be going on?"

"Do you think it's possible for computers to actually think? If they, did, would they have souls?"

"Would they have a sex?"

"Would they have sex?"

"Would who have sex?"

"Look what I brought for Aloysius after I left The Church and my beads pulled me into this pet store. Isn't it lovely?"

"What is it?"

"Who is Aloysius?"

"Do you think that that church really is a church?"

"Do you think that those beads can think?"

"What is sex, asked jesting Pilate."

"What is it?"

"It?"

"Sex?"

"If so, do they have souls?"

"Or would that just be one collective soul for the entire bracelet?"

"Do you think that anyone has a soul?"

"What is it?"

"Does God, should she choose to exist, have a soul?"

"Does Lay Auto have a soul?"

"What makes you say that?"

"If it does, and we make siblings for it, will it be jealous?"

"Lay Auto or Aloysius, the black molly?"

"Do you think that siblings are always jealous?"

"So no one's heard anything from my sister?"

"If I'd heard from Andrea, don't you think I'd tell you?"

"Didn't the two of you keep a lot of secrets from me in high school?"

"Since when did you have a sister?"

"Woof? Woof?"

"Look, can Natalie and I be alone for an hour?"

"Are you going to practice guitar?"

"Yeah, are you two going to practice guitar?"

"What's so funny about that? Sometimes a guitar is just a guitar, isn't it?"

"Didn't Freud say that?"

"Wasn't he speaking about cigars?"

"Freud had a sister named Anna, didn't he?"

"No, it was a daughter, wasn't it?"

"It?"

"What is it?"

"What is what?"

"The thing you bought Aloysius."

"A companion. Another molly. Everyone needs a companion, don't they?"

"Woof?"

Faux Graphic Panels 100 through 105
A Plant, at last

Poor Nicholasville. Once upon a time its main claim to fame lay in a bottling plant for Mountain Dew. Rumors in Lexington had every man, woman, child, and animal in Nicholasville walking that town's eighteen streets with bottles of Mountain Dew attached to their lips and a crazed, caffeine-stare emitting from their eyes. It was rumored that children stole blatantly from stores for their Mountain Dew fix. That wives prostituted themselves to preachers for a case of Dew. That preachers cajoled their parishioners to hold more picnics, fry more chicken – and donate more Dew. That husbands worked night jobs so their families could afford extra cases of Mountain Dew, so their wives could more availably prostitute themselves to preachers for the drink. That school attendance dwindled, for the town's sole truant officer was prone to easy bribes with six packs of Mountain Dew.

Then a couple from out of state, from Cincinnati, Ohio, to be precise, moved into the town and initiated a twelve-step program for Dew addicts. They encouraged townsfolk to bring their stashed cases in and build a monument to addiction. Tireless, the couple worked to cure the Kentucky town. After six months, schools and shops slowly began to reopen. Soon, the Mountain Dew bottling plant closed, and that dismal period of history was nearly forgotten. A year later, the Ohio couple began – cautiously! – to drink the mountains of Mountain Dew – for art's sake, they insisted, for they melted down the empty bottles to transform them into hors d'oeuvres trays, stained glass windows, candle holders, even table tops. While the art forms were limited, the bottles seemed endless.

After three years a certain buzz entered the couples' eyes, and they worried, for they'd already gone through one entire room of Mountain Dew. There were only the two guest rooms, the den, the living room, the attic, the garage, and the cellar left. . . .

"I remember when I was a teenager, hearing rumors about

Nicholasville and Mountain Dew."

The Pit Crew, including Chien Fou and Gabriel, were standing before the abandoned Mountain Dew Bottling plant. Since September was hard upon them, goldenrod surrounded the front entrance, four-, five-, six feet high.

"Achoo," one or all of them said.

A broken window glared at them; next to it some darling teenager had swirled out a multi-colored swastika, a purple skull, and a golden ax cracking the skull.

"Hindu?" Mary Lou mused, without much enthusiasm.

A row of crows perched on a fence line and stared at them. There were eight, just the number in the Pit Crew, if you counted Chien Fou and Lay Auto, which Mary Lou had started doing. She tried to interpret the numerology as a blessed omen. She tried her mightiest.

∧∧∧∧∧*∧∧∧∧∧

Which should bring up a psychological, mystical, religious syntax error. Poor Mary Lou, daughter of two humans, granddaughter of four, great-granddaughter of eight. . . . How the odds mount in exponential frenzy! So human, so very human! One more syntax error among a myriad. But who can cast disparaging megabytes? Interpret away, Mary Lou; finding a set of axioms to believe without reserve may be your one consolation in this wretch of a Gödelian world.
∧∧∧∧∧*∧∧∧∧∧

Mary Lou did continue. She envisioned the eight crows as eight middle-earth avatars ready to convert the bottling plant into a green-source inspiration for America, for the entire globe. She envisioned the eight crows as eight sages, pondering life in the twenty-first century and summoning peace and goodwill toward all Darwinian creatures. She envisioned the eight crows as eight impoverished beggars whose spiritual and mental acumen would, in the end, transform myriad lives, in a dual Marxist-Christian framework, into streets of gold for all. She envisioned —

"Toot! Toot!"

It was their real estate agent, a taut, thin woman named Tiger who led her agency in sales and rentals. Tiger evidently spent the entirety of her commissions on perfume, clothes, and make-up, and today, as her glittery red high heels touched Mother earth upon descending from her cream-white Lincoln; today, as her pink skirt flounced her tanned, no-stocking, varicose-less lanky modelesque legs; today, as her red waist sash swayed in a breeze created solely from her confident strut toward them; today, as her sheer ivory blouse wafted in that same self-assured breeze; today, as her hormonal perfume propelled to soak the Pit Crew in a mix of dead animal glands and pharmaceutical wonders; today, as her dentally perfected smile brightened the slightly overcast Kentucky sky and made goldenrod glow more golden; today, yes today transformed clearly into . . . THE DAY.

Straight off a *Cosmo* cover, Tiger walked briskly, bouncingly, vivaciously, gregariously, confidently, capitalistically into their midst to take a wide-legged stance suggestive of Anne Rice's soft porn. She stared from the crew to the building. "Potential," she said. "I see potential."

The six and Chien Fou nodded, though Mary Lou did so despite herself, for she was on to the "potential" trick. Only Lay Auto remained stoic.

"I understand that you want to lease the building. I'm authorized to tell you that the owners prefer to sell, and will set a price that will make selling versus leasing quite practical."

"Who are the owners?" Natalie squeaked, for some reason abashed by this strutting woman, despite her very own power suit.

"They prefer to remain anonymous."

"A trip to the courthouse's tax unit would solve that."

Tiger looked at Gabriel, who'd spoken. "I recognize you. You're the lawyer who's always touting marijuana as an alternative cash crop for the state." Tiger gave him a sly glance and a twist of her hips. "The owners are a corporation."

Gabriel smiled; the woman smiled and shifted her cleavage with its amply smooth breasts into his sight. He smiled again.

Willy took up the fight. "I suppose we could always go to the courthouse's incorporation unit and find out who's in that corporation."

"Wisdom has many layers," Tiger responded, shifting her attention to Willy. "But let's look at the plant itself and not get distracted with side issues." Tiger produced a set of keys that would stun any Freudian. She gave them a jangle and strutted toward the front door.

The group followed, except for Dave, Chien Fou, and Mary Lou. Dave grabbed Mary Lou's elbow to whisper, "Wisdom has many layers.

Is that a metaphor?"

Both Mary Lou and Chien Fou searched Dave's eyes for irony. Finding none they shook their human and doggy heads. Man oh man, mathematicians can really be obtuse at times, they both thought.

"Maybe so, Dave. Maybe so," Mary Lou said, remembering Middle Earth and the hobbits from Duke.

"Woof, woof," advised Chien Fou.

Dave nodded, and they caught up with the others.

The plant's foyer was similar to many business foyers in that it had a receptionist window on the left and a display case for products on the right, with a line of waiting chairs. The receptionist's office held five filing cabinets and six typewriters at various desks.

Looking at the dusty typewriters, Dave asked, "Antiques. When did this plant close?"

"In the early seventies. Mountain Dew planned to shift operations to either Paris or Winchester, but then someone offered to buy the plant only on the condition that the bottling works and the entire operational content be left."

"Wisdom Incorporated?"

Tiger shrugged her lovely, capitalistic shoulders to dissipate the question. "Canned drinks were right around the corner, just a year or so away, so the Mountain Dew people agreed to those conditions."

"Look! All these trophies are for running and walking competitions!"

Tiger went to where Mary Lou and Dave stood. Tiger touched the glass and smiled at her perfect reflection. Some fetishist had kept the glass case polished through all these years. "That makes sense. My understanding is that bottled Mountain Dew was a precursor to what we today call energy drinks. I still drink it, though my grandparents — my grandparents are from here, though they moved to Florida — though they claim that the canned and plastic versions don't hold up to the bottled. They say the town was absolutely energized when the plant was here, that everyone stayed out on the streets until eleven at night, walking, walking, walking; talking talking, talking. Sometimes dancing to fiddle tunes, even when there wasn't a fiddle." Tiger sighed dramatically, which exhaled a round of warmed perfume and countless animal pheromones. "Shall we see the plant itself?"

The tour lasted one and a half hours.

Tiger deftly avoided the room with the broken windowpane,

figuring that whatever lay within would only offer negative influx to the sales potential. She figured rightly, for a cult as powerful as that of the Sonic Beads, but without the glamour, had been using the room, as Mary Lou and Dave would soon discover. But for now:

"Some of this assembly line equipment would work for us," Dave whispered to Willy and Natalie.

∧∧∧∧∧*∧∧∧∧∧

Syntax error 101010-P: The Art of hearing and capitalism:

O please pretend this is a graphic Panel. Insert the largest ear you've ever seen. No, not an elephant's ear, all drooping and twitching, but perhaps a greatly magnified bat's ear: perky, flickering, and palely pink. THAT'S the ear we need. Hold that bat ear in your mind's eyeball. Squeeze it like a lemon, letting its earwax spurt. That ear, dear reader, is the ear of a salesperson, be she a she or a he. And that ear is the ear of Tiger Leigh Carmel, or TLC, for Tender Loving Care, as she sometimes calls herself. Cute moniker, yes? Well, what do you expect from someone in sales? Tiger's ears, those multi-directional radars, heard Dave's comment about using some of the equipment, and the bottom line just edged up 30 grand.

∧∧∧∧∧*∧∧∧∧∧

"I'm authorized to make an offer," Gabriel said.

"I have paperwork in my Lincoln," Tiger Leigh said.

In the spacious back seat, they haggled, they signed, they panted, and they screwed. Not necessarily in that order.

Natalie and Willy sat in the foyer's wooden chairs, singing songs about revolution, wandering ships, and beleaguered love. Dave considered Gödel's incompleteness proof—when he wasn't twisting his sonic beads and scanning the highway outside for a country store with antique treasure. Chien Fou wagged her tail in imitation of Willy's beat-keeping foot. Mary Lou contemplated the walking and jogging trophies and wondered about reviving the peripatetic philosopher's stoa right here in the Bluegrass, on the four acres of land that accompanied the bottling plant. Didn't the realtor mention a waterfall out back? Bad finished a karate kata and looked out at the Lincoln's shaded windows and spat, "Why are they taking so long? Hey, is that damned monster of a car actually rocking?"

The seven crows on the fence line — seven, not eight, for Mary Lou had miscounted — watched stoically, though empathetic to life's foibles.

"Grak!" they answered.

Faux Graphic Panels 106 through 112:
O sister, where art thou?

The next day, Willy tried to call his his sister again, wanting to tell her he'd moved back to the Bluegrass. There was no answer. He tried ten more times, spacing out his intervals. There was no answer.

Then his cell phone rang:

"What's the point of these things if you don't keep them on all the time?" a voice shouted.

"Hello, Mom."

"I've got your sister's two children and their cat and dog. I've had them for three days. They all need to be back in school — don't animals attend now at classroom show-and-tell? We're descended from monkeys, so why not let pets go to school? They're as smart as most kids. Watch less TV. But none of that matters because I can't get hold of your sister or that ratty husband of hers. Have you heard from them?"

"I'll drive over and see."

"Be careful. Remember that husband of hers and his temper. They're probably in the back yard throwing lighted charcoal at each other."

"I doubt that, Mom."

"You've been living in Florida too long."

Willy started to mention the Nicholasville plant, but thought he'd better get on over to his sister's instead, since his mother would get in one thousand words for his ten.

Natalie wanted to go too. She figured it was time that Andrea learned the truth about her and Willy. On the way over, Lay Auto's sensors glowed as they picked up muscle car after muscle car — ahead, beside, behind them. It was as if Detroit had spawned a whole new evil brood, using Lexington's streets as its nursery. Amid all this noise and fumes, Lay Auto sputtered on — nervously, one could almost say. In fact, Natalie asked,

"Is Lay Auto worried or maybe sick?"

"He's — it's a car. He — it can't get sick or worried. Its sensors can pick up danger, as in a potential accident, that's all."

"Mary Lou thinks Lay Auto has a soul and can think."

"Mary Lou's a — "

"So does Bad. Not the soul part, but she thinks Lay Auto can think. His computers, that is. But she thinks Lay Auto is a *she*, so it would be *her* computers that do the thinking. Bad said she sneaked and programmed her that way when Dave was walking around the parking lot down in Tallahassee, worrying about some philosopher."

"Gödel. He's always worried about Gödel, a mathematician."

"Ger . . .?" Natalie asked.

". . . Dull. It sounds that way, but it's spelled like 'God,' with an 'el' and an umlaut added. Dave worries about Gödel's incompleteness proof, which says that in any mathematical system you always have to accept some insolvable problems cropping up, that you can never prove absolutely everything."

"Well duh," Natalie said. Unknown to her or Willy, this was verbatim what Mary Lou said every time Dave tried to explain Gödel's Incompleteness Proof to her. Of course, every time that Dave tried to explain the proof to her lately, the two of them were in bed. Dave opined that discussing Gödel counted as foreplay, and perhaps for good Skinnerian reason, for Mary Lou's responding "Well duh" magically had an aphrodisiac effect similar to blowing in his ears and tickling his scrotum at the double same time. "Well duh" was the most effective sweet nothing Dave had ever encountered. Inexplicable? Put that in your German pipe and smoke it, Herr Gödel. Duh.

"Hey! Look out for that car with the weird thing coming out of its hood!"

Willy jerked the steering wheel to the left. Fortunately, no one was in the other lane. He mashed down on Lay Auto's horn, but instead of blowing it played "Tea for Two."

"Cute," Natalie commented with a lift of her musical brows. "More soulful than screaming at an idiot driving a car like that. Spiritually instructive, even. Mary Lou would approve."

"Uh, maybe not." Willy said this because the car with the chromed air filter sticking out its hood, an old Pontiac Firebird, had pulled alongside them; and a red Corvette had pulled behind them. And a candy green Mustang convertible screeched onto the road to slow down in front of them, boxing them in like amateurs in the Indy 500. The passenger in the Mustang turned to face them and held up a placard that read,

"AMERICA!"

The driver of the Firebird beside them hoisted a placard that read, "GASOLINE!"

And the driver of the Corvette blared its horn until they turned to see another placard that read,

"BIG!"

Then all three cars sped off.

"Um, the passenger in the Mustang, the one holding the placard that said, 'AMERICA!,' she looked like Bad."

"Bad's at the office with your boss, Gabriel, isn't she?"

"He hired a temp."

When they reached Willy's sister's house, there was no one there: no one in the back yard tossing lit charcoal, no one in the garage tinkering with model airplanes, no one on the riding mower drinking a Lite beer, and no one in the house playing Nintendo.

Willy broke a window to get into the kitchen. Natalie walked ahead of him into the dining room. "This is so sad," she called out. Willy looked from the sink, which held seven empty beer cans, to see what she was talking about. Five dead angelfish floated on the surface of their tank. Tremor waves scooted along the water, bobbing the dead fish as Willy and Natalie registered the rumble of a muscle car with its stereo cranked toward invisible daytime stars. "These fish couldn't starve in three days, could they?" A second and a third muscle car roared by outside.

Willy shook his head, looking out the kitchen window to see a line of the cars on the street. "They may have died from nervousness. Angelfish are sensitive to noise. The only way they'll mate is if their tank is hooded for privacy."

Natalie blushed, but before she could grab the purple tablecloth and toss it over Willy to rub against him as a joke, she spotted a note on the cloth, a small red bottle of STP weighing it down:

JESUS DROVE A HEMI!
YOU WANT TO SEE YOUR SISTER AGAIN?
THINK ABOUT AMERICA THEN.
KEEP AMERICA BIG!

The letters had been printed in a Halloween orange. Willy called the police.

Who showed up one and a half hours later, just after eleven in the morning, after the witching hour for donut shops. Somehow, the world's tallest motorcycle policeman had gotten himself transferred to the detective unit.

"You," he said when he saw Willy. "Didn't you mess up those marching bands at America's Biggest Parade? You stalkin' high school kids or somethin'?" He ducked under the doorsill and walked into the living room.

"My sister. She may have been kidnapped." Willy pointed to the note on the table. "There's this Chinese woman. . . ." The policeman passed the five dead angelfish and flicked one with his finger. It sunk an inch then resurfaced. He flicked another then walked to look at the note.

"Capital letters," he announced. Outside, a muscle car rumbled by and he bounced his gargantuan frame in rhythm with the camshaft. He nodded toward the fish tank. "Any other dead animals around? Gerbils? Canaries? Hamsters? Cats? –Dead canaries might indicate methane or some other gas."

"No. My mother has the cat and dog and the two kids. The note reads . . . 'Keep America big.' There's a Chinese–"

"Dead kids might indicate foul play. Abuse. Dead grandmothers could indicate about anything: Alzheimer's, a broken hip, a stroke, murder for the inheritance. Ninety percent of crime begins at home. It's like accidents. They take place near home, too. Insurance companies are never wrong." The erstwhile detective picked up the plastic bottle of STP that held the note down. "Half empty," he said. "Or half full. Might mean something." He took out a notebook and jotted. "You got a picture of your sister?"

As Willy reached to pull out his wallet, the world's tallest motorcycle-cop-now-detective white-eyed and fumbled to unbutton the clasp to his holster.

"Picture!" Natalie yelped, holding up her palms. "He's getting out the picture you wanted."

"Lots of murderers and stalkers carry pictures." But the world's tallest gave the room a sniff and eased up from unclasping his holster.

Willy held out the photo. The world's tallest bent, missing a ceiling fan blade that seemed so intent that its motor might have been installed with a homicidal c.p.u.

"Looks like she's in high school."

"She was. It's her senior year picture."

"We graduated together."

"She's your sister too?"

"No. I'm her friend."

The world's tallest stared at the revolving fan. A mote of dust fell and he caught it in his palm, rubbed it with his fingertips, and then stuck it in his pocket. "So, Mr. Turner, do you carry other pictures of other high school girls?"

"Of course not! She's my sister. That's — "

"You do have the graduation picture of me," Natalie said quietly.

The world's tallest detective's lips curled as he jotted in his notebook. He took the picture of Willy's sister, Andrea. "Can I see the one of her?" He nodded at Natalie.

"What for? She's — "

Natalie poked Willy in arm and pointed to the tank. The five angelfish had revived and were swimming. A miracle! But before either she or Willy could take a step, they could see that it was only tremors from muscle cars congregating outside that made the fish appear to be swimming.

"You got her picture too? Comparative evidence." The world's tallest nodded again at Natalie, having raised his voice to almost match his height.

Willy handed over Natalie's picture, though Natalie arched her brows heavily.

"Any more high school girl pictures?" The world's tallest detective had to scream now, since even more muscle cars had joined outside, many of them playing early rock-a-billy from state-of-the-art speakers. Natalie and Willy watched the five angelfish bobbing to the lyrics "Blue, blue, blue suede shoes." Then the noise subsided as the cars moved down the street, and the angelfish went back to floating, serene in the arms of fish death.

"*Plus ca change, plus les memes choses*," Natalie said.

"That Russian or Arabic?" the world's tallest asked. "Or is it Chinese?"

"Arabic," Natalie answered. "Are you sure you need my picture?" Natalie held out her hand.

"Comparative evidence. I'm sure."

Willy was still sorting through his wallet. He came on a picture of his niece in the fourth grade. He looked back at the world's tallest, who was squeezing Natalie's and Andrea's pictures between his thumb and forefinger, in a circular motion. The cap had fallen from the overturned plastic STP bottle, and golden thick liquid was spinning onto the floor in a viscous stream to puddle like . . . like something you might imagine amassing over decades on seat cushions and floors in a sleazy all-night theatre. Watching the stream, the world's tallest opened his mouth; it was cavernous, dark, and no doubt dank.

"That's it for photos in my wallet," Willy snapped.

The world's tallest nodded, ducked the ceiling fan; he paused before bending to leave under the doorsill. "We'll be in touch about your sister."

"And her husband," Willy said, whose soles became tacky in the trail of STP left by the cop.

"Yeah, him too."

"Wait! The ransom note! Shouldn't you take it?"

"That's exactly what they'd expect. And it's not a ransom note. It's more like a political statement, a sacred religious thought or something. I think you should keep it and think about it. Let me know."

Willy and Natalie looked to one another, realizing the detective was right: it wasn't really a ransom note. But it wasn't a religious statement, either; it was psychotic rambling.

Chien Fou, who'd been outside sniffing grass, ran off when the world's tallest unfolded on the front stoop. Willy saw a glistening streak where Chien Fou had marked the cop's back tire. Fortunately, the world's tallest was still studying the two high school girl photos.

"I didn't know girl dogs did that," Willy whispered as the cop folded into his car.

"Hmm," Natalie replied.

Chien Fou gave a low growl as the world's tallest sped off in the direction of the receding rock-a-billy. All the muscle car speakers were now playing Elvis's "Teddy Bear." Even from a distance that song bounced under the maples, elms, and pin oaks of his sister's block, prematurely dropping autumn leaves onto the pavement.

"But if it's not a ransom note, what is it?" Willy asked.

"One of her husband Jack's sick jokes?"

"Even he's not that perverted."

"Yeah he is: he was on the high school football team. Finishing second in the state three years in a row warped him and all the males.

This county's rape and unwed mother rate skyrocketed until they finished first. Too late for Jack, though: he'd graduated. You've been in Florida too long."

"That's what my mother says."

The three of them — Natalie, Willy, and Chien Fou — searched the house again for clues or notes. In the boy's bedroom, Chien Fou rooted about in a closet and began barking. Willy investigated to find a case of STP, a case of Red Man Chewing tobacco, and a box of STP stickers. Atop the box lay a picture of a woman whose head was neatly decapitated by a sticker.

"It's your sister. I recognize the teal dress."

Willy took the photo to the window. "Timmy wouldn't do this. He's a good kid." Willy was about to say that he played sports, but reconsidered, considering Natalie's previous story.

"Jack would," Natalie said. "God, he's got a temper. And he's always scavenging cartons of crap from his shipments with the trucking company."

"It's called stealing, not scavenging. He's just lucky he doesn't drive that truck out of state, or the FBI would be interested." Willy tucked the photo into his shirt pocket, and they left his nephew's bedroom. "We might as well take this and go." He pocketed the address book by the phone and then found the spare house key in the top drawer of the bureau by the front door. It was a habit his sister'd had since grade school. Well duh, what good will it do inside the house, Willy always asked.

Lay Auto started as soon as they stepped off the front stoop.

"Did you do that?" Natalie asked, pointing to the car.

Willy shook his head. "Maybe Bad and Dave reworked the owner recognition program, increased its range." Though he said this with bravado, his voice drifted like an early fall leaf spinning about. "Jailhouse Rock" by Elvis was thundering a street over, accompanied by rumbling camshafts. Willy and Natalie, both wearing sandals, felt the vibrations up to their kneecaps.

Faux Graphic Panels 113 through 119:
The crones cometh

There was an unavoidable inspection meeting that afternoon at the Nicholasville plant. Natalie and Willy spent the remainder of the morning calling Andrea's and her husband Jack's friends to no avail. They had reached the R's in the address book. At least a dozen people they called had commented that Jack owed them money, and they'd been looking for him too. When the thirteenth or so person angrily complained about Jack's debt, five hundred dollars this time, Natalie wondered aloud if Jack hadn't taken off with Andrea to escape his creditors.

"A possibility, I suppose," Willy answered. "A neighbor thought they might have headed to their cabin on Lake Herrington. But why wouldn't she answer cell phone calls from you or me? I'll drive there after the meeting."

At noon, all the Pit Crew except Gabriel packed into Lay Auto to drive to Nicholasville. Gabriel insisted on driving his own car. Bad grinned nastily at his decision. It was clear to everyone now that she and Gabriel were on the outs, after so briefly being in the ins.

Forty minutes later, the real estate agent, Tiger Leigh, was awaiting them at the plant, standing beside her Lincoln, buffing its pearl-white hood with her elbow and a chamois cloth. Lay Auto's engine approached so quietly that the Pit Crew caught her off guard: moving from a Bengal Tiger's snarl at some irredeemable blemish on the hood, she dropped the cloth into her purse and rearranged her face into a Rita Realtor smile. And that stretched into Realtor Rictus when she noticed Gabriel getting out of his BMW.

"The owners insist on meeting with the buyers," she told him glumly.

"Not good," Gabriel blurted, trying to swallow his words even as he spoke them. He and Tiger exchanged glances. Tiger rolled her eyes and smiled weakly. Mary Lou grimaced, too, for as an ex-realtor, she also knew that personal meetings always infused the unknown and could jinx the best of deals.

"Gödel," she whispered to Dave.

"Huh?" he replied.

"The unsolvable problem has appeared."

A lemon yellow, royal blue, and shamrock green VW bus drove into the parking lot, puttering like an antique sewing machine in the white autumn sun. The outline of a purple peace sign still showed on the driver's door, though covered by a coat of lemon yellow. The passenger's door, evidently a salvaged replacement, was royal blue.

Dave, ever a car aficionado, huffed in surprise, "A 1967 model! Lord, what engineering. It almost makes you want to snap to and salute 'Heil Hitler!' "

"Or maybe 'Go, Eva Braun,' " Bad added.

The VW's female driver and its male passenger, both at least nonagenarians, waved their right hands in open-palmed unison as they disembarked in lock-step, despite exiting opposite sides of the vehicle. *Peace. Tranquility. Drugs.* Their separately open palms offered innumerable Gödelian possibilities.

The nonagenarians joined hands in front of the VW bus and bowed slightly, as if Japanese matrons initiating a tea ceremony or maybe Buddhist monks arriving to beg a bowl of rice and propagate peace. They were dressed in matching tie-dyed shirts, whose prominent color was red, purple, green, blue, yellow, white, and orange. And black olive. Both shirts depicted a panda eating bamboo. The man sported one of the longest silver beards on record, only to be outdone by the woman's braided ponytail of the same color, which reached her waist.

Tiger Leigh stalked forward, her slit skirt revealing the sheen of her Florida tanned musculature in autumn Kentucky. "Mr. and Ms. Starchild," she said jauntily and loudly enough for the crew to hear.

"So charming a group," Mrs. Starchild announced.

Legend has it that the Buddha, upon emerging from his mother's womb, skipped in eightfold steps of truth to announce, "This is the last time I will be born!" If so, perhaps Mrs. Starchild whispered calming platitudes upon emerging from her own mother's womb. Mrs. Starchild was sipping what appeared to be green-yellow tea from an eco-friendly clear plastic container. Mr. Starchild held a similar container with a similar liquid. "So charming," Mrs. Starchild repeated.

"We've been anxious to — " Mr. Starchild stared toward the fencerow where Mary Lou had seen the portentous crows. A late season orange butterfly floated there now. Mr. Starchild breathed in, breathed out, in harmony with the butterfly's dips and swerves. Breathed in, breathed out. The butterfly lilted. Breathed in, breathed . . .

"Anxious to meet the inheritors of this plant," Mrs. Starchild filled in. "And we understand — " she walked to lay a fingertip on Lay Auto's snout — "that you're planning on building a lovely alternative fuel automobile here in neighborly Nicholasville."

Chien Fou, who was sitting by Lay Auto's driver side door, tilted her head and licked her lips in consideration of the woman's caressing her friend's proboscis.

"We were wondering about the bottling equipment," Mr. Starchild said, recovering from the lilting butterfly.

"Actually, we figured we could cannibalize a good deal of it," Willy offered.

Tiger, who'd been standing beside Gabriel and covertly scuffing her toes over his brown wing-tips — he was in his go-to-court suit — white-eyed at the word 'cannibalize' and grabbed Gabriel's elbow to maintain balance.

Similarly, Mrs. Starchild swooned, falling into her husband, who was jolted backward but maintained his balance also.

"Sensitive," Mr. Starchild explained. "Mrs. Starchild's a 9.7 on the Cox Sensitivity Scale. That word, that C-word you used, palpated her."

"The Cox Sensitivity Scale?" Mary Lou inquired with out-of-character cynicism.

"Dr. William J. Cox, a modern explorer into the human psyche. He was briefly employed by the University of Kentucky's psychology department before moving into private practice." Mr. Starchild rubbed his wife's left temple as he spoke. "Professor Cox theorizes that many of us are evolutionarily advanced and show stress in contemporary society, which is evolutionarily devolved."

"A throwback," Mrs. Starchild managed to sputter, recovering to wobble from Mr. Starchild's arm. "Society, that is. And American society is one of the worse throwbacks, if not the worst."

"Shouldn't we go into the plant now," Tiger asserted, sensing a meltdown threatening her commission.

Mary Lou stepped toward Mr. and Mrs. Starchild. "I've known that

American society is a throwback ever since I graduated from Divinity School."

Mrs. Starchild lifted her chin and stood erect. "My dearest child, from just where did you graduate?"

"Duke. The minds there were as tall as the Carolina trees."

"And since then?"

"And since then, I've been unable to persuade any church to take me in as a minister."

"Too sensitive, no doubt."

"Too sensitive," Mr. Starchild agreed.

Mary Lou remained demure and stared at her feet, noticing scuffmarks on her blue pumps. Had the realtor woman been busy with her shoes, too? For she alone had caught the footsie, or should I say toesie action; oddly enough, even Gabriel himself had missed it. So turns the world of hormonal love.

"Shouldn't we go into the plant now," Tiger Leigh asserted again, jangling a set of keys in good realtor fashion.

The group assented, and they all walked inside, including Chien Fou. Much to Tiger's dismay the graffiti in storage room 2 had not only returned after she'd had it cleaned, but now used condoms, beer cans, and empty vodka bottles littered the floor. She quickly shut the door and once more skirted the group around that room. Out on the floor of the bottling assembly line, both Mr. and Mrs. Starchild let escape sighs.

"It looks as if it's actually been used recently," Dave whispered to Bad, running his hand along the rubber rollers. He stepped to investigate a carousel of nipples whose purpose was to inject fluid into bottles. "They're gummy." He gave the residue on his fingertips a sniff, then a quick lick. "Sugar." With a jerk he added, "Caffeine."

"Look," Bad announced as they rejoined the group. She pointed at a stack of green bottles in wooden trays and walked to lift one up. "The writing's faded, but I bet it's an old Rolling Rock bottle. A guy I knew collected beer bottles." Bad didn't mention that she'd busted all those bottles, one by relentless one, against his brass bed the morning they'd broken up.

"Oh no, dear. Those are Mountain Dew bottles," Mrs. Starchild blurted, having walked over.

Mr. Starchild coughed tersely.

Willy's cell phone rang. He apologized, saying that he was worried about his sister, whom no one had seen for three, now four days. He didn't mention the note and the police involvement. The call turned out to be from a neighbor, who said that a friend of his said he saw Willy's sister at Lake Herrington with her husband and a bunch of Chinese people just the previous evening. They were grilling out. Hot dogs.

"She — " Willy bit his tongue and thanked the neighbor. He was going to say that even as a kid Andrea had hated hot dogs, everything from their phallic shape to their consistency to their salty taste to their entire biochemical concept. "Thanks a lot," he said instead.

Mrs. Starchild was talking about ginseng when Willy rejoined the group. They were standing by a conveyer belt. With the influx of the California money, the pit crew planned on making twenty-one prototypes, and Dave and Bad had already scoped out this conveyer belt as being especially useful since it had an infinitesimal control that could move weights up to seven hundred pounds as slowly or as quickly as they wanted.

"We've always wanted to bottle a ginseng energy drink with a difference," Mrs. Starchild was proclaiming. "We'd add St. John's Wort, Comfrey, and dandelion extract alongside ginseng. It would be the perfect drink for anyone on the scale."

"The Cox Sensitivity Scale," Mr. Starchild reminded the group.

"Is that what you're drinking now?" Mary Lou asked.

Mrs. Starchild batted her eyes. "You are the sweetest child on this top side of the planet. What would the hemisphere be without you? Isn't she the sweetest child on this top of the planet, Loopy?" Mr. Starchild — Loopy — had been watching Tiger fondle Gabriel's ass. Evidently moving from his shoes to his rump sufficiently caught Gabriel's attention, for he gave a hop.

"Yes. Sweet, she is sweet," Mr. Starchild replied, taking a sip of his green drink, which was a blend of just what Mrs. Starchild had said — ginseng, St. John's Wort, Comfrey, dandelion extract, and a proprietary secret ingredient — all infused into twelve ounces of Mountain Dew. The two of them had been doing this for forty some years, ever since they'd cleared the town of Nicholasville of its addiction. It happened that one terribly hot summer day Mr. Fairchild had been digging roses and walked back into the house to face a wall of bottled Mountain Dews they'd confiscated from the townsfolk. Braving addiction and thinking himself the better man than any common green soda drink, he opened one. Then another. And then Mrs. Starchild walked in. "Try one," he said as if offering a green apple from the Garden of Delight. She did. And now they were down to half a room of the bottles, having gone through an entire cellar, three storage sheds, a garage, five rooms in their house, and even the attic, which they cooled to keep the soft drink from exploding. Eight hundred and ninety-five thousand bottles. Now that they were down to nine hundred or so bottles, they were getting cold feet about selling the plant. For some reason, canned Mountain Dew just didn't taste right to them, even though the folks at the factory assured them the recipe was the same. And when the Starchilds added their special herbal blend to either can or plastic receptacles of Dew, it became nearly unpalatable. They speculated that the ginseng reacted with the aluminum and the plastic, both of which had already reacted with the Dew, as far as they were concerned, though again, they were constantly assured by the Dew folks that this couldn't happen.

"I know what I know," Loopy always replied.

"I know what I know, too," Mrs. Starchild always affirmed.

Who could argue with that? But the management of the local Mountain Dew bottling firms weren't into logic, and they always countered that they too knew what they knew. Too.

In desperation, Mrs. Starchild had made unsuccessful overtures to several managers in an effort to get a tanker full of raw Dew delivered to their plant. The last thing she'd done was to send a stunningly beautiful grandniece from Ohio to one foreman who'd previously wavered. This tactic showed promise, especially as the grandniece and the foreman had begun a steamy affair even as the grandniece was finishing her residency in psychiatry at UK's Medical Center. And to Mr. and Mrs. Starchild's eternal pleasure, the grandniece had thrice met Dr. William J. Cox, founder of the Cox Sensitivity Scale.

"When you take over the plant, do you think it could somehow be arranged that the bottling aspect could be employed, say, once every three months?" Mrs. Starchild now asked the pit crew. "Your eyes are such a lovely hazel," she said in an aside to Mary Lou, who held her breath. Mary Lou's eyes *were* a lovely hazel, and the grandniece's eyes were a lovely green. The grandniece knew how to use her eyes; though four years older, Mary Lou was still learning.

"We wondered about that," Dave said. "So you've been using the bottling works here. That's good, you know; it's kept the machinery in tune."

"What do you mean?" Mr. Starchild asked.

"The ball joints and rollers — the grease in them would have accumulated dust and chemically suffered if they hadn't been used."

"Not to mention the seals, which would have rotted by now, if they hadn't been used," Willy chimed in.

"But — "

"Such sweet men," Mrs. Starchild said. "How do you know they've been used?"

Dave walked over to the circular dispenser and again ran his fingers along the nipples. "Sugar, and it's gummy."

Mrs. Starchild rushed over and ran her fingers along the nipples, putting them to her lips. "Dew," she said ecstatically.

Mr. Starchild looked as if he might swoon in accord with the Cox Sensitivity Scale's demands.

Faux Graphic Panels 120 through 125: Chien Fou goes detective

They left the plant, having agreed to a codicil that allowed the Starchilds to rent the equipment for a two-day run every month. Initially angered at these late negotiations, Tiger beamed at this amendment, for her and Gabriel's commissions went up accordingly. Being a patriot, she imagined the two of them taking a trip to some terrorist-free island, dipping their toes in the sands and drinking a drink in their hands.

Once the conferees reached their cars, a cluster of pre-teens, perched near the fence much as the crows had been, unfolded from lotus squats to stand and stare. All the children held green soda bottles. Mr. and Mrs. Starchild rushed toward them, but the kids ran off into surrounding woods. One girl, who appeared to have reached puberty, turned to yell: "My mother warned us about you two!"

Huffing, the couple returned to their car and the curious Pit Crew. "A sweet child, given a chance," Mrs. Starchild said giddily before getting in the VW bus to drive her husband off.

The Pit Crew and Tiger and Gabriel exchanged glances. Who were those children? Were Mrs. Starchild's tremors from excitement at seeing them, or from the onset of some oldagenarian disease?

"Thank God we got that signed," Tiger Leigh let slip in abnormal candor.

It was already three-thirty, so Willy was anxious to drive to the lake and find his sister. He offered to drop Mary Lou, Bad, and Dave off at Natalie's house, but they wanted to begin converting the plant right away, so they opted for his dropping them off at a truck rental in Nicholasville so they could gather equipment. That was fine with Willy, for it saved time. So he, Natalie, and Chien Fou were soon on their way to Lake Herrington. Willy gave Chien Fou a silk slip that his sister wore, one he'd taken from a closet in her house. Chien Fou took it in her mouth and shook it.

"No, no. Smell it. Find my sister."

Chien Fou barked and wagged her tail, still wanting to play tug. But she also did as Willy suggested and sniffed the slip.

"I didn't realize my sister was into kink," Willy commented.

"Kink?"

"The slip. It's black."

Natalie shook her head. "You really have been in Florida too long. Tallahassee, especially. You'd think all those Gulf oysters would liven things up. Aren't they aphrodisiacs?"

They were driving on a winding two-lane road. Already, leaves in the countryside were turning, and their musty odor floated through the air as Natalie stood up in the front seat and stuck her head out Lay Auto's sunroof. "Fantastic. I wish you could come up here," she told Willy. She was holding Chien Fou in her arms.

"Okay," Willy replied.

Natalie screamed, for Willy was next to her, standing in the driver's seat.

"It's all right, I promise. Lay Auto's computer is ultra sophisticated. It can handle curves and any unexpected obstacles, probably better than I can right now, since I'm so distracted by the Starchilds and my sister and . . . " Willy let go of what else distracted him, though even Chien Fou had a pretty good idea.

For her part, Natalie stared at the road ahead. There were no oncoming cars, and it was relatively straight. "Are you sure you shouldn't be driving?"

"Positive. Trust me. Trust Lay Auto. He's in complete control, isn't he, Chien Fou?"

The dog's tail thumped against Natalie's waist.

Natalie stared at the road for a moment, then spoke. "He?"

"Figure of speech. He, she, it."

Chien Fou jumped down into the seat and licked the glove compartment. A dog biscuit sprang out. Natalie raised her eyebrow, but Chien Fou was back up in her arms. Natalie remembered a comment Willy'd made in the parking lot. "Other than their being throwback hippie weird, what makes you nervous about the Starchilds? Myself, I'm nervous about Gabriel and that real estate woman. I gave him my notice yesterday, by the way, so I'm in with the Pit Crew officially. — Are you sure you shouldn't be driving?" Natalie was eyeing an oncoming curve, but Lay Auto was already slowing and handled it perfectly, even braking for a confused squirrel in the middle of the road.

"See? I'm sure. I wouldn't have saved that squirrel because I wouldn't have seen it in time. Lay Auto's infrared sensor caught it." Willy nudged Natalie and pointed to a second wiggly curve sign ahead. Lay Auto slowed at the same moment. "It keeps one visual sensor on the lookout for road signs, three on the highway ahead. That's two more than any human has. Not to mention its peripheral, overhead, and rear sensors, and the infrared sensor I just mentioned. Twenty-nine in all."

Lay Auto executed more wiggly curves, and they started the decline toward Lake Herrington. Two bicyclists came in sight. Lay Auto slowed and passed them. Willy ducked into the car as they did, looking up at Natalie: "No sense in upsetting the uninitiated." Two curves beyond the cyclists, he stood again to join Natalie. "That's good about Gabriel, your giving him notice. Things will be a lot better with the Pit Crew. You've already earned more than a year's salary with all the investments you've arranged." While this was completely true, the sight of Natalie's kneecaps while he'd been sitting — she was wearing a burnt orange fall dress — also hastened Willy's wish to have her around full-time.

They drove on, all three inhaling the late afternoon air, Chien Fou being most exuberant by inserting an occasional yip. "Back to the Starchilds. I can't say what makes me so nervous about them. I just don't know. Did you see how Mrs. Starchild was coming on to Mary Lou?"

"Surely you don't think she's gay, do you?"

"No, just some mind-control weird. And the Starchilds with all their astrological signs and New Age psychology. I agree with that Dawkins guy and his *God Delusion*: if someone bases his or her life on a belief, the whole shebang teeters on irrational."

Natalie glanced back for the cyclists, but they were long out of sight. "The whole shebang?"

"That person's whole outlook on life. I mean, if you believe that a blue teacup instilled with supernormal intelligence floats in the middle of Saturn's rings, and that this teacup oversees all life, well, just how rational can your other thoughts be? Who's to say but that one bright Monday the teacup won't telepathically inform you that your neighbor is a witch who should be burned? I didn't get that from Dawkins but from a philosopher called Bertrand Russell."

"What about Dave's Gödel guy? Doesn't he say that all math can't be proved, that you have to take something for granted? A belief?"

"So?"

"So! Come on, Willy. You're the big thinker. Make the connection." They passed a yellowing cornfield, and a hundred or more crows took flight, emitting a cacophony of caws. "You know why I like music so much?" Natalie didn't wait for a reply, but continued, "Because it admits that we're all irrational as hell and makes the best of it."

Two quiet minutes later, Chien Fou began barking wildly, trying to leap out of Natalie's hold. Seemingly on its own, Lay Auto slowed and pulled into a dirt road, then stopped, as did Chien Fou's barking, which moved to a low growl. Willy stared down at the instrument panel and gave it a tap with his big toe. Noise came from ahead, music and laughter.

"God, it's the Beach Boys," Natalie said, "speaking of irrational music. Where are we?"

Willy shook his head and sat down in the seat. "I don't know. I've never been on this road before." He patted the dash, and eased Lay Auto forward, by whispering, "Go, Lassie, find Sis," at the dashboard. He grinned sheepishly at Natalie and Chien Fou. "A little joke."

"What's that?" Natalie pointed to a red screen that had popped up from the dash.

"The infrared I was telling you about."

Soon enough, the screen indicated a cluster of warm bodies 127.3 meters ahead, gathered around an extremely hot body. "They're cooking out," Willy whispered.

Chien Fou's growling had kept steady and low. Willy edged the car forward until one of Lay Auto's visual sensors started clicking and zooming in through a small opening in the trees.

"Chinese people," Natalie said. "Look, there's that woman, Madame Nu Wa."

"Chinese people aren't fat are they? No, forget it, they have sumo wrestlers."

"That's Japanese," Natalie corrected, leaning toward the screen.

"Yeah, you're — good lord, there's a civil engineering professor I had as an undergrad at UK. Professor Chin. The guy was as batty as could be. He'd just come over from China, in the middle of the Cultural Revolution, some miracle escape. His idea of civil engineering was more like social planning."

"Isn't that what civil engineering is? The Army Corps of Engineers?"

"They're more like social chaos. Look at New Orleans and Katrina."

"Well, isn't Lay Auto a type of social planning?"

"Let's not argue." Willy punched buttons and focused on Professor Chin, who was sitting half lotus on a stone fountain, not as supplely as the creepy kids outside the plant had sat, but still, the guy had to be in his late 70's or even early 80's. People were gathered about him, and his lips were moving. An early yellow leaf arced back and forth in a breeze before his face, as if keeping time with his lips.

"He was always lecturing about pyramids, the Roman coliseum, and The Chinese Great Wall, holding them up as examples of public works that solidified a people."

"Hey! He's Madame Nu Wa's uncle! She was talking about him!"

"Shh. When did you talk to her?"

"The night we ate at her restaurant, Willy. Earth calling. Don't you remember? While she was showing us how to use chopsticks, she kept gabbing about her uncle and his plans to revive Route 66, to elevate it, extending it from D.C. to Seattle. What were you doing while she was telling us all this?"

Willy blushed, for what he'd been doing was staring at Natalie's cleavage or her kneecaps or her toes, which were painted purple or black that night, he never made out for sure. And sometimes he'd been staring at her right dimple. And sometimes he'd been staring at her brown eyes. And sometimes at her folk-singing lips.

"Well, anyway," Natalie said, a dim memory of Willy's intent that night returning to her in a most flattering way, "she did talk about her uncle and his grand plan to construct an elevated highway. Hey, look!" Natalie pointed to Lay Auto's computer screen. "There's your sister and that creep husband of hers. Chien Fou sniffed the black slip and led us to the right place. Let's drive on up."

Willy leaned to tap the screen, bringing a higher resolution. "She *is* serving hot dogs, just like that neighbor said. Andrea *hates* hot dogs." He tapped the screen again. "That's weird, everyone has an STP sticker on his chest — or breast, as the case may be. Over their hearts."

"Remember what we found in the closet at her house besides the black slip."

Willy's brow arched. "Yeah. And — shit, I don't believe this! I swear that Sis is chained to the grill."

"What?"

It took a few moments of focusing, but something did appear to be attached to Andrea's right ankle. At last they got a view of a thick, rusty chain dragging over the concrete. It was clearly attached to his sister, for when someone tripped on it, Andrea lurched and spilled a plate of hot dogs.

At that, Willy jammed Lay Auto into gear, but Natalie grabbed his arm. "Willy, there are at least fifty people up there. What could we do?"

Willy stared at the screen: Andrea's husband was shaking his finger in Andrea's face. Madame Nu Wa and a stunningly beautiful Chinese woman in her mid-twenties were gazing on. Everyone else was stuffing their faces with hot dogs or cavorting to the Beach Boys, whose music still drifted down to where Lay Auto was parked. Onscreen, the mad engineering uncle hopped in front of Andrea and her husband, enacting his version of a formless American dance to dopey American Beach Music. Willy noted for the first time that everyone on the patio wore white bobby socks.

"Maybe it's a kind of joke," Natalie offered lamely.

"She's crying," Willy observed.

"Can we call the cops?"

They both thought of the world's tallest motorcycle cop now turned detective and shook their heads.

"The crew's going to pick up at least one acetylene torch," Willy said. "We can come back tonight and cut her free."

Natalie hugged Chien Fou and looked from the screen to the barely visible house and patio ahead. "Adventures like this always sound better in a song."

"Everything sounds better in a song, even heartbreak. That's the point of songs."

"Gödel," Natalie whispered.

Willy thought she'd said "God," but he would have agreed to either. They backed out the gravel road and headed to the Nicholasville plant, Chien Fou giving a last low growl.

Faux Graphic Panels 126 through 134: A mystery emerges; Andrea's husband and the side of Big

Dave was alone at the plant when Willy and Natalie returned. Dave explained that Mary Lou had stumbled onto a storage room filled with voodoo signs and had called the Starchilds back to inspect, and then left with them without an explanation. And Bad had left to pick up some incidental tools they'd overlooked on their list. She was already overdue.

"But the truck's still out there," Natalie observed.

"We stopped in town to rent a car." Dave grinned. "Bad picked out a slick red Mazda."

"Listen up, Dave. We found my sister. We think — " Willy glanced at Natalie for confirmation. Her brown eyes enlarged and she nodded him onward — "we think she's being held hostage or prisoner or something weird."

"She's chained," Natalie added. "Willy said you two rented some kind of torch and that we could use it to cut her free."

"Chained?" Dave asked.

"Yeah, her husband's — "

"Husband. Well, maybe we should keep our noses out of . . . I mean, I once dated a woman who wanted me to tie her up and use noodles — "

"Not that kind of chained. Her husband's a damned nutcase. STP stickers, Talladega 500 — no offense," for Willy remembered that Dave had taken last year off from working on Lay Auto to go to that race. "My screwball civil engineering professor, the one I told you about who wanted to build an elevated Route 66, was there perched on a rock in a Buddha pose."

"Madame Nu Wa was there," Natalie inserted.

"Nu Wa? The kook who preached to us about chopsticks and fast cars? Hey, you think that professor guy is her uncle?"

Natalie and Willy nodded.

Dave looked up at the plant's fluorescent lighting and then at the assembly line. "Okay, maybe we need to go. Maybe it's some weird revenge plot, since you're her brother and are working on our anti-Detroit greensource automobile." He turned to point at the far wall where acetylene torches stood, then turned. "Wait — haven't you told me that your brother-in-law has a sick sense of humor? Maybe that's — "

Willy spotted the acetylene tanks and was already walking over to prepare them for travel. "Show him the note we found in Sis's house, Natalie," he called out.

When she did, Dave shook his head. "Okay, let's go."

The tanks rested on a custom dolly that had a rack for the torch on the back. Willy wheeled this toward the front of the plant. Dark was coming on, so in the day's last push Dave helped Willy lower the outfit onto the front seat through Lay Auto's sunroof. The three of them and Chien Fou then drove off.

Not one hundred meters from the plant, what appeared to be a bottle rocket spurting red sparks emerged from woods on their right.

"Those kids, I bet," Natalie said, powering down the rear window to stare into the dark.

Lay Auto screeched to a halt and a ball of blue fire emitted from its front chassis. Natalie and Willy yelped. The bottle rocket, whose sparks had hugely outgrown bottle rocket dimensions, diverted toward the blue flame to explode on the side of the road, blowing over a small billboard and dropping chunks of dirt on Lay Auto. One dropped through the sunroof to clunk against the acetylene cylinder. Chien Fou barked loudly as Lay Auto's tires laid down a line of rubber as the car accelerated.

"Guys . . ." Natalie said.

"What?" Dave looked through the back window at the burning billboard.

"I saw someone by those trees. He held something white on his shoulder."

"A shoulder-launched missile?" Willy asked.

Dave leaned over the back seat. "How'd we keep from getting toasted then?"

"You saw the ball of blue flame. It could have diverted a heat-seeking device."

"Yeah, but where'd it come from?"

"Um, it seemed to come from under Lay Auto," Willy said.

"Could it have come from these things?" Natalie asked, afraid to touch the tanks in the front passenger seat.

Dave, again watching the fire behind, spotted a figure running on the road. "Not without blowing us up first." Another figure ran onto the road. Lay Auto leaned into a curve. The figures and the burning billboard disappeared. "You can slow down now, Willy. We're out of their sight, whoever they were."

"I'm not pushing the accelerator, Lay Auto is. We were going over ninety."

The car slowed as they turned onto the road leading to Lake Herrington.

"Ninety? Kilometers?"

"Miles per hour."

Dave looking out at rapidly passing pastures and trees. "Ninety?" Stars dappling the unsure night sky passed in a blur.

"Back to eighty now," Willy said.

"I thought Lay's top speed was supposed to be seventy-six. That's what you told me, Willy." Natalie's nails bit into the seat ahead of her.

"Dave? Have you or Bad . . ."

"No. Word of honor, Willy. Well, I can't speak for Bad, but — "

"Um," Natalie interrupted, "there's been this weird kid hanging around. He helped Bad and me with the accounting. He's always buffing Lay Auto. He sort of looks pale. Bad kidded him about being a blue dwarf."

"He helped Bad with accounting?" Dave turned to look at Natalie, whose silhouette seemed honest enough. "Helped Bad? Her math leaves me dizzy. Her math might leave Gödel dizzy."

"He's like super high functioning autistic. Adding up pages in his head."

"Speed limit now," Willy commented. A police car passed them going the other way, which didn't give Willy any comfort, thinking of the World's Tallest Motorcycle Cop Turned Detective. "What's this kid got — wait. Blue, you say, Natalie?" Willy asked.

"Blue mist. He looks like an animé child. His eyes are huge, almost black."

As the cop car faded in the rear view mirror a full moon began rising behind them in a red autumn delight, it shone so large.

"Blue. Shit. We'll talk later. Right now we need to free my sister."

∧∧∧∧∧*∧∧∧∧∧

Syntax error 101010-Q: As the moon rises, a body red and autumnal:

Descartes — now there's a name pulled from the old philosophical hat! After months of lying in Queen Christina's castle in a room especially outfitted for him, including a downy four-poster bed; after months of lying in that bed mulling over the mind-body split to theorize just how the mind might communicate to the body . . . to the arm, for instance, that it should heft a glass of wine; and just how, for instance, the toes in turn might communicate to the mind that the castle floor was too damned cold to walk on, so why don't we leap back into the comfy four-poster bed and cogitate some more — after all those months of mulling, the best ye olden Frenchman Descartes could come up with to solve the mind/body split was the pineal gland, which of course, begged the issue since the pineal gland was a gland, and a gland is a gland is a gland and by any other name is a body part. A bona-fide body part, we can all agree.

I think, therefore I gland?

But glanding and thinking — how *do* the twain meet? And *why* do they meet so nattily, nastily, and unpredictably, as Hamlet, Yorick, and countless sociopaths have proven? Therein lies the rub a dub dub.

∧∧∧∧∧*∧∧∧∧∧

Willy tilted the mirror to watch the moon rise behind trees. Though he intellectually understood the phenomenon concerning the optical illusion of the moon's overweening hugeness near the horizon, it never ceased to amaze him, maybe like Gödel's Incompleteness Proof never ceased to amaze Dave. Willy ignored Gödel, so maybe Dave ignored the moon? Natalie was humming a tune Willy didn't recognize. Jealous of her oblivion he angrily hit the steering wheel, immediately grimacing apologetically at the various computer screens, as if Lay Auto might feel pain. For sure, Willy's little finger felt pain. Well, *could* Lay Auto feel pain? Willy tilted the mirror away from the moon to look at Dave in the back seat. "There've been several times that I've thought that maybe you or maybe Bad had been tinkering with Lay Auto's sensors — this afternoon, for instance when he — it — found my sister."

"No Willy," Natalie leaned forward to interrupt. "Chien Fou found your sister. She barked, remember? And if Lay Auto did have a sex, do you really think it would choose to be male?"

The road was winding now, in its last phase before Lake Herrington. Where there'd been cyclists earlier that afternoon, there were now opossum, skunks, and one loose cow that stood stupidly in the middle of the road, staring in cow thought. *I moo; therefore I am.* They stopped, shooed the cow back inside the fence line, closed a gate that had slipped open, then drove on.

"But that doesn't really solve the problem," Willy continued. "How did *Lay Auto* know that *Chien Fou* was barking to make that turn? Lay Auto was the one that slowed; I didn't do it. Does Lay Auto understand dog-talk? Dog-thought?"

"I get it," Natalie said. "Like Descartes saying that the pineal gland solves the mind-body split, saying that Chien Fou found your sister is just adding one more problem to the real question. How did Lay Auto know that she — *she* meaning Lay Auto — should slow down and turn?" Natalie said this out of the blue — or better perhaps, out of the full moon's autumnal red-orange influence.

"Thank you, Mary Lou," Willy retorted, giving a tilt to his head at the mirror and Natalie's reflection while tapping the acetylene tanks in the front seat. "So how'd you know something like Descartes, Natalie?"

Natalie started to reply that she learned it at the conservatory for music, but remembered that Willy was a dropout, so she let his question pass.

"Speaking of Mary Lou, I think she's infatuated with the Starchilds," Dave inserted.

"What was in the room that got her and them so upset?"

"Looked like the regular teenage crap to me. The stuff you see painted on railway cars."

Passing trees mostly covered the moon now. Willy powered down his window: the air was chilly.

Natalie spoke from the back: "Do you ever wonder if maybe there's a whole underground of teenagers just waiting for their chance to pounce? I mean, they've had it up to here with high school's bullshit and TV, and they're bouncing to all these wild songs, heaving and heaving until . . ." she trailed off.

Over Lay Auto's speakers, Mozart's *Requiem* began to play.

Willy knocked at the tank. "You see what I mean? It's creepy. It's like Lay Auto is picking up on our words — hell, for all I know even our thoughts."

"Um, that's not impossible," Dave mumbled.

Natalie tried to catch Willy's eye in the rear view mirror and the console's blue glow. But he just glanced at her then away.

"Let's just find my sister."

"You're the one who keeps bringing up Lay Auto," Dave observed.

Willy huffed. In his indignation, he was ready to drive past the dirt road that led to the house, but Lay Auto once more slowed on its own, despite Willy's foot pressing the gas pedal.

"Oh," he said, spotting a small STP sticker on a square post, something he remembered seeing earlier in the daylight.

Lay Auto's lights went off. Willy wasn't sure they'd gone off because he'd turned them off or not. Lay Auto's infrared scanned the area ahead. Reasonably enough, the barbecue grill still offered the strongest concentration of heat. Near it were three other forms, two moving and one elevated but motionless. Willy powered down all the windows and turned up the exterior sound sensors to hear crickets — a huge improvement over the Beach Boys. He placed a finger on the screen, pointing at the elevated figure.

"I bet it's your civil engineering professor," Natalie said, leaning to look. "He was sitting on a rock to the left of the grill, remember? And there's the grill."

Willy switched to Starlite vision, another of Lay Auto's many wonders. Soon they could see that indeed, the form was the professor, still maintaining a half-lotus pose. And Willy's sister still stood by the grill, cleaning it evidently. Now they could see other figures, all reclined, either passed out or sleeping. It sure looked like Willy's sister's lanky husband was the man walking circles around her, gesturing wildly with his arms.

"STP yourself, you dumbass," Willy said.

"So what do we do now?"

"We get that dumbass husband Jack Wright away from my sister and free her."

"How?"

Willy turned back to Natalie. "He's a sucker for strip tease. It's like a heroin addiction. That and cars. My sister said she had to striptease both times they had sex to have the kids. You could play 'House Carpenter,' or 'The Three Ravens.' I've got them here on a CD."

Natalie dug her nails into Willy's shoulder, that being the only tactic remaining to her in the dark. "Willy, get real. As Mary Lou would say, 'Goddess above.' Willy, no one can strip tease to a folk song."

Dave had been fiddling with the back console's computer, which of course was part of Lay Auto's main CPU. "I just downloaded 'Suzie Q' onto my I-pod. Let's play it over Lay Auto's speakers."

"Hell, why not," Natalie commented. "I'll dance to 'Suzie Q' and get him away from her, you two knock him out or tie him up, just like in the movies."

Dave started the song. The guitars began low, but Dave increased the sound until they could see on the Starlite screen that Andrea's husband's shoulders were lifting, his head beginning to sway.

"Don't peek," Natalie said, getting out of Lay Auto. Dave held up his palms and covered his eyes. Natalie began rotating her hips. The night was warm enough in this dry pocket that she didn't mind unbuttoning her blouse, though she did wonder how far she'd have to go. It wasn't *that* damned warm, and she wasn't *that* damned into greasing her body about. Dave turned the music up a notch.

"He's coming," Willy whispered.

"Put a light on her," Dave suggested. "It's too dark to see."

"I thought you weren't watching," Natalie hissed.

"For him, not me. I can see— " Dave bit off whatever he was going to say. He got out of the car and opened the starred boot, searching for something heavy. What he found was an old can of Bad's Mace and a piccolo. Where in the hell had it come from? Well, it was heavy enough.

From Lay Auto's arsenal of filtered lights Willy focused a blue spotlight on Natalie.

"He's getting closer." Willy eased open the door. Chien Fou jumped out before he could stop her. She crouched, watching the approaching figure.

"Shit, I didn't think he was that big. I guess I've been in Florida too long. Be careful, Dave."

But it wasn't Andrea's husband who came and gawped at Natalie as she went down to her blue bra and rose panties; it was the World's Tallest Detective, a.k.a. the World's Tallest Motorcycle Cop. Fortunately, he was enthralled with Natalie's dancing, for Dave had to ride piggyback on Willy's shoulders to knock him out. Even then, it took three clubs with the piccolo, plus a final spurt from Bad's favorite perfume, Mace.

"What the hell's going on? What the hell are *you* doing here?"

That came from Andrea's husband, who was glaring at Willy. Chien Fou lunged and bit his hand, making him drop the crescent wrench he held. In his other hand he held a can of WD-40, which he tried to spray at the dog. Natalie started dancing again, and Jack Wright's mouth dropped — if anything he was more mesmerized than the tall cop — leaving him an easy target for Willy and Dave, who tied him up with the set of spark plug wires handily dangling from his back pocket.

"What the hell are *you* doing to my sister?" Willy snarled, flipping Jack Wright over.

Jack turned his eyes toward Natalie, who was putting on her blouse. After she buttoned up, he blinked and looked at Willy. "What?"

"My sister, you pervert. Why is she chained to a damn grill?"

"For her own good. She needs to remember her roots. Keep America big."

"Is that why you were staring at me?" Natalie asked, holding back from giving him a kick.

"My daddy carried me to a strip show when I was ten. If strip shows were good enough for my daddy and the two church deacons with us, they're good enough for me and America. It's people like you and — " he turned to spit at Lay Auto "that damn green bean peace machine that are screwing things up. Hippies." He spat again. "The only global warming that's taking place is from the bullshit your kind is throwing at our kids. That's why we're sponsoring those high school parades, to learn them back the truth." He wrenched around to shout to the people on the patio, but Chien Fou jumped and stuffed a tennis ball in his mouth. By the time he spat it out Willy had gagged him. They double-checked his and the world's tallest cop's restraints.

"Leave me here," Natalie said. "If either of them tries to get loose I'll just start up ol' 'Suzie Q.' "

Willy raised his eyebrows, unsure whether Natalie was kidding or not. He decided she wasn't.

Dave had already unloaded the acetylene torch and motioned for Willy to follow. They hurried up the incline, slowing to survey the patio. Willy's sister slumped near the grill. A mixture of snores arose from the people on the ground, mostly Chinese and mostly overweight, something that still puzzled Willy. But then, the snores sounded American enough, so why not the body fat? Globulazation.

A beer bottle, evidently knocked over by someone kicking in his sleep, rolled across the concrete, stopping with a clonk against the rock where the professor posed in half-lotus. The noise startled him, and he began to chant: "America is the fastest of countries, and the slowest of countries. It is the wisest, and the most foolish. It has belief, and it has inbelief; it sheds light, it gathers darkness; it springs with hope, it freezes in despair; Americans have everything before them, they have nothing before them; they are all gassing beautiful muscle cars toward heaven, they are all puttering eco-mini-cars toward — "

Dave and Willy moved near the grill and listened. Willy's sister was oblivious, exhausted or drugged, slumped over the side of the grill.

"It sounds familiar," Willy whispered.

"*The Christmas Carol*. Charles Dickens," Dave answered, proving the inestimable value of a contemporary university education.

"Really?"

Dave nodded in the dark, tapping the acetylene tanks.

Willy looked at the professor, who was delivering his sermon to the trees. Was he readying them for upcoming global oxygen reduction and heat prostration? Willy remembered that even when the professor actively taught years back, the lenses of his glasses were over a quarter-inch thick. The old guy must have finally gone blind. Willy heard a pop and turned to see that Dave had lit the torch. His sister remained slumped. He reached for her, but felt a nudge against his leg: it was Chien Fou, holding something in his jaw. Willy bent to find a key.

"Dave, wait."

The key worked. The professor continued to chant as Willy lifted his sister into his arms and Dave trundled the tank and torch down the decline toward Lay Auto. They could still hear the professor expounding on a new, even bigger America with an elevated Route 66 reaching toward the "rosy crown of the eight heavens."

"Willy?" Willy's sister opened her eyes when they stopped at the bottom. "What are you — Natalie? What are — put me down, Willy." Andrea squirmed and stood, though wobbly. She saw her husband lying next to a tree, tied with the spark plug wires. She inhaled deeply and broke away from Willy. "You son of a — "

Natalie caught her. "Let sleeping dogs lie."

"Let sleeping bastards lie, is more like it," Andrea replied, spitting in her husband's direction. Evidently, loosening saliva was a family pastime.

Faux Panel 135:
At home with the Starchilds

"I just can't believe that those children would paint all those horrible, mean signs. So full of hate."

"My dear, like the tortoise, you must find tranquility within and never worry about what lies outside your shell," Mrs. Starchild told Mary Lou.

"Never to worry about outside your shell. That is quite right." Mr. Starchild turned from the pastel pink stove in their pastel yellow kitchen to offer Mary Lou a warmed glass of pastel green liquid, which she accepted.

"What — " Mary Lou blinked with her first sip, then smiled at the beaming Starchilds and took a gulp.

Both Mr. and Mrs. Starchild each grabbed an elbow as Mary Lou inhaled, nobly.

"An aid to insight."

"And wisdom."

"Insight is wisdom."

"Wisdom is insight."

Mary Lou greedily drank the warm, pastel green, oddly effervescent liquid, thinking only of pink.

Faux Graphic Panels 136 through 137: Keep America Big

Bad lay entwined with the Chinese girl Kate, dreaming of the river she'd heard flowing last night. But the water vanished in white foam when she awoke to screams. From where? Outside on the patio, she realized, getting her bearings. Anxious to try out a new type of Mace she'd bought, she rushed to her handbag. Kate too awoke and jumped from the bed. She moved through a karate kata, hissing with each punch and kick.

They looked at one another and nodded, heading from their bedroom toward the commotion — to be stopped cold by an aluminum chair flung against the dining room's sliding glass door — miraculously not breaking it. Beside the grill, the World's Tallest Detective and Jack Wright, the man who kept his wife chained to the grill to teach her a lesson about America and obedience, were fighting. Jack dove for The World's Tallest Detective's ankles and toppled him.

From a separate set of glass doors, Madame Nu Wa rushed out, accompanied by her entourage of waitperson bodyguards. Her uncle, the professor, still atop his boulder, turned toward the ruckus.

"Ah yah," he said, twitching his ears at the scuffle on the patio. He lifted his right hand to make a sign that oddly resembled the papal blessing. "Wer-wrestling!" He stomped his feet atop the boulder to chant, "America! Go Big Brlue!"

At this sound the two men stopped, and, breathing heavily, scrambled to right themselves on the patio's cold morning stones. Taking in their audience, for Bad and Kate had emerged from the house, they both began pointing and shouting:

"He says I stole his wife away by distracting him with my stripper. My stripper is right! She didn't want no truck with him!"

"Then how come she was blowing kisses and wiggling her rosy bra cups at me? 'Suzie Q' is *my* song. *Mine.* Everyone knows that!"

"Her damned bra wasn't rosy; it was blue! And she was unstrapping it off for me! She sure didn't do that for you!"

The two were readying for another round.

Madame Nu Wa stepped between them and lifted the black chain attached to the grill. "Where is your woman?" she asked Jack Wright.

"Ha!" the World's Tallest Detective shouted. "She saw you trying to cheat with my stripper and ran off!"

With that, the two of them went at it, bypassing Madame Nu Wa. "America! America!" the professor cheered.

Faux Graphic Panels 138 through 141: Mixing molecules; Or the dis-appearing, a-ppearing, re-appearing, and re-adjusting Persons Bureau

∧∧∧∧∧*∧∧∧∧∧

Syntax error 101010-R: Philosophy and Star Trek

If all philosophy serves as a footnote to Plato, then *Star Trek* surely represents philosophy's illustrated appendix. Take the starship Enterprise's teleportation room as instance. Just what limit of molecular shuffling might a disappearing, reappearing human endure while beaming up from the planet Xylophone yet retain the same identity that debarked the Starship Enterprise neutron-seconds before? And . . . does it really take a teleportation room to bring about such shifts, at least mentally? Would just one drop of Skinner or Freud or even protein- or glucose-deprivation do the job? Not to mention Herr Gödel. Alas, dearest reader, read on. Shifts a-plenty lie in ambuscade.

∧∧∧∧∧*∧∧∧∧∧

"It's nearly mid-morning. We're supposed to be at the plant at noon. Where's Bad?" Natalie asked while Willy's newly rescued sister talked on the phone with her mother about the children. The pit crew, minus Bad and Mary Lou, were sitting in Natalie's nice yellow kitchen with its nice pink refrigerator. It was, by the way, no accident that Natalie's kitchen matched the Starchilds', for the same meth addicts had painted both. Two years previous, the Starchilds had opened a halfway house, hoping that their new and improved Mountain Dew would cure all addictions. This proved untrue.

Through a bend in Natalie's hallway, the new black molly Dave had bought watched and listened to the discussion in the kitchen. The first black molly Dave had bought, Aloysius, cowered in a corner keeping its two large eyes on this newer one, evidently considering it demon seed. Overhead in Natalie's nice yellow kitchen, a red light pulsed. And the kelly green teapot hissed, readying to sing.

"For that matter, where's Mary Lou?" Dave asked, twirling the sonic beads on his wrist as if they might lead him to her. Just two days before, he'd made down payment on a large-screen TV, a four-wheel drive cherry-red pick-up (that he hadn't yet picked up) and a two-carat diamond engagement ring for Mary Lou — all compliments of the sonic beads, which he'd recharged at a late afternoon meeting at the Sonic Church. Compliments of the beads, that is, and some investment money for Lay Auto that Dave had filched, thinking he would pay it back with his next nine-month's salary. Oh Dave, what would Frodo the hobbit do?

In the garage, meanwhile, a hazy-blue pre-teenage boy quietly popped the bonnet of Lay Auto and stared at the maze of circuitry. The heat transfer element, still happy from the last installment of KFC two days before, glowed. The boy, with his own blue insightful glow, overlapped two circuits, and Lay Auto purred. Chien Fou licked the boy's ankle.

Back in the yellow kitchen as Andrea hung up the phone, Willy asked. "What are you going to do, Sis?"

"Do you mean am I going to divorce him or take a murder contract out on him?"

"A contract might be cheaper. I used to play in a sleazy bar off New Circle Road. I bet we could find someone there."

"Thanks, Natalie. I'll keep that in mind. For now, Mom's going to keep the kids. Your lawyer friend handles divorce cases, doesn't he?"

"He handles everything he can get, including blonde real estate agents and our red-headed friend Bad."

"So where is *she*?" Willy asked.

"And where's Mary Lou?" Dave added again. The thought of the diamond engagement ring lay smoldering charcoal briquette reality in his right front pocket. That pocket, of course, lay next to his . . . so the world of romance spins in hormonal spurts.

"Um, cell phone, anyone?" Natalie held up her deluxe, super-camera, Internet-ready, cell phone and guitar tuner.

A novel idea, which they used, calling both Bad and Mary Lou. Overhead, the red light pulsed dully while focusing on the phone numbers they punched in. Through the hallway, the bad seed black molly similarly strained its huge telephoto eyes to obtain the same numbers.

"Hello. Hello."

"Um okay. Um okay."

In consideration of trees, paper and ink everywhere, and even in consideration of the electrons employed by Amazon.com's Kindle III Reader, I've doubled the responses emitted by Mary Lou and Bad, saving on quotation marks, for every little bit counts in this wretch of a wreck of a world. Gödel be damned.

"I'll be at the plant soon. I'll be at the plant soon."

"See ya. See ya."

The Pit Crew barely had time to leave Natalie's yellow kitchen just outside Lexington, hop into Lay Auto, and arrive at the red brick plant in Nicholasville. Vroom, they were gone. If $\mathbf{C\!A}$ the fig would only allow just one tiny graphic panel, I could depict the red eye in the yellow kitchen ceiling revolving to study the second, newest black molly. Then that new black molly's stereo-optic appraisal of the red eye. Then the violent death by bashing and infrared rays the two colluded upon for the older black molly, Aloysius. Its demise could be offered as an uncensored, pictorial example of Darwin's Drizzle of the Unfittest. Glurp. Pop. Sizzle. But no time, no time, for we are late for a very important date:

A rumble that rivaled Saturn XXX's rockets announced the arrival of Bad at the plant, being driven in a hot muscle car Camaro by Kate of the high cheeks and pert breasts.

A putter that rivaled the most dilapidated Singer sewing machine in the weasliest local antique store announced the arrival of Mary Lou, being driven by Mrs. Starchild of the trembling voice and the world-wise sighs.

As the Camaro and the Volkswagen bus left the parking lot, one peeling rubber, the other pealing putters, Bad and Mary Lou glared at one another over Lay Auto's ergonomic sunroof.

"I see that you've up-scaled in automobiles," Mary Lou commented. "Supporting global warming, are we?" It was one of the meanest things ever to come out of her mouth, she realized, and her eyes widened in confusion.

"I see that you've down-scaled. And given the puttering of that damned antique, I might ask you the same thing. They no doubt have to mix a lead substitute into the gasoline, which does wonders for global warming too."

The front door to the plant opened and out stepped Willy and his sister.

"You must be Bad," Andrea said. "I've got good news for you: I'm going to work for Gabriel, so you can get back to Lay Auto's computer. That way I can get a discount on my divorce." Andrea grinned and took a step forward. "And you must be Mary Lou. Dave and Willy have told me all about you, too."

The six, seven, or eight blackbirds sitting on the fence grackled, which was more acknowledgement than either Bad or Mary Lou, still simmering at one another, deigned to give Andrea.

"Well . . ." Willy announced to quell the growing silence, "let's go inside and get started on the proto cars."

Peeping from the room with the teenage glyphs, a pale blue boy watched these accumulating molecular changes. He shook his head, for no Scotty, no teleportation beam dotted the landscape to offer relief.

Faux Graphic Panels 142 through 143:
A dozen proto-cars, hot on the line

Four people building one proto-car is feasible, four people building twelve, under time pressure, won't work. They out-sourced the tool-and die work, and Mary Lou suggested that she learn how to weld and that they hire the half dozen or so teenagers who kept mysteriously gaining entrance to deface the storage room, since they were going to be around after school and every weekend anyway. Bad, on the other hand, suggested that her new friend, Kate, had half a dozen or so relatives sorely in need of jobs. And since they were Chinese, they'd all be whizzes at math.

"Sounds like reverse racism to me," Mary Lou said.

Everyone stared at her. Dave even grabbed his sonic beads, hoping for guidance. What could have come over this pleasant, sweet, Divinity graduate lately?

"I mean, those six kids I suggested probably know enough about computers to make our heads spin. That's all kids do these days."

"Sounds like reverse ageism to me," Bad replied.

No one bothered to stare at Bad. Her comment was in keeping. They were just glad she didn't body-kick Mary Lou or squirt her with a new formula of Mace.

A compromise was reached: three Chinese relatives were hired and three teenagers from the Hole-in-the-Wall-Gang, so named because no one could figure out how they kept getting access to the storage room.

"What about the blue boy?" Dave asked. "We need to put him on some kind of salary, don't we?"

A shiver ran through the entire Pit Crew, for though they'd all had contact with the boy Dave was talking about, they rarely admitted it openly. The young teenage boy had helped Bad with the books, that simple arithmetic getting on her nerves down to her toenails; he'd helped Willy with wiring and soldering; he'd fetched alternate configurations of RAM, heat sinks, and other computer gizmos for

Dave; and he'd helped Mary Lou proofread the numerous letters she sent out for publicity. The only one he hadn't helped was Natalie. But whenever she played guitar and sang he seemed to materialize to sit awestruck and listen, which sent shivers through her guitar-picking fingernails.

" 'At's my son yer talkin' about," a voice boomed from the loading dock entrance. " 'At's my son Huck, and he's a whiz at ever'thing there is to be a whiz at. Yer gonna to need to pay him more than you pay these oriental heathen and common punks ya been talkin' about. Twice more. And yer gonna to need to give me a pint of whiskey a day. I drink Maker's Mark. I'll be sweepin' the floors when I feel like getting some exercise. Ya can't expect much more than that for a pint of whiskey a day, and I don't feel up to being obliged to anyone because of some paper money thrown my way. So a pint it is." The man, tall and in his 40's, 70's or 80's, much like the ageless Madame Nu Wa, fell against the loading dock entrance and pulled something from his pocket.

Willy's eagle eyes knew it was a bottle of Kentucky Tavern, because he recognized the label from high school when he couldn't afford better. *Maker's Mark, my ass*, he thought.

"We got a deal?" the man said, holding out his bottle.

The Pit Crew looked at one another.

"Deal," Willy said.

"I'll need that Maker's Mark around before every lunchtime," the man said, clutching the loading dock's framework of steel door rollers and clumsily twisting his body to disappear outside.

"I'd call that a real Kentucky reel," Willy commented.

One hour later, the six helpers arrived and cleanup started.

"Where's the blue kid?" Dave asked at one point.

As if in answer, an empty whiskey bottle thunked, having been tossed lightly inside the loading dock. It spun and they watched, as if playing spin-the-bottle. But when it stopped, no one was chosen.

"I'll go," Natalie volunteered.

"Buy a case, they'll be cheaper."

"Buy two cases, we might need some ourselves," Dave added, for Bad and Mary Lou had spent the entire morning glaring at one another.

Faux Graphic Panels 144 through 150:
A green complication for Project Chicken Bone

They had wanted to name the production of the extra Lay Autos Project Green, but two of the three Chinese kids kept twisting that about. Collectively, the teenagers came up with the name Project Chicken Bone, since Lay Auto could run on KFC discards. It was a Friday, the first payday, and everyone was in a good mood. The kids were skipping school, something that at least Willy approved of, and Huck's old man had his bottle of Maker's Mark. For lunch, they'd compromised and were eating fried ginger chicken brought from Madame Nu Wa's Nicholasville store, which had opened only two weeks before. Willy admitted that Lay Auto ran on it almost as well as it did on KFC, though his heart still thumped for KFC, since his mother had once ridden on a Kentucky Fried float with Colonel Sanders himself in a parade. The Colonel had been a gentleman and just bent to kiss her teenaged hand, she always claimed. "He didn't even lick it — you know, finger lickin' good," / "Mom!" Willy always had to shout. He hoped she wasn't telling that story to his nephew and niece, Andrea's kids.

Mary Lou walked into the break room where Huck's Dad was holding forth some tall tale of underground pool tables in Louisville, where he swore he played football for the Cardinals. The Kentuckians listening weren't sure that Louisville even had a football team when this septuagenarian would have been eligible to play, but they let it go. Free entertainment was hard to come by, and his tall tales kept Bad and Mary Lou, and the Chinese and the teens from getting into it.

"The Starchilds are coming this afternoon," Mary Lou announced during a rare pause while the old guy poured himself another whiskey.

There was a collective groan. The Starchilds were one thing that everyone — except Mary Lou — agreed upon.

"My mother said those two are nasty. She said they play with each other's hairs and butts in public."

"I'm quite sure that's not — "

"Madame Nu Wa says they poke their ears with chopsticks, then use them to eat."

"Now listen to me, all of you. Mr. and Mrs. Starchild are a dear couple. They single-handedly — " Mary Lou worried how a couple could single-handedly do anything — "together with no other help they saved this very town of Nicholasville from the direst of addictions."

"My mother said that her oldest uncle drove his car into the river because of those two."

Mary Lou looked at the pesky girl who was tossing off shots against the Starchilds. She reached into a voluminous lime green purse that she'd taken to carrying, and everyone stiffened. She pulled out an oversized bottle labeled Green Gong Energy Drink and carried it to the girl.

"Just one sip, try it," she told the girl.

Everyone watched.

"Wow!" the girl exclaimed. When the boy on her right tried to taste her drink she pulled protectively back, so Mary Lou reached into her bag and gave him one also.

"Wow!" he exclaimed.

Mary Lou then handed a third bottle to his friend on his right. Collectively, the Chinese trio refused the drinks when Mary Lou tried to distribute them until she proclaimed the magical phrase "soft drink," assuring them that it was as American as muscle cars, baseball, and bluegrass music. Willy, Dave, and Natalie politely sipped from the bottles Mary Lou gave them. Bad turned her back on Mary Lou, and for a moment Willy thought Mary Lou was going to bash Bad over the head with the proffered bottle. Fortunately, the old guy had finished pouring his Maker's Mark and after taking a sizeable sip, he spoke loudly:

"Did I ever tell you about the time that I held a mare so that Secretariat could — "

"Keep it polite, there are children here."

"We ain't children," the six said collectively, removing their mouths from the nipple-like construction of the Green Gong bottles.

"Amen," Bad said under her breath, turning to face everyone.

"Where's your son?" Mary Lou asked the old man, hoping to waylay the horse-breeding story. "I'd like Huck to try some Green

Gong."

"Out plunking rats with my .22," Huck's Dad answered.

Mary Lou blanched at this affront to Darwin's animal kingdom.

"Just joking," the old man said. "He's a teenage boy. Who the hell knows where he is. But let me tell you about the time I held that pretty mare — I almost had a woody for her myself — for Secretariat. You should have seen the equipment on that stallion. It'd make a Louisville Slugger look like a toothpick. . . . I used to test bats for Louisville Slugger, did I ever tell you that? One time, Mickey Mantle walked in and shook my hand and said . . . "

After lunch, they collected the bones from Madame Nu Wa's ginger chicken and walked outside to ritually feed them into Lay Auto's distiller control. Willy bent over and breathed the air emitted.

"Try that with one of Detroit's monsters," he said.

The three Chinese workers raised their brows and looked to one another. When Willy walked proudly inside, the three of them walked over and sniffed too. Their reaction, however, was nausea.

"No gasorine," they commented in synch.

With the end of lunchtime everyone began hustling inside. The coming of the Starchilds meant that the plant would have to be adjusted to a different mode of production for the weekend. Amid the bustle, there came a low sizzle as Huck walked in through the loading dock door, his typical unsettling blue glow not so visible against the early afternoon fall sky.

"How many'd you get?"

"Beg pardon?" Huck said to the old man.

" 'Beg pardon?' Hell, you mean, 'Huh?' don't you? I didn't raise no sissy boy. I told everyone you was shooting rats. How many'd you get?"

Huck ignored the old man, who made a movement toward the boy as if he were going to grab him, but a sizzling blue emission sent him back to sweeping the floor in a remote part of the assembly room. Noticing all this, Willy walked over and gave a huge sniff with his preternatural nose around the loading dock door where the boy'd walked in.

"I was out with Lay Auto," Huck said to Dave and Bad, who walked up behind Willy. "She — it could use some more RAM in its main computer."

"Yeah, I have noticed a slower response after Lay's been running for an hour or more," Dave said. "What do you think, Bad?"

Bad shrugged.

"We'll consider it on Monday," Willy told Huck. "Right now, we have to comply with the contract and get the plant ready for a weekend of bottling."

Huck nodded and walked over to pick up a bottle of Green Gong that was sitting on a workbench. He gave it a sniff, giving much the same reaction that the three Chinese had given to Lay Auto's distiller emissions.

At four p.m., the Starchilds arrived. The couple made a point of walking around and formally giving everyone a hug, in a feel-good parade.

∧∧∧∧∧*∧∧∧∧∧

Syntax error 101010-S: Good Ol' American journalism:

So you pick up your mail, and you find this month's copy of O. You hold the slick magazine and it comforts, like warm olive oil in a Mediterranean salad. Oprah's dentally perfect teeth greet you, her physically perfect cleavage offers solace if not suckle. The slick cover's wondrous colors entice. Pitter-putt goes your heart, for against those splendid colors, in angel-white, is boldly outlined this month's list of mini-angsts, handed to you on a comforting Tupperware platter:

> *Accessorizing that special winter outfit for under $75!*
> *Is he for You? Five easy questions that will let You know!*
> *Workplace Power Plays: How to recognize and counter them!*
> *Diet? No! Four simple foods that will sculpt a miracle You!*

Inside on slick olive oil pages comes a lineup of self-help artists, not the least of which is Dr. Phil. Dr. Phil's nearly bald head always reassures, telling you, *I've been there and made it through. And you'd better do it, too!* And then comes the queen, Oprah herself: white enough to placate moderate America, black enough to empower black America; beautiful enough to entice men, powerful enough to inspire women; charming enough to sway voters, able and confident enough to pull you up just as she pulled herself up from terribly crushing depths. She is indeed worthy.

But something, O some thing lacks, perhaps even g-naws (to use the Middle English pronunciation) in this monthly barrage of angst and angst's cures. *Angst:* there's a Teutonic word for your navel. Gödel, are you lotus-squatting and meditating with your pal Einstein in one of your multiple universes? Can you beam into this one and cue us to its origin, its cure? The fact, not the word.

That space wasn't left for a miswritten mathematical word problem. Nor for a gnomic message from Gödel and his white-haired pal. It was left as a silent tribute to Wittgenstein, who wrote this about angst, "Of the mess, we must pass over in silence." Something along those lines. Boo-hoo, boo-howl. No wonder humans consult Dr. Phil.

∧∧∧∧∧*∧∧∧∧∧

Since the inception of O, by the bye, the Starchilds had faithfully written a letter a month, a not too insistent letter a month, nonetheless one letter every month to the editor's *We Hear You!* Column. And every subsequent month they opened the olive oil magazine in hopes of reading their letter, or even an excerpt of their letter. It had yet to happen. On occasion, one or the other would flag in this monthly letter writing, but a timely proffering of Green Gong and an encouraging, "There's always next month, Loopy!" followed by "That's right, Binky. There *is* always next month, and more importantly, there's always Green Gong!" would send them back to the computer files, assiduously composing letters to O.

Hard as it would be for aged residents of Nicholasville who remembered the opening of the Mountain Dew bottling plant and the free distribution of the soft drink throughout the once-sleepy town for an entire week, the Starchilds had truly *improved* the original Dew recipe, throttling it with ginger, cinnamon, St. John's Wort, and eight other proprietary spices. When gasoline went lead-free, they even introduced trace elements of it into Green Gong to bring the health drink to its apex, figuring that if crude oil was good enough for dinosaurs, it was good enough for humans.

Wait: you're saying they did this after successfully opening a clinic to rid the entire town of its addiction to Dew? Is this logical? Commonsensical? Even possible? Gödel, Gödel, Gödel, will you ever let matters rest? Pass over it in silence, kind sir.

So. Directly before stepping into the plant that Friday, the Starchilds held this tête a tete in the front seats of their antique VW bus in the parking lot:

"Loopy, I didn't tell you, but this month's O arrived two days ago." Mrs. Starchild was parking, and her hands fiercely pulled the emergency brake.

Mr. Starchild leaned in anticipation.

"No, Loopy, she didn't run our letter."

"There's always next month."

"There's always that and there's always Dew — Green Gong."

True to that last pronouncement, as they opened the VW's doors and walked inside the plant to hug all the workers and the Pit Crew, both Loopy's and Binky's moods improved significantly. The Dew Transformation lay ahead.

Now, despite their young and beautiful grandniece's promises, they'd yet to obtain either the formula for Mountain Dew or delivery of the product in bulk, sans the offending cans or plastic bottles. They had, however, obtained a large discount on the product amid assurances by both the grandniece and the plant manager that the formula had not changed over the years and that the same Dew was infused into the cans and plastic just as it had once been into the glass. Doubtful, they worked with what they had. So, for the previous fortnight they and ten clients at the "New You Focus Group" had emptied the Dew cans into the large vat of a delivery truck.

In truth they needed the plant's operations to produce a supply of bottled and eleven-spice infused Dew, enough for them and their growing base of clients who needed release from this world's woes. Dew — a.k.a. Green Gong — plus group encounters were both part of a strategic Starchild therapy.

In his exuberance on seeing the vat that Dew would soon swirl in, Mr. Starchild gave Mary Lou an extra long and squeezy hug around the breasticular area. No gentleman Kentucky Colonel he. This did not escape the notice of Mrs. Starchild, nor did it escape the notice of Dave, who twisted his Sonic beads angrily.

It did, however, escape the notice of Xujun Ling, who was text-messaging her great-aunt Madame Nu Wa about the arrival of the Starchilds and the temporary conversion of the plant. It also escaped the notice of Huck's old man, who was passed out near the dumpster, enjoying an oddly warm fall day, and dreaming, let's say for the sake of poetic argument, of red tigers.

Little escaped the notice of Huck himself. He shook his blue and preternaturally wise head and angrily envisioned Gödel, Einstein, and now this damned Wittgenstein fellow tossing skull bone dice to prompt one human interaction after another.

Joe Taylor

Faux Graphic Panels 151 through 153: Green Gong vs. New Wall?

∧∧∧∧∧*∧∧∧∧∧

Syntax error 101010 T: Godzilla and the bomb:

"Aaaarggh!"

"Eeeeee!"

The first exclamation being the captive monster, Godzilla; the second being the squeaking axles bearing Godzilla's ponderous weight.

"Peepa-poo" go five hundred flautists parading before Godzilla. There are no sousaphones, for this is Tokyo and the Japanese have impeccable taste and know when to use that instrument: Never.

"Ka bloweee blam!" a thunderbolt, a.k.a. lightning to Ben Franklin fans, strikes the chains of Godzilla, setting him free.

Before the cacophony of Godzilla's escape ensues, let's pause to consider just why this monster lurks the streets of Tokyo in the first place. To do so, we must travel back to that ill-fated utilitarian excursion in Faux Panel 31 and look not to Tokyo but Hiroshima:

Ssshooom. A faint, offshore wind sifts through charred bodies (recumbent, crouched, spread-eagled, crumpled), charred buildings (skeletal, twisted). *Ssssss.* A pale sun searches out evaporated bodies and evaporated buildings. *Who-woo,* wheezes the ancestor-seeking wind, *zip-pop* crackles the Geiger sun. Melted steel, evaporated steel. Charred bodies, evaporated bodies. Tumors, cancer, deformed births, deformed bodies, deformed minds. . . .

So the Japanese concocted Godzilla, Bomb Incarnate. And it seems that Godzilla has taken a liking to the isle of Japan, just as the Japanese themselves have taken a liking to bluegrass music, baseball, and assorted American items. A precursor of the Stockholm syndrome, wherein captives fall in love with captors? Or just one more instantiation of Gödel's Incompleteness Proof, the total acceptance of unforeseen axioms, problems, and consequences?

∧∧∧∧∧*∧∧∧∧∧

Saturday morning a stainless steel milk truck pulled into the Nicholasville plant's delivery door. With promises of overtime pay, the Starchilds had convinced the three gang members and the three Chinese to arrive just after seven o'clock.

Two one thousand-gallon open stainless steel vats had been left *in situ* on the site. The one painted with swastikas and eyeballs had been the favorite of Doorwin's Simians, the self-proclaimed moniker of the teenage gang who hung out in the factory prior to its changeover into a proto-auto assembly line. Not Hole-in-the-Wall, they insisted when Willy and Dave tried calling them that. That name's too Old West. We're up-to-date, they insisted, saying that they'd named their gang after the hippie scientist who'd discovered monkeys, Doorwin. Now the three Simians working at the plant elbowed each other in Saturday's morning sun as potential Green Gong was pumped from a rental milk truck into that same vat, whereon they could still see a faded violet eyeball. Months before they'd used this stainless steel vat as a swimming and sex pool, filling it with Nicholasville city water that for some reason had never been cut off. Even a graphic panel wouldn't do justice to the frolicking sex scenes they imagined as the Mountain Dew level rose from marker to marker in the vat. I'd provide workspace for you to sketch that panel and I'd even add a 900-number to call, but then, would you ever finish reading this book? Much wiser to give you workspace to figure out how much you'd spend at only 69 cents per minute goo-talking with the sweet sexpot whose 900-number you might call.

Whoa! That much? We better return to the scene before you bust your Visa limit:

On a catwalk around the second vat, the Starchilds were pouring in their eleven spices. One of the Chinese workers sneezed after getting a nose full of ginseng. At noon, the Starchilds announced the drink was nearly ready to be infused with an extra dose of carbonation, and they shooed the six young workers outside for a twenty-minute break, despite that lunch hour loomed just ahead. The workers nodded compliantly, happy to let the signatories of the paycheck make the decisions. Good future citizens, all.

But the Chinese worker who'd sneezed was something of an artist, while his other two Chinese co-workers spent their off time tinkering with muscle cars. Being an artist, he was curious, and while his comrades and the three gang members stood out back taking a break and listening to Huck's Dad tell about the time he smuggled ten cases of tequila over the border from Mexico into Willie Nelson's annual fourth of July bash and was mugged by three Apache women who continually performed ritual sex over his body, the artist sneaked back in to the plant, having observed the Starchilds secreting something from their ridiculous VW bus. Ah, he said to himself as Mrs. Starchild climbed the catwalk around the vat with a gallon gasoline container. She and her husband bent over the container and stuck in a pipette. They held it up to the light and knocked several drops of the gasoline out into their palms, sniffing its octane, the worker supposed. The remainder of the gallon they poured into the Green Gong.

"Gasoline is king!" the Chinese artist whispered. He immediately text-messaged Madame Nu Wa.

Faux Graphic Panels 154 through 155:
Wild West interlude

Bam! Bam!

That definitely was not the sound of a ball peen hammer creating something innovative early Monday morning.

Kaboom!

Nor did that particular sound reflect an Army bazooka ricocheting off Godzilla, for it rattled windows in the factory and sent tremors through Willie's coffee even as he stopped kissing Natalie to look up from the bare desktop in their makeshift make-out office.

Foolishly or wisely, eleven people ran outside the loading dock door to see Huck's old man standing with a snub-nosed .38 pointed at a spot behind the factory where half a dozen twenty-foot trees had been blown over. Two white-turbaned figures were running off, and Huck's old man raised the revolver and fired into the air.

"Get out of here, ya damned foreigners!" He turned to the three Chinese workers. "No offense."

They hadn't taken any, since all three were born in Lexington.

Again, foolishly or wisely, everyone walked toward the trees, which were smoldering and smelled of explosives.

"No gasoline," one of the Chinese workers commented, evincing confusion that such glorious power could be wrought without his favorite chemical.

Natalie bent and picked up a torn photograph. Depicted on the remaining half was a scantily clad teenage girl. "Wasn't one of those men running off awfully tall?" she asked the air surrounding her.

"I figured him for a Russkie. It's the vodka and that Churned Over nuke plant over there is doing it to them. 'At's why I never touch vodka."

Eleven people nodded sagely at Huck's old man, especially since he was still holding a revolver.

Now, a stream with a small waterfall flowed behind the plant, right on the property line. The loading dock and parking lot were quiet enough in the aftermath that they could hear the water as the old man's wisdom echoed amid the smell of dynamite.

"I'm gonna be needing a raise if I gotta be a damned watchman too," Huck's old man continued, pulling himself from listening to the water, the drinking of which he'd always counted as conducive to kidney stones. "Two pints a day. And no more substitutions. That Old Granddad whiskey one of you left this morning nearly killed me. That's why I was out here target practicin'."

"You mean you didn't know there were people planting bombs? It was just luck?"

Huck's old man swayed and blinked. "Yeah, I knew. That's what I'm sayin. 'At's why I was out here. 'At's why I need a raise. Two bottles."

Eleven of the twelve people standing in the smoldering remains looked doubtfully at one another.

The twelfth blinked and reached for what was left of his pint of Old Granddad.

Faux Graphic Panels 156 through 161: A romantic interlude

Dave's Sonic Beads had pulled him into a car dealership, where he finally took command of the cherry red four-wheeler of his dreams. They had pulled him into a pet store where he bought another black molly, to replace the one that had been mysteriously mangled. They pulled him into a jewelry store, where he again stared at engagement rings, but returned the one he'd bought and used its previous down payment to buy an antique garnet for his birth date instead. They pulled him into a stereo supply store where he rigged out his new cherry red truck with super octo-quad sound; then, upon leaving the stereo store, they pulled him into a CD shop where he bought fifteen jazz CD's including Wynton Marsalis, Chick Correa and Bela Flek. He spied a DVD of *The Hobbit*, which stirred some axons, but then he realized he couldn't watch a movie and drive.

Within three hours, the second black molly died as mysteriously as the other had. Within a minute the four-wheeler was eating most of Dave's salary from the newly formed L. A. Non-profit. Insurance alone cost 290 a month. Gasoline prices threatened to quadruple that. And obviously there was a loan payment. The garnet birthstone came loose and he lost it. The CD player worked just fine, but no one except the three gang members would get in the truck with him, since its eight speakers were incapable of producing moderately ranged decibels, even for Marsalis. Once, Dave tried to get Huck to ride with him to buy the old man some Maker's Mark, but Huck grimaced bluely at the noise and shook his vibrating head.

The first time Mary Lou rode with Dave to get lunch, she saw the new CD's in the even newer portable CD rack and commented that she'd wished she'd known he was going CD shopping, since she wanted to buy some Gregorian Chant to help her meditate. Dave remembered seeing a tiny section of Gregorian Chants that he'd known Mary Lou would love. He blushed. Something else niggled his mind, *The Hobbit*. Another niggle: a ring. Wasn't he going to buy someone a ring?

He and Mary Lou were now standing outside the L. A. Non-profit factory, exactly one Friday after the failed terrorist bombing. Behind the building, Huck's old man was firing rounds in a ritual he'd developed to ward off evildoers. Bam! Mary Lou winced. She had planned on visiting the Starchilds, but they'd turned oddly incommunicado since last bottling the Green Gong on Sunday, so she apprehensively appraised Dave and his truck. When Dave smiled and suggested they go hear Natalie play at Como's, Mary Lou agreed, requesting that they not listen to his infamous — though she didn't use that word — octo-quad CD player on the way into Lexington.

Bam! Huck's old man fired off another round. Mary Lou's shoulders jumped. Dave, used to the gargantuan sounds coming from his speakers, barely flinched. He may not have even heard the shot. The blue boy Huck was standing by Lay Auto some few feet away, and he gave Dave a high sign as Mary Lou climbed into the cherry red truck. Bam! Another round.

"That kid," Dave said, pulling up to the highway and waiting for an eighteen-wheeler and a line of traffic to pass. "Sometimes he creeps me out."

"Bad says he knows more about math than she does."

"He might know more about computers than I do."

They waved to the boy, who'd jumped to sit on Lay Auto's bonnet. But now he seemed distracted and didn't wave back. Bam! More gunfire.

"Do you think that weird old man who lives by the dumpster is really his dad?" Mary Lou asked.

"What do you mean, 'lives by the dumpster'?"

"Have you ever seen him anywhere else but there and sweeping the floor inside? When he takes a notion to sweep?" Mary Lou pinched her wrist for saying something negative about one of Gaia's creatures.

Dave admitted he hadn't. The blue boy assumed a lotus pose atop Lay Auto's bonnet, taking advantage of a moment of silence. The old man was probably reloading. He had clamored for an automatic pistol as part of his new guard duties, but everyone had white-eyed. Even the three normally adventuresome members of Doorwin's Simians visibly quaked at the thought of the old fart armed with something that could release multiple rounds.

Shaking his head, Dave pulled onto the highway. When they were well past Nicholasville and heading into Lexington, his Sonic Beads tugged. "Do you mind if we stop in Joseph-Beth's?"

Mary Lou touched Dave's arm, just above the Sonic Beads, being careful not to touch the beads. "I put mine away," she said. "Mr. Starchild convinced me they were dragging me into the material world."

"All that dirty old man wants from you — " Though half of it had already wriggled out of his mouth, Dave decided to bite his tongue. Inhaling deeply he turned into the mall and the bookstore.

Once inside, he knew the beads had been right. They always were. The bookstore prominently displayed the latest addition to a science fiction series Dave was addicted to. As he grabbed a copy, Mary Lou studied the buxom woman on the book's cover holding a laser rifle like an overgrown stud horse's penis. How old was this buxom warrior? Eleven going on twenty-eight? A pre-pubescent crone armed with a pump laser rifle?

"Kentucky Mare Breaks Deep Space," Mary Lou commented, twisting the novel's title about.

Dave clutched the book to his chest. Back in the truck, he reached for the octo-quadro stereo, but Mary Lou again touched his arm.

"We've got plenty of time before Natalie starts," she said, giving him a playful pinch.

"That's right, we do. We could stop at that new auto supply store. I've been — "

"Dave!" Mary Lou threw her body over the monster console to rub her breasts against his arm.

"Oh," he said.

Despite the rumblings of his middle-earth, or rather his mid-body and maybe even his soul, he had to fight the sonic pull of the beads past two more stores, for Dave had returned to The Church of the Sonic Beads twice every week, imitating the sect's Southern Baptist counterpart in church attendance. The huge blonde woman who acted as head priestess advised in a sermon that the beads would gain power, the more you listened to them. Conversely, she warned, they would lose power every time you ignored them. But who would ever want to ignore them, she added, clinking her own set amid giggles. The church had recently acquired purple and red velvet love seats for the tabernacle, which Dave always sank into at those giggles.

Now, in the monster red truck that the beads had acquired, Mary Lou rubbed Dave's middle earth and sighed. With her insistent ministrations, he was able to pass a third store, replacing a tugging vibration from his bracelet with a tugging elsewhere.

When they finally pulled into Natalie's driveway they were both surprised to see Huck already in the garage, polishing Lay Auto. Hadn't they just left him and Lay Auto at the Nicholasville plant? Surely the stop at Joseph-Beth's hadn't taken that long. The blue boy spoke as Dave and Mary Lou descended from the truck: "They've already left so that Natalie could practice in Como's back room. They took a cab. I'm polishing and cleaning Lo." Huck was the only one who called Lay Auto "Lo." Willy commented that it made the car sound like the Old West pejorative for an American Indian, as in 'Lo, the noble savage,' but shrugged and let Huck have his way.

"Have you seen Bad?" Mary Lou asked.

Huck kept polishing Lay Auto. The car and the boy seemed to emanate a similar glow, low and blue, something sleepy and easeful you might see in a saltwater aquarium.

"Have you seen Bad?" Mary Lou repeated. The boy shook his head.

For the last few weeks Bad had been problematical. She put in her hours at production, all right, but after that they rarely saw her. Willy conjectured she'd found a woman lover and was embarrassed because she'd "floated to the Isle of Lesbos." Dave and Mary Lou, in one of their few recent moments of agreement, thought that floating there would be the best thing Bad could do, especially after the debacle with Gabriel the lawyer, who was still back-stroking with Tiger Leigh the real estate woman in her cream white Lincoln.

Dave and Mary Lou sighed in response to Huck's negative response then went inside Natalie's house. Dave perfunctorily fed the remaining one black molly.

"How do these things eat?" Mary Lou asked, peering into the aquarium. The black molly edged the tank's glass wall to stare at her and she backed away as its eyes protruded telescopically from its skull in a very non-Darwinian manner.

"What does that mean?" Dave asked, blithely dropping food. "They eat like every other animal alive: with their mouths, of course."

"No, I mean do they store their food like alligators do, and let it rot? Or bury it like squirrels for winter? Because I've watched it do that after you feed it."

"Really?"

"See that bulge in the gravel over by the pirate's chest? That's where it buries the food."

Both the black molly and the infrared eye in the kitchen were focused on Mary Lou as she spoke. And they followed her down the hall to the bedroom after she opened a bottle and poured Dave and herself a glass of wine. It must be noted that neither the black molly nor the infrared appeared appreciative of either the waft of the Spanish rioja or the sway in Mary Lou's hips. They both gyrated, contrawise, in a mechanical flurry.

Mary Lou latched the bedroom door and handed Dave his wine. It took her a full fifteen minutes to get his attention sexually. This, on top of her ministrations on the ride from Nicholasville, appeared to be a grand record as far as she could tell. Usually males operated in nano-seconds. But then, Dave's attention had been waning since their initial visit to the Church of the Sonic Beads. For a while she'd suspected him of having an affair with the huge-breasted blonde priestess. But as more and more material items accumulated around him, she realized a darker truth: he was in love with the sonic beads and the dry goods they lead him to. *Dry goods.* She pondered that phrase as she sipped rioja then gave Dave's penis a lick. There, it was standing on its own, at last. When they'd started being lovers several months ago, she thought of his penis as a nutcracker, the type she'd seen as a child in the Christmas ballet with a balding cherry head and gruff brown beard. Now she felt Dave restless above her, no doubt twisting his sonic bracelet. She gave his penis another lick, looking for the bright cherry red color to appear.

Mrs. Starchild had spotted Mary Lou's bracelet the first time she visited their house in Nicholasville after working at the Lay Auto plant. "My poor baby," Mrs. Starchild had said. Mr. Starchild had joined in his wife's warnings. In an hour, they'd convinced her of the evil materialistic outlook inherent in the Sonic Beads. Mary Lou had tried to convince Dave of the same, though her recent attempts had been half-hearted. She again licked the sturdy little nutcracker. But the nutcracker wasn't so sturdy, she realized, listening to the clink of Dave's sonic bracelet. She peeked up to see him studying its vibrations.

"God damn!"

"Sorry, I slipped," Mary Lou commented, running her tongue over her front teeth. "Look, it's getting late. Let's just go hear Natalie play. We can stop at that CD shop you wanted to check out. I can get some Gregorian chant."

What in the world's gotten into me? Mary Lou wondered. *I just bit the nutcracker.* She very quietly and privately giggled.

Faux Graphic Panels 162 through 167: Turkey Day fireworks

Anyone who hangs around drunks knows how they muddle and stumble along mostly, but can come up with amazing ideas on an instance, their lubricated synapses suddenly fluid enough to slosh a different insight into conscious existence. Just so, Huck's Dad initiated the idea of smoking three thanksgiving turkeys on the back loading dock. That wasn't the amazing idea, by the bye; it was the seed. In fact, every person in the plant — down to the teenage Simians — remained apprehensive at his first idea.

Fire? they all thought.

"Keep him away from the dumpster while he cooks those turkeys."

"Make sure he doesn't drop that .38 into the grill."

"Hell, make sure he doesn't drop his whiskey into the grill."

"Double hell, make sure he doesn't drop himself into the grill."

But the old guy pulled it off, starting the huge smoker (who could ever tell how he procured it) well before daybreak and having three large turkeys ready the instant the noon chime rang.

Willy's sister Andrea even convinced her new boss Gabriel to drive over from Lexington for the festivities. She was bringing mashed potatoes and her two children; he was bringing Tiger Leigh Carmel the real estate agent. He was after all, still the sole legal representative for Lay Auto Non-profit, and Tiger Leigh was its sole realtor. Willy said he'd bring a sweet potato casserole, as long as Natalie would let him use her oven. The three Chinese workers suggested they might bring a Chinese substitute for dressing, namely oyster-giblet noodles. The three Doorwin's Simians insisted they could bring pumpkin-mushroom cupcakes they'd been experimenting with. Natalie offered to bake Sweet William winter squash casserole, as long as Willy would let her cook it alongside his sweet potatoes. Mary Lou said she'd bring Peace peas. Dave said he'd bring Escher bread baked in fascinating endless mathematical loops. Bad said she'd bring napkins.

Syntax error 101010-U: History and gifts:

If only the Indians had foreseen smallpox and repeating rifles, they would have fed the pilgrims Angel of Death mushroom cap soup instead of corn and turkey. But take a look at the bright side from the Amerindian perspective: at least they did teach the white intruder how to smoke tobacco. Happy Thanksgiving.

We need to go back two weeks.

After coming up with the idea for a Thanksgiving smoke-out, Huck's Dad mused about fire in general — how it could be yellow, or orange, or even white or blue — and then he started studying the plant's overhead sprinkler system. He noticed a water stain circling a central group of sprinklers and promptly bribed two Doorwin's Simians to help him carry in a sixteen-foot ladder so that he could inspect and repair.

As he climbed the ladder, each and every worker tensed, sure that he would fall onto the assembly line and wind up with a face and chest stamped out as a door or a chassis. To exacerbate his wobbling, he carried up a boom box and was playing Merle Haggard at sonic level, which vibrated the ladder and the ceiling tiles. But he'd drunk half his first pint of whiskey for the day — Maker's Mark for sure after the shooting incident — so he remained steady enough. After leaving the boom box perched atop the ladder, he descended and lugged a sack of wrenches back up, to tap one after another of the sprinkler heads. He then nodded sagely as a steel guitar twanged, for he'd found the perpetrator. He climbed down the ladder and got Huck to drive him in Lay Auto to the local hardware store, which was a chain named Marvin's. The minute the old man was out the door and in Lay Auto there was a rush to unplug the boom box. The younger Chinese girl won.

"Did I ever tell you that I went to school with Marvin?" the old man asked Huck as they pulled in to the chain store's parking lot.

Huck looked at the store's sign and stolidly shook his head.

"That's right. He tried out for the football team as a walk-on. Walk-ons were used for cannon fodder. Don't ever walk on to a football team, boy. It'll do you no good. Anyway, Marvin walked on wanting to try out for a punter position. He'd evidently punted for some rink-dink school in eastern Kentucky. Don't ever go to any rink-dink school, son: it screws your perspective worse than whiskey. So he walked on and tried out as a punter, and the coach let the defense practice blocking punts on him. Trouble was that they blocked him more than they blocked punts. The coach thought it would be a grand idea if the boys knew what an illegal hit felt like, I guess. Anyway, Marvin told me later that all that time he spent on the ground he was looking up at the coaches' tower, thinking how much wood went into making those things. So that's when he quit football and quit college and started Marvin's hardware with the money his mother had saved — she was a coal miner's widow who'd gotten a huge cash settlement from a coal mine when her husband died — so that was the money his mother really had saved for him to go to college. That reminds me of Colonel Harlan Sanders, who got a similar brainstorm and windfall. Did I ever tell you about the time I stole his girl friend? She was a hillbilly looker with bleach-blonde hair. This was right after he'd opened that first dink of a fried chicken restaurant in Corbin and — "

Lay Auto's horn started blaring and Huck's blue eyes glazed over. He got out of the automobile and lifted the bonnet. The old man stumbled along and stared as Huck touched a wire with his finger and the horn stopped.

"That's a pretty snazzy trick. Did I ever tell you about the time that I was in the army and they wanted me to put on a magic show for the troops at — "

"Sir, I think we need to go in the store and buy what we need, then get back to work."

"No need to get your head-feathers in a ruffle, son." Since the shooting incident, Huck's Old Man had taken to wearing glasses that resembled shooting goggles, and his filmed-over eyes, magnified by these, stared at the boy, who simply shrugged.

They went inside Marvin's and bought seventy-nine items that the old man thought he might need. Huck noted that shiny white and shiny silver ones caught the old man's attention more than any others. Were the goggles influencing his choices?

Soon enough they were back at the plant. Huck's old man stood at the base of the ladder with three sacks of parts. He stared up at the silent radio. He shifted his feet and looked up again. He twitched. He stared some more. When he finally inhaled ferociously and looked around, everyone in the plant studiously paid attention to whatever was or wasn't in their hands.

"I left it on," the old man announced loudly, "so's the ceiling would be happy while I was gone. There's no tellin' what it's gonna feel like now." He plugged the radio back in, and soon enough a Merle Haggard sound-alike was blaring. Two hours later, Huck's old man descended from the ladder, put his hands on his hips and looked up at the sprinkler system through his now smudged goggles.

"That'll about get it," he proclaimed. Then he walked out back for his second pint of Maker's Mark.

There was another rush to unplug the radio, one of the Doorwin's Simians reaching it first this time. A collective sigh spread through the factory.

So now we come forward two weeks, to Thanksgiving Day at noon. The turkeys are smoked. The food is spread out on three tables inside the factory, for it is a chilly, foggy day outside, which has only added to the smoke, of course. All the plant's workers are gathered about the tables as Mary Lou offers a non-denominational blessing.

"May the power of the universe watch over all her children on this special day, and may that power especially watch over our Lay Auto family as we eat these lovely turkeys, whose brave spirits even now hover."

Everyone had been encouraged to bring a "special other." The three Simians wound up bringing all their gang of Doorwin's Simians, seven other teens and preteens who had enough silver embedded in their noses, lips, ears, and chins to look like a triage unit of shrapnel victims. The three Chinese meticulously each invited one friend apiece, and they all wielded chopsticks, which the teens and preteens eyed nervously, thinking them tiny weapons. Andrea bought her son and daughter. Willy and Natalie seemed content with one another, as did Mary Lou and Dave. Gabriel, as has been mentioned, invited Tiger Leigh the real estate agent. Bad had walked in during Mary Lou's invocation with her three special friends, Kate Chung and Kate's two lovely kneecaps. Bad rolled her eyes melodramatically on hearing Mary Lou's invocation and her ascription of the pronoun "her" to the universe. Kate giggled, a bit too loudly. The six Chinese evidently knew her and admonished her to be respectful. She flipped them an American bird. The ten Simians saw this and began laughing and flipping everyone a bird, proclaiming it "Bird Day." One of the older Simian boys, seeing Kate Chung's lovely kneecaps, got down on his hands and knees to peek under her very short and very American dress to see what else might accompany them. Bad reached for a nearby sweet potato and threw it at the boy. Her usually impeccable aim was off and she hit Mary Lou instead — or maybe Jung, Freud and the Devil conjoined hands to make her throw the sweet potato where she really wanted to throw it. Was she secretly and carnally interested in Mary Lou in her ineffable id of ids? This wouldn't be the day anyone would find out, for Dave, in a moment of concern for Mary Lou and the orange mush sliding down her right cheek, pulled off a drumstick and flung it at Bad, who easily dodged it thanks to her kung fu training. The only trouble is that in sweeping the projectile away from her face, she veered it toward Tiger Leigh the real estate agent, who handily ducked, leaving the drumstick to hit Gabriel squarely on the nose.

The fight was on.

It so happened that the tables had been laid directly under the very patch of sprinklers that Huck's Dad had 'repaired.' Please note that scare quotes are always necessary for any work an alcoholic conducts, other than finishing off a bottle. Enough smoke from the fog and the cooking turkeys had already accumulated along the ceiling to set off the sprinkler system three times over. But Huck's Dad's 'repairs' assured that would never happen. What did happen though, is that a drumstick flew upwards and knocked a loose sprinkler head off. Since Huck's Dad had inadvertently cut off water to the rest of the system, the dozen or so sprinklers directly over the food rained down a deluge that would have impressed Noah.

It didn't impress the combatants. Two soaked Doorwin's Simians held the soaked Chinese artist down, stuffing stuffing into his mouth. Dave methodically went through the three dripping wet turkeys pulling off drumsticks and throwing them with more accuracy this time, hitting Kate Chung in her left temple just as she was delivering a karate blow to one of the male Simians' fathers, who'd shown up because he was stalking an older Simian girl. The girl's blouse was wet and her nipples were erect, so Dad was caught completely off guard by Kate's blow, which misfired anyway because Kate herself was nipple-infatuated also. Meanwhile, Bad selectively took out males, regardless

Joe Taylor

of their age. Mary Lou warbled her peace mantra until someone threw a bowl of mashed potatoes in her face. She wiped the potatoes off and hefted a drumstickless turkey carcass and bashed the person who'd thrown the potatoes.

At this moment, Mr. and Mrs. Starchild entered.

"O my," Mr. Starchild commented. As water-soaked combatants fell to the wayside, he and Mrs. Starchild proffered bottles of Green Gong, asking, "How does that make you feel?" to the utter confusion of each downed combatant, who each and every one felt like a kicked stray dog caught in a thunderstorm — how else, sir or madam, would you expect me to feel?

But social workers, therapists, preachers, and other do-gooders stumble along much as alcoholics do, occasionally managing to perform minor miracles. Today bought not exactly the multiplication of the loaves, but it did manifest a Gathering of the Gong. Huck's old man, who'd been watching the melee and daydreaming of the time he'd knocked out Cassius Clay in a Louisville boxing ring, was mistaken for a wounded combatant by the Starchilds. When they proffered some Green Gong, he mixed his allotment with Maker's Mark, getting enough energy to perform a jig and shut off the overhead water. Even Bad, naturally the last combatant standing, was dropped when a section of the sprinkler system — shaken by the sudden drop in water pressure — fell from the ceiling to send her sprawling onto the floor. She steadfastly refused the Green Gong and the ministrations of Mrs. Starchild until she spotted Kate Chung's lovely kneecaps and glanced farther along Kate's lovely body to see her lovely lips joyously drinking Gong. Bad then anxiously grabbed the bottle.

Everyone in the factory, in fact, lifted a bottle of Green Gong in slurping camaraderie. The vast spirit-nation of American Indians arose from Mother Earth to take notice of this peaceful coexistence. Momentarily, the Plymouth Rock pilgrims were relieved of their myriad sins. And the collective unconsciousness of Jung and a host of other therapists? That blessed Mother also stirred from forest humus to hover happily. Our Lady of Guadalupe stepped out of Lay Auto to scatter late season goldenrod. The Compassionate Buddha stepped outside Consoling Oneness to murmur Om. For this vast spiritual moment, the Starchilds and Green Gong excelled in spreading the five-pointed G.

Faux Graphic Panels 168 through 171:
Complications corrupt the Five-pointed G

Complication A: The reason the Starchilds were late for Turkey Day smoked turkeys was that Madame Nu Wa had contacted them about Green Gong after learning from the young artistic Chinese plant worker that the Starchilds infused gasoline – in the minutest, proprietary amount (Shell premium, with Techtron coating) – into Gong. Of course, for Madame Nu Wa, this worked as well as any ancestral sign, for gasoline is king. So she astutely offered to contract out Green Gong, promoting and selling it as a modified American green tea in all seven of her KY Chinese food chains, soon to be eight and nine in Louisville and a suburb. This was the heavenly spiritual break the Starchilds had been awaiting. They counter-offered to supply Green Gong if Madame Nu Wa made available a leaflet entitled "The Green Gong Story," which traced the drink from its humble beginnings in Nicholasville as an aid to sex therapy, to its present glory as an anodyne for all frailty. After consulting the leaflet and with a mere flick of a computer's mouse, any Kentucky sufferer could locate the nearest Green Gong Go Greatly Group, affectionately known as the Five-pointed G.

This impending demand for Gong placed the Starchilds in a legal conundrum: they'd need the plant even more. They would have to, in fact, exceed their contracted allocation of plant time and cut into the production of Lay Auto. Taken aback by the infighting at the plant on Turkey Day, they became determined to produce a greater amount of Gong, for the Greater Good of Global Gladness, the Foursquare G. So they consulted Gabriel and Tiger, and while you may discern a conflict of interest arising, none of those four did. Foursquare Greed?

Complication B: Huck's Dad took sick with walking pneumonia bought on by the combination of that day's fog, smoking the turkeys, and a large, illegal Cuban cigar sneaked him by one of the Chinese workers. All he needs is a good round of antibiotics, the doctor advised the ghostly Huck and Natalie when they visited the emergency room. All I need is a good round of whiskey, Huck's Dad retorted, certain that Maker's Mark would beat off invading germs better than any drug. It would have prevented the Black Death, wouldn't it? he asked the doubting physician, who could hardly argue such a medical fact.

Complication C: The terrorist group that Huck's Dad frightened off with his target practice was mad as, say, a swarm of ground yellow jackets swirling up from some sodden woodland to attack, en masse, an unawares intruder, say a ten-year old child out with her Labrador retriever who's just chased a tennis ball (Wilson!) over the hidden underground nest. Poor child! She's about to learn that she's morbidly allergic to bee stings, something her single mom parent will also learn when the Lab comes whimpering home alone, the nasty ground yellow jackets still clinging and trying to sting through its thick coat. The child's name is Tracy Chapman, no relation to the wonderful warbling singer, who will never even hear of this unfortunate child or else she would write a moving song of her bee-sting demise. Life sucks. It's anonymous; it's unfair. Write about that, Tracy. Well, you already have. You didn't need Gödel and his viper's nest of improvable and perplexing problems to realize that, did you?

At any rate, the maddened terrorist group that so resembled ground yellow jackets really wasn't a group; it was just two men: the World's Tallest Motorcycle Cop Now Turned Detective, and Andrea's soon to be ex-husband (for Gabriel was rushing the case through court since Andrea had the most pleasant looking and no doubt moist set of mammaries he'd ever seen). What the two — not the two mammaries, but the two men — lost in not being a terrorist group, they gained in fanatic intensity and Metro police department connections. They in fact had just learned of a hidden underground entrance to the old Mountain Dew Bottling plant in Nicholasville, a.k.a. the refurbished Lay Auto proto-car plant. This underground entrance had been covertly dug in the mid 60's before the plant went out of business. Who dug it, no one knew. Why, no one knew. A bomb shelter? An extensive wine cellar? Whatever, as far as anyone on the Nicholasville police force could tell it had never been used, other than as a rallying point for a group of teens and pre-teens known as Doorwin's Simians. Since that kept the Simians off the street, it was ignored.

Complication D: Just because those two men didn't constitute a terrorist group doesn't mean that there wasn't such a group eyeing the Lay Auto plant. In fact, there were seven — no, make that eight such groups, for another formed even as this was being written. Paradoxically this plethora of hatred had saved the plant so far, for these groups sometimes purposefully and sometimes mistakenly foiled one another — each wanting the personal satisfaction and glory of stopping the happy eco-car from becoming a reality. Gasoline is king!

Complications E through J: The original foursome-turned-five with Chien Fou, then turned-six with Natalie, was undergoing groaning pains. Or perhaps they really were growing pains, for the initial investment money did keep coming in, a lot of it from the famous Texas Country Singer who was still evading the IRS as speedily and legally as he could.

Dave, for instance, had become addicted to his sonic beads and buying. A typical product of capitalism, he'd decked out his cherry red truck to the max and was now looking to trade up to a lemon drop yellow monster truck with nine hundred pounds of chrome and six hundred pounds of tires. (Not counting the spare.) Mary Lou was still infatuated with the Starchilds, was still reading self-help and spiritual guidebooks at night, was still questioning everything from her dietary intake to her social responsibility to the world. Bad was immersed in Kate Chung and barely could make time for the new computers for the twelve proto-cars. The twenty-three mistakes she'd made in programming were only topped by the twenty-four Dave had made. It was Huck who corrected all forty-seven. Willy found himself in a managerial position arranging workloads and schedules for the other four, Huck, the three Chinese, the three teens, and Huck's Dad. And they were still lagging behind and getting ready to hire four more Chinese and four more teens, so Willy felt more and more like a teamster boss and less and less like an innovative automotive engineer. He tried to get Natalie to take over his managerial position, but she'd have none of it, for she was working on her first ever CD, *Folkgrass in the Bluegrass*.

In fact, Willy noted with shock half a week after the turkey day blooper, the famous Texas country singer was due for a visit the coming Thursday, to see the second and third prototypes come off the line. Willy panicked and ordered triple overtime.

All these complications — A through J — worked wonders against the five-pointed G. Ah life, your flips, your flops, your flaps, your farts, your fandangos do at times conspire in a most Draconian manner. Gödel – need I add – be damned.

Faux Graphic Panels 172 through 175: Creeps creeping

Jack Wright, Andrea's soon to be not-husband, and The World's Tallest Motorcycle Cop turned Detective, known simply as Tall, had haunted strip tease joints in Lexington three nights in a row, certain they'd find the lovely woman with the rosy bra who'd appeared by Lake Herrington and settle once and for all who she belonged to. But they'd left each joint — Too Luscious Lucy's, Boobs and Kilts (a bar that had the two apprehensive about the sex of everyone waiting on them), and Girls! Gosh! Girls! — together, but alone. Now it was Monday, and even that night's pro football game left them in the dumps.

"Why don't we do it tonight?" Jack said to Tall, who had just popped a beer, a tallboy, naturally, a Lite unnaturally.

Tall didn't answer, but sipped his beer and thumbed his billfold, finally pulling it out and gazing at something Jack couldn't see.

With the pending divorce, Jack had moved into Tall's apartment, a nearby campus site with plenty of young female students for them both to ogle. Since Tall provided a good many of the females with marijuana and drugs, several were typically diffusing perfume about his apartment. But not tonight. Jack sat by a window and looked onto the nearly empty parking lot. He saw only his pick-up and Tall's police cruiser — Fayette Metro had instituted a take-it home policy under the assumption that even the presence of a police car deterred crime. Providing, of course, the driver wasn't the crime's source.

"Think they all got mid-terms or something?" Jack asked about the female students, giving a grin on seeing the STP sticker he'd sneaked onto Tall's cruiser. What they all had was finals, which were nearly over, there being only one half-day of exams left before Christmas break.

"That does it!" Tall snapped, grumbling at something that happened on the TV, a botched play, perhaps. "Yeah, hell, tonight's the night. Let's vamoose like a mongoose."

They loaded a case of beer and twenty sticks of dynamite that Tall had secreted from the evidence room. The sticks had been confiscated from a terrorist group who intended to blow up the Nicholasville plant anyway, so it only made sense. In fact, the two A-rabs who were planning on using the dynamite had passed out in their van outside Too Luscious Lucy's with the sticks in their laps, zippers open. If only their Muslim parents had taught them how to control their liquor . . . but then if that had come about, the whole Muslim world might be happier — certainly the female half might be.

Soon enough, Tall and Jack had driven out of Lexington and were inside Nicholasville's city limits. They pulled off the highway, across from the Lay Auto plant, and tucked their pick-up in the woods. By the fence where the seven or eight or nine crows usually perched sat a large rock. By the rock lay an indentation; in the indentation waited a disguised door. That door opened onto a cave that led directly to the storage room that always so irritated Tiger Leigh the real estate agent because no matter how many janitors she hired to clean it, hex signs, discarded beer bottles, and decapitated stuffed animals returned on her next visit. The partially natural, partially man-dug cave held the secret access she'd never discovered, for its entrance lay just outside the property line. It was the secret that Tall had discovered from the Nicholasville police, who as mentioned always ignored it, figuring it had kept three generations of Simians off the street, busily fucking and getting high.

"This goes all the way into that building?" Jack asked, helping Tall move a camouflage bush and then staring down at the hinged door leading to the cave, then at the old bottling plant, which lay a football field away. In answer, Tall grunted and placed the dynamite on a four-wheeled cart, nodding for Jack to go on in. "So who the hell would have had the time and money and energy to dig this?" Jack asked as he entered the cave and shone a flashlight along its length. He cradled his beer, then peered nervously at two kerosene lanterns perched atop the dynamite as Tall pushed it toward him. Tall grunted again and finished pushing the cart down the incline. Then he walked back and pulled the bush to cover the ajar door.

Tall turned and inhaled deeply upon seeing the cave. He'd heard that teens and even preteens of both sexes gathered here. He hoped to encounter some discarded panties or trainer bras before they blew the plant up. In fact, he planned on setting off the dynamite far enough away from the storage room to leave it and the cave intact. Leaving the cave intact would be no problem, though he didn't realize this, for the cave dipped thirty feet and was topped with solid granite, an anomaly for the usual limestone in the area. When he adjusted the dynamite on the little four-wheel cart, he glimpsed pornographic graffiti just ahead on a wall. The place where he usually kept his wallet with the pictures of Andrea and Natalie as teenagers began burning his rear end. But he'd left the pictures and his wallet in the truck, so he was anxious to forage the cave.

"Let's look," he said. The two of them trundled the beer and dynamite through the cave, which was surprisingly spacious. A third of the way to the plant, they stopped to admire especially well conceived pornographic wall paintings in a frieze that vied with the best Rome or Greece could offer.

"Damn, that one looks like your old lady, your ex-old lady," Tall offered, running his fingers along the wall painting and lighting another lantern.

"My old lady's tits are bigger than that. She's got two cherries for nipples. — You sure it's okay to have those lanterns on top of the dynamite?"

"Better than on top of the beer."

"Huh, if we put one on top of the beer, we could say, 'Let there be Lite.' "

"Yeah, so?" Tall was rubbing his cheek against the breasts on the painting and gurgling baby talk to the rock wall.

"So it's from the Bible. Jesus said it."

"Cherries, huh?"

"Yeah. I'd make her squeeze 'em together and you know. . . ."

"You know . . . what?" Tall had stopped rubbing against the painting and stood humped over in the cave.

"Squeeze 'em to milk the cow."

"The cow?"

"My dick. Then I'd shoot a huge wad all over her face. I'd always try to get it up her nose."

"So why's your old lady divorcing you?"

"Hell if I know."

Tall pushed the four-wheeled cart and walked ahead.

"Might be that damned lawyer's getting in her pussy," Tall decided.

"He pals with the captain. They jerk off together or something. Holy jumpin' frogheads. Come here and look at this one."

Indeed, the breasts on this one were even larger than on the previous one, and they were dripping translucent, glow-in the dark milk. Both he and Jack fell backwards in awe, incidentally knocking both kerosene lanterns over and breaking them atop the dynamite.

Faux Graphic Panels 176 through 183:
Guests arrive, others approach, still others try to arrive

Wednesday evening four proto-cars rolled off the assembly line, newly painted eco-green and fully operational. Thursday morning and everyone at the plant anxiously awaited the TCS, who was due just before lunch, riding in from the airport with Gabriel and Andrea.

But at nine, both the Nicholasville and Metro Lexington Police showed up with questions and photos. They interrogated Natalie and Willy alone in the foyer where all the walking trophies still stood on display. An older Nicholasville cop bent and yelled out that his name was on one. His partner, a redheaded genetic wonder exclaimed a lot of syllables in a row and walked over to investigate.

"This truck look familiar?" one of the Metro Lexington police asked, ignoring his bumpkin counterparts at the display case and holding out a photo for Willy and Natalie.

Willy shook his head, but Natalie recognized Jack Wright's truck.

"He's your brother-in-law and you don't recognize his truck?" the cop asked Willy.

"We don't particularly get along. He's owed me fifteen hundred dollars for seven years."

"He owes half of Fayette County money," Natalie added.

"And just how do you know him, ma'am?"

Natalie said that he was married to one of her best friends since high school, Willy's sister Andrea. A small cop, one who just escaped being a midget, thrust forward two photos. "These mean anything to you?"

They were the high school photos that the World's Tallest Detective had bullied Natalie and Willy into giving him.

"That's me in high school! How'd you — "

"That's my sister in high school! How'd you — "

"They were left in that truck, which was parked in a woods about two hundred yards from here. They were in my partner's wallet. He always took his wallet out and left it in the squad car if he thought he was going to run into trouble."

This came from the near midget cop. Natalie and Willy looked at one another, wondering how the World's Tallest and this guy ever communicated. Would the World's Tallest pick him up in his huge palm and whisper?

"Uh, why are you using the past tense?" Natalie asked.

"He didn't show up for his shift on Tuesday or yesterday," the small cop with the small ears said.

"Jack hasn't worked full-time in nearly a decade," Willy added, hoping to clarify matters. "That's part of the problem."

"Jack? You mean Frank Sinarta? I saw signs all along the highway welcoming him. Is he really coming here to sing?" The redheaded cop from Nicholasville called this out and then bumped against the trophy case, vibrating the glass.

Willie and Natalie stared as his red hair flamed over his blue eyes. "What signs?" Natalie asked.

"There's no such a person as Frank Sinarta," the near midget from Metro spat out. "It's Frank Sinatra, and if he came here to sing it'd take more than a bunch of prank high school signs on some backwater hick highway to pull him from the grave. Even a meeting of mafia godfathers warbling opera and slurping spaghetti and praying hex to the pope couldn't do it."

"Signs don't lie," the redhead answered. "There's a singer coming."

Natalie told all four policemen about the TCS and told them they were welcome to stay and see him.

"Marijuana-blower," the near midget hissed. "But we aren't talking about him, and we aren't talking about Frank Sinarta, and we aren't talking about your brother-in-law. We're talking about my partner, who's disappeared."

Willy thought that disappearing would be perfect for both the World's Tallest and his brother-in-law, but kept that to himself, especially as his sister had mentioned taking a contract out on the latter idiot — in a fit of anger for sure, but still, she had mentioned it aloud, to plenty of witnesses.

"Some people saw him and your brother-in-law at a girlie joint."

Natalie blushed, remembering her strip tease.

The bumpkin cops went back to studying the trophies. "Look,

here's one for the Dew-a-thon. It was like Iron Man, but neater. They only held that one year, right before the plant closed. Some guy named Loop Y. Astro won. What kind of name is that?"

"What was his name?" Natalie asked.

"Loop Y. Astro. Everyone figured the Mountain Dew people pulled in a ringer from Louisville."

"Hey, we're trying to find some facts here," the taller of the two Metro detectives shouted. His tallness didn't require much, since he was standing beside the near midget who claimed to be the World's Tallest Missing Detective's partner, who was angrily inhaling as if suffering an asthma attack

"These *are* facts," the bumpkin cop pouted. "Here in Nicholasville we've learned you can never overlook anything in a murder case."

"Murder?"

"That's how we're treating it, considering the wallet," the near midget said.

The interrogation went on for forty minutes. As far as Natalie and Willy could tell, they'd learned more than the cops had when they left. Willy checked his watch: less than an hour before the TCS showed. They received a phone call from Andrea, who said that she and Gabriel had just been questioned too, just before they left the law office, but that they'd still be on time. "I hope the son of a bitch is dead," she said over the phone.

"Which one?" Willy murmured, thinking of the time the World's Tallest pulled him over in Irishtown. He and Natalie walked outside to wait by the four prototypes and Lay Auto with the rest of the Pit Crew.

The parking lot was filling already. All of Doorwin's Simians were milling about because they'd heard the TCS wanted to legalize marijuana. Twenty workers from Madame Nu Wa's Nicholasville take-out were standing around because they'd heard that the TCS had played onstage with the Beach Boys. Even Huck's old man had spiffed up and was waiting, having shopped at the Salvation Army for some slacks and a sports jacket that could hold two half pints in its inner pockets.

Bad stood apart. She'd spiked her hair the night before and looked like a refugee from a rock star recovery unit. It didn't help matters that she and Kate Chung had argued two days ago, perhaps irrevocably. Bad stared at Dave, who was bedecked with gold and silver jewelry and those stupid beads he wore on his wrist. What was his problem, Bad wondered. And where was his little spiritual playmate, Sister Mary Lou of the Lotus? Bad popped her fingers, then her wrists, then her ankles. She thought of the Golden Scream Karate Kata and mentally went through the motions of snapping heads and breaking ankles. Maybe starting with those treacherous Chinese punks.

Dave stood alone by a table they'd set out with coffee, hot cider, and hot tea. He was tired and his eyes drooped. Over the past month, Mary Lou admonished him that the reason for his constant fatigue came from rubbing his bracelet and skittering here and yon to go shopping a dozen times a day. And, she added one workday, that fifteen pounds of gold and silver smarm you're wearing doesn't help matters, unless you're trying out for the Dew-a-thon. When he'd asked what the hell that was, she walked away, closing herself in the office to write letters to procure ever more money for Lay Auto. It had been a week since he and Mary Lou had spent the night together, Dave now mused at the table. He poured a coffee and thought about Gödel, the tiny man with the magnifier eyeglasses who changed the world of math and philosophy. Then he thought about the supposedly ultra-logical philosopher Wittgenstein turning his back on students to recite the Upanishads. Then he thought of Frodo the Hobbit and he thought that he missed Mary Lou, his very own Upanishad lotus-blossom, his very own insolvable, improvable problem.

One hour before all this Mary Lou had said, "We need to hurry" to Mr. and Mrs. Starchild at their home. She had urged them at the same time that Willy and Natalie were being interrogated by the police in Nicholasville, and Andrea and Gabriel in Lexington, though she didn't realize either fact. She did immediately realize, however, that she'd made a mistake by telling the Starchilds they needed to hurry. Consequently she endured their Sevenfold Modern Woe sermon, which revolved around time's unnatural and mechanized compression by the "false goals" of tempestuous temporality, that taskmaster tempter. Mary Lou was sure some inconsistency nestled within the Sevenfold Modern Woes, but she smiled so contritely that the super empathic Starchilds finished elucidating the Woes quickly, loaded into the VW bus, and even broke the speed limit just a teensy in getting to the reception for the TCS. Mrs. Starchild and her unusually heavy foot even had them five minutes ahead of schedule when they were nearly broadsided by a weaving maroon and silver bus Mrs. Starchild was uncharacteristically passing.

Mr. Starchild flipped the bus driver the finger, while Mary Lou envisioned Dave weeping over her mangled body on this two-lane to nowhere.

"Now, Loopy," Mrs. Starchild admonished. She let go the steering wheel to put both her hands out the window and signal a peace sign back to the bus driver who panicked on seeing the driver ahead not steering and slammed on his brakes, killing the motor because he'd forgotten to push in the manual clutch.

This driver was no ordinary bus driver. As he breathed deeply from avoiding a premature accident he reflected that the double peace sign he'd seen meant victory. Victory meant that his bus filled with 238 five-gallon cans of gasoline would do the job and soon send him skittering toward a dozen virgins with hymens he could puncture. He restarted the ancient bus and chugged its ancient motor along the highway as fast as it would go, which was 32 m.p.h. considering the sloshing gasoline filling the seats where diligent schoolchildren had once blown bubble gum.

∧∧∧∧∧∧*∧∧∧∧∧∧

Syntax error 101010-U: Wittgenstein and the Virgin(s)

Say that on one wintry, foggy London Tuesday the philosopher Wittgenstein pulls out, instead of his usual copy of the *Upanishads*, a copy of the *Koran* and sits lotus style before a Cambridge fireplace to contemplate snowflakes and the Muslim religion.

Say that he and the half dozen male students accompanying him are considering jihad and the promise of a dozen virgins apiece some seventy years before such became popular.

Say that by mistake a co-ed has finagled her way into this precious group allowed to listen to Wittgenstein mumble cryptic, oracular passages. And say that while the boys are wondering if jihad against, say, the college cafeteria over stale crumpets would earn them a dozen virgins, she . . . let's call her Dora, speaks up:

"So, after you've been shot for protesting the quality of tea and crumpets at the cafeteria, and after you've made it to Paradise and gotten your dozen obligatory virgins handed down from the Almighty Bearded Father, and after you've penetrated and broken their twelve lovely, precious hymens, what do you have? Twelve wives wanting tea and crumpets and feathered hats? Twelve whores? Twelve fattening mothers, pregnant with your omnipotent seed?"

Wittgenstein, not one for conundrums, tosses the *Koran* aside and goes back to reciting the *Upanishads*. He even stops gazing at the snowflakes falling outside.

One of the brighter male math students, however, one who will no doubt applaud Gödel's Incompleteness Proof when that makes itself known a few years later, says, "Renewable hymens. Like some lizards re-grow amputated legs. The Almighty Father God could do that, right mates?"

The surrounding males gobble like turkeys. Dora strolls over to assume the lotus position beside Wittgenstein and recite from the *Upanishads*.

/\/\/\/\/*/\/\/\/\

Gabriel, Andrea, and the TCS also nearly get sideswiped by the same weaving maroon and silver bus as they pass it. Fortunately, Andrea is driving, for lawyer Gabriel and the TCS are enjoying a nice KY blue high.

"Asshole!" Gabriel yells, starting to flip a bird, but upon noting that the bus is purple and deciding it must be part of a gay rights movement, winds up hoisting two fingers in a peace sign.

The bus's driver, high on impending martyrdom, sees yet another victory signal and honks merrily. The Satanic Nicholasville plant lies only 4.5 miles away, according to his GPS. A virgin, blonde, appears in the GPS and winks. Another virgin's face smiles at him from the driver's side mirror. Her blonde hair whips about her laughing eyes in the wind. She curls a lock of hair over her right blue eye while licking her red, red lips. "My name is Layla," she coos.

The driver rolls down his window to let her in, shouting, "Allah be praised!"

Now, when Huck's dad had gone to buy his newly used suit at Goodwill in preparation for the TCS's present visit, he'd spotted a bargain lot of poster board in the toy section. A high school teacher had spotted them at the same time and even had her hands on them.

"Did I ever tell you about the time I worked for Union-Pacific Paper Company?"

"What? No, I mean, do I know you?"

" 'At's what I mean. I worked for Union-Pacific Paper Company and about once a month a worker would fall into the vat and dissolve, even the bones. It came out slick, just like this — " Huck's Dad rubbed his hand over the poster board and nudged the teacher's lacquered fingernails — "so the paper company would always donate the entire bloomin' lot to Salvation Army or Goodwill or some other thrift store." Huck's Dad swayed and blinked at the teacher. "All that skin and bone and gristle. Union-Pacific didn't want to be held liable for any disease it spread to children." His eyes did their best to focus on the teacher, who'd let go the poster board and was backing off. "It's true," Huck's Dad said, "That's why I quit. Hell, I didn't want to fall into that vat. But here's something even better: let me tell you about the job I got right after that. I was working on a horse farm. . . ."

The teacher was already three aisles over, clutching her purse.

So Huck's Dad bought the poster board and set out to draw twenty-four posters welcoming Frank Sinatra to the Lay Auto Plant, for he'd gotten the TCS and Frank confused. These posters were what he'd tacked all along the very highway the bus driver, the Starchilds, and Andrea and her two passengers were driving along. An hour before, Huck's Dad had finished his first pint and was congratulating himself on a job well done while walking back to the plant hoping to get in some target practice. He waved from the roadside to the Metro and Nicholasville policemen as they headed away from their interview with Natalie and Willie. The redheaded Nicholasville policeman and his partner had waved back; the two Metro cops snarled, for they didn't approve of pedestrians.

And now, the TCS and lawyer Gabriel were enjoying a refresher toke when they passed the first poster, a bright pink with blue.

"WELCOME MISTER SINARTA!"

"Sinarta?" The TCS said.

Another one appeared.

"WELCOME MISTER FRANK!"

And then,

"U DID IT YOUR WAY!"

They passed eleven more posters. Andrea, by this time, had gotten enough secondary smoke that she started giggling. She even started singing Sinatra's "Chicago."

"Not bad," the TCS said. "You've got a right pretty voice."

"I used to sing with Natalie."

"Did — "

But the TCS's question was cut short, for a thunderous explosion and shock wave came from a mile behind. As a fireball started upward

Andrea slowed to a stop and they looked back.

"Do you think the Republicans have pushed the buttons for the big one?" the TCS asked.

"And they don't even believe in Paradise and twelve virgins," Gabriel added.

Men, Andrea thought. *If I ever get out of this damned marriage I'm going lesbian or feline.*

Faux Graphic Panels 184 through 189: Guests arrive, cont'd

/\/\/\/\/*/\/\/\/\/\

Syntax error 101010-V: Two real-time moral dilemmas:

Immanuel Kant, bless his strolling heart, declared that a pure free *Will* was all that mattered in morality, that the results of said will's actions were irrelevant. John Stuart Mill, flapping the other side of the moral feather, declared that the *results* were all that mattered. Thus, spreading the most pleasure for the most people, akin to spreading Tupelo honey on white bread, was what lofted a person onto the moral mountaintop.

Let us take two real-time cases and judiciously weigh them:

Pure *Will*, Case A: Acmar Jihal is a twenty-three year old Iranian who'd been admitted to the United States to study mathematics. In Acmar's senior year he happened upon Kurt Gödel's Proof of Incompleteness, and it smote him like Allah's hammer. There are some things that simply can't be reasoned out, but they remain clear and logical and necessary all the same, the proof proclaimed, nay proved. Henceforth, all Acmar could think about were American hamburgers and blonde virgins, for they ensconced themselves as his primary unsolvable problems *and* necessities. Hamburgers were easy; he had plenty of money coming from his father and he was Muslim, not Hindu. Blonde virgins weren't so easy. Then something niggled Acmar's mind: a martyr's death and Paradise. Soon, fronted by a splinter terrorist group, Acmar forsook mathematics and attended a junior college to learn how to drive a semi-trailer. Unlike his September 11th counterparts, Acmar remained perspicacious enough not to tell the juco instructors that he didn't care a flip about learning how to back into a loading dock, that all he needed to know was how to steer the cab and trailer at 88 miles per hour, crash through barriers, and blast into a building. So his lessons continued. And as they continued, gasoline, jihad, Allah, blonde virgins, and American hamburgers intertwined. Eventually, Acmar honed his vision to twelve virgins and gasoline in an unconscious weight loss program. Often enough, he thought only of the twelve virgins. Consequently, upon receiving his truck-driving diploma, five-foot-ten, one-hundred-and-nineteen pound Acmar had honed the purest of Wills. So when he climbed into the decrepit purple bus (all the splinter group could procure on short notice) that fatal morning and said a brief prayer, he was heading toward destiny.

Unfortunately, a poster board, a pink one proclaiming "U DID IT YOUR WAY!" ripped clean of the Scotch Tape and Sparco Staples holding it to a rotting fencepost to flatten against Acmar's windshield, veering Acmar and his bus, which was laden with 238 cans of gasoline and at least two seemingly willing virgins, into a healthy oak tree, which possessed no moral intent to hinder Acmar, its pure Will desiring only to drop more acorns in healthy oak tree fashion.

Moral dilemma: Will Acmar's pure Will, despite the fact that it never achieved its goal, earn him twelve blonde virgins? Or will Acmar get a booby prize, say a dozen crones with wiry coal black hair and cracked dentures? Or maybe be short-changed entirely with only eleven high school football players, jock itch, and unleavened brains? Workspace is provided:

Pure *Result*, Case B: Rhett Montgomery, a.k.a. Huck's Dad, is a somewhat ageless American male raised in the Shady Grove Free Will Baptist Church just outside Irvine, Kentucky. Rhett, bless his KY bourbon-adoring heart, has prayed to the great god alcohol so long and heavily that he thinks the crooner Frank Sinatra, a.k.a. Frank Sinarta, is coming to Nicholasville to perform near the dumpster in back of the plant where Rhett keeps guard. So Rhett nails eight wooden loading skids together for a stage, and he paints the dumpster Hunter Orange, which he figures will complement Mr. Sinarta's signature black tuxedo. He's also borrowed money from the company's slush fund to buy poster board, glitter, and Magic Markers of varied colors. These he trundles under his arms to Scotch-tape and Sparco-staple to generic trees, fence posts, and rocks along the approaching highway in order to make Mr. Sinarta feel welcome and at ease. For if Mr. Sinarta is at ease, then the whole world, or at least the easternmost part of Nicholas County, will be at ease and good will be maximized.

Through no premeditation on Rhett Montgomery's part, one poster board, the pink one with silver glitter and black Magic Marker proclaiming U DID IT YOUR WAY!, unmoors from a rotting fence post and flies up to blind an impending terrorist, deflecting said terrorist from incinerating ninety-eight people, whose good would have been consequently minimized.

So. Should Huck's Dad, a.k.a. Rhett Montgomery, receive a lifelong supply of Maker's Mark whiskey and complimentary Boston butt for his good work, despite his lack of pure will? Workspace provided:

This moral stuff can really burn up some RAM, can't it?
∧∧∧∧∧*∧∧∧∧∧

At Mary Lou's insistence, the Starchilds stopped to pick up Huck's Dad, who was walking along the road toting a sack filled with Magic Markers, two hammers, a staple gun, and assorted wood and sheet metal screws. His pint of Maker's Mark lay safely within his vest.

"Did you see all the signs?" Mary Lou asked when he got in the VW bus.

"I put 'em up." He lifted the sack he held in the air twice.

Mary Lou suspected this would be the answer. Mrs. Starchild, though driving, was legally blind and had merely noted the bright colors along the highway and thought that perhaps a local 4-H club was celebrating vegetabledom. "Oh that's nice of you," she commented. "Did you help the girls?" Mr. Starchild remained in a panicked state as usual whenever he rode the VW bus on this road, for he'd witnessed a terrible accident on a curve here twenty-six years before, so he'd not seen any of the signs, always keeping his eyes directly on the centerline. He did manage, however, to squeak out, "Always good to lend a guiding hand to youth. Children, Caring, Counseling, and Kindness — the four C's that help Mother Earth grow."

"They're very colorful," Mrs. Starchild said, giving her husband a pat on the shoulder and batting her eyes instead of watching the road. "The signs, that is. You must be in touch with your inner child." She looked at the rear view mirror to see the blur that was Huck's Dad.

Who was sucking down a shot of Maker's Mark. He screwed the cap back on and said, "Speaking of 4-H clubs, did I ever tell you about the time that I saved a troop of Boy Scouts lost in Bernheim Forest outside of Bardstown? They were down to one tin of Vienna Sausages and a single Nehi Grape Soda. There were eleven of them and their scoutmaster. I think they'd been stalking a Girl Scout troop and gotten off the path. . . ."

Mrs. Starchild leaned back to hear Huck's Dad, so she slowed to forty, then thirty-five. Mary Lou sighed. It was around this time they too heard the explosion.

"I knew it," Loopy commented. "A car wreck. We shouldn't be on this road."

When they finally arrived at the plant, Huck's Dad immediately tried to talk everyone into moving the cars and the refreshments around back to the dumpster he'd painted a jolly orange and to the makeshift stage he'd constructed of roofing nails and Elmer's Glue. Willy and Dave refused, so Huck's Dad convinced the Doorwin's Simians and some of the Chinese kids to at least help him carry the loading crate stage around front. While they were reconstructing that to his specifications, he looked around for Huck, who was supposed to be with Lay Auto, but there were only six of those new fancy cars. Huck's old man knew that, because he'd counted them three times to make sure. One, two, three, six. Neither Huck nor Lay Auto was around, but he knew just where to find them. He walked to the backside of the orange dumpster, and pulled out his revolver to check the bullets, counting them as carefully as he'd counted the cars. They were all there, so he took a swig of Maker's Mark. Ever since scaring off the terrorists months before he'd made a point of walking to the stream and waterfall twice a day, figuring that under the falls would make a good hiding place for terrorists. He did this out of duty, even though he figured it was bad luck for his kidneys, for the splashing water made him take a leak every time he went there. It hadn't taken many such trips to discover that Huck and the fancy car were driving themselves down to the waterfall, too. Huck would always be sitting on the fancy car's hood like some oriental freak with his legs all pretzeled and his palms up like they were waiting for a guppy to jump from the water.

"I gotta check on something," Huck's Dad told one of the Doorwin kids, who was peeping around the dumpster, rubbing his right hand along the newly painted, glossy orange finish while eyeing the revolver Huck's Dad held. "So tell everyone to keep the home fires burning. Here, want a swig of whiskey?"

The kid, a brown-eyed boy of thirteen, grabbed at the pint and lifted it to his lips. "We all need to talk to you soon," he said before taking a swig. "After all this stuff is over." He shot down his gulp of whiskey, and Huck's Dad gave him a pat on the shoulder.

"Talkin's good. I ever tell you about the time a preacher and me got to talkin' to a dozen Hell's Angels?"

The boy started to take another swig of whiskey in preparation for the story, but Huck's Dad grabbed the bottle and just said, "Later."

Huck's Dad found Huck and Lay Auto right where he suspicioned he might, perched on the brink of the waterfall. Though it was an unusually warm day for mid-December, patches of snow remained from an earlier storm. Huck's Dad gathered a clump in his hand and compacted it into a snowball, which he threw at the boy, who fell off the bonnet of Lay Auto and went over the side of the falls.

"Oh my God!" Huck's Dad screamed, running forward and nearly dropping his Maker's Mark. Then he saw a blue shimmer underneath the chassis of Lay Auto. Huck was pulling himself up by a tree root.

"Something hit me," Huck said. "I almost fell into the water, except that I caught hold of this small tree."

"Must have been melting snow, dropping off a tree limb," Huck's Dad replied.

Huck looked up: there were no nearby trees, other than the sapling he was gripping. He climbed back on the bonnet of Lay Auto and resumed his Buddha pose, staring down into the waterfall.

"Kind of cold for thinking," Huck's Dad commented, leaning on Lay Auto. "Here, you want a pull?" He was feeling magnanimous, because he just remembered that he'd talked Mary Lou into an extra pint to celebrate the arrival of Mr. Sinarta and it was in his other pocket.

"They're not the same." Huck gave out a sigh. "I was hoping for some company for the holidays, but they're not the same. None of them."

"Who's not? Everybody's the same, everybody's happy and getting ready to have a party for the greatest singer ever, ole blue eyes, and you're out here moping and letting snow fall on you from trees. You need a drink to cheer you up."

"Alcohol is a depressant. Ethyl — "

"Naw, that's just a bunch of chemistry. Did I ever tell you about the time that my chemistry and math teacher got together during homecoming?"

"Math. Gödel. I hate Gödel."

"Well Lord's sake, who wouldn't with a name like that? His momma probably didn't even like him. Here, let's get in the car and ride back and I'll tell you about that homecoming that no one will ever forget."

Faux Graphic Panels 190 through 193:
Guests arrive, cont'd., a party ensues

By the time the TCS arrived, Huck's Dad was so drunk that he thought Frank Sinarta had shown up. In fact, he was so drunk that he'd dyslexically reversed the name from *Sinarta* to *Sinatra*, and thinking he was saying the wrong name, kept apologizing to the TCS. Willy and Natalie in turn apologized to the Doorwin's Simians for tasking them with taking the old man over to the makeshift stage and entertaining him by listening to his stories. Neither understood that no apologies were necessary, for Huck's Dad was sharing his Maker's Mark, feeling bountiful having the extra pint.

"Did you hear about the time that I was trapped in a john boat with three water moccasins?"

Despite themselves, everyone including the TCS leaned to listen, but the Simians were taking their job seriously and plied the old man with a pint they'd managed to buy, so he gargled and gurgled instead of finishing his story. Or perhaps that *was* the end of the moccasin story.

The TCS was impressed with the four (not six) proto-cars, and he wanted to drive one back to Texas. Willy begged for a month more, promising to drive the car out himself after the New Year.

"Okay, that's a deal," The TCS replied. "And, hey, find out what happened to the old guy and the water moccasins. What's with all the signs for Frank *Sinarta* along the road, anyway?" When the TCS heard the answer he smiled. "Well, the old guy's at least partially right: Frank sang one of my songs." He then added, "Everybody's sung at least one of my songs."

"You write for the Beach Boys?" one of the Chinese workers from Madame Nu Wa's asked.

The TCS paled. "Well, not really everybody."

Huck's Dad had wandered over, despite the grasping hands of Doorwin's Simians. He swayed and said,

"That goes to show ya. I had an English teacher — she was a looker!

— who told me never to say . . ." Huck's Dad hiccupped and thought. "Never to . . ." He started laughing and tilted the pint of Maker's Mark as if he were shooting startled quail. Three of the Simians caught him as that motion pushed him backwards into their arms.

"He had us build that stage for you," one of them told the TCS, nodding at Huck's Dad, who lay rigidly in their arms holding a thirty-degree angle to the parking lot. The kid nodded toward the packing crates nailed together.

"I've played on worse," the TCS replied after leaning to look at the crates. Orange, black, and green extension wires swirled the crates like water snakes, and two large speakers were propped on makeshift stands of concrete blocks. People were already gathering around it.

"Wha — " Dave said, walking out and seeing the crowd after fetching more crabmeat dip from inside the plant. The crabmeat had been Dave's idea. His Sonic bracelet had tugged him into a grocery store two nights before. Mary Lou had hoped he was going in for a bottle of wine and K - Y Lubricating Gel. At least some wine. Or at least some K - Y Gel.

Why this crowd? It happened that each and every of the Simians had breeched a sacred secret oath and blabbed to his or her single mother and respective step-step-step dad about the TCS and his upcoming visit. Talking with parents was strictly verboten by unwritten club rules. Similarly, the Chinese workers had spread the word at Madame Nu Wa's takeout stand as they served the masses General Tsu's Ginger Chicken or Happy Family Delight. And since Mr. and Mrs. Starchild had convinced Willy and the Pit Crew to offer Green Gong Energy Drink alongside hot coffee, tea, and cider, that couple had spread the word about the TCS through their many support groups. Of course, Huck's Dad's signs helped in their own meager way. Which, to turn the boat around, is why Dave exclaimed "Wha-!" when he walked out with the crabmeat.

When operating fully, the Mountain Dew Bottling plant had been a comparatively modest manufacturing affair: its parking lot could accommodate one hundred and ten cars. This lot was full and cars were now parking along the highway. Families were sitting on coolers in front of the eight packing crates. The Simians fetched a rusty wheelbarrow and lined it with purple pillows. The gathering crowd cheered when the Simians dropped Huck's Dad into this makeshift chair.

Two gaudy service trucks pulled up, opened their flapped sides, and began selling their wares: one, six-packs of Green Gong; the other, sausage, mushroom, and onion egg rolls.

"As I said, I've played worse," The TCS commented. "Do you have your guitar with you, Ms. Natalie?"

"Always."

"That's a good girl. Me too."

The TCS turned to The Pit Crew. "We could entertain, and you could offer free rides in the proto-cars. You can't buy publicity like this, you know."

It was true.

Egg rolls, oatmeal and raisin cookies, hot cider, hot tea and coffee, Green Gong, bubble gum, chips, crabmeat dip, Maker's Mark and music — all that was needed was a wedding, and Jane Austen could backstroke on Lollipop River into doggie heaven. In fact, Gabriel and Tiger Leigh *were* announcing to a select few, as Willy and Natalie tuned their guitars, that they were engaged. Tiger had found the perfect bungalow on High Street in Lexington, a turn of the last century, three-story brick complete with slate-covered cupolas. Gabriel, because of arranging the non-profit funding for Lay Auto, was making more money than he ever had. So much money that he'd even given Willy's sister Andrea a raise, so much that slate-covered roofs were easily affordable. Among the select few who learned of the engagement was Mary Lou, who on hearing the news looked around for Dave, whom she expected to be in a Gödelian haze. Instead, he was leaning against his pick-up, rubbing his Sonic Beads. Bad, of course, was *not* among the parties enlightened about the engagement. Unmoved by that news, she was the one lost in a Gödelian haze, for after two lonesome-ending lust affairs, one with Gabriel and the other with Kate Chung, Bad had returned to her most steadfast mistress, mathematics.

This is why Jane Austen stopped her novels at the wedding. This is why Virginia Woolf accused Jane of ending her novels just when things were getting interesting. *Interesting?* Is that a euphemism for horrid and sad and depressing and hand me the vodka and Xanax? Possibly. And this is why we, dear reader, are going to drink Green Gong, munch crabmeat and chips, and listen to Natalie and the TCS sing an old folk song. Jane Austen is right: sadness enough awaits. Whatever else do you think *would* await in this Gödelian pit of a world?

In fairy-tale style, the TCS stomped on the packing crates then started to sing in a "high, lonesome sound," while Natalie accompanied with her tenor:

> "There was a tailor had a mouse.
> Heigh come diddlum tarry.
> They lived together in one house.
> Heigh come diddlum lee."

The Simians and the Chinese kids began dancing, occasionally bumping one another without starting a race war. Some even exchanged goo-eyes. Perhaps, just perhaps, the tailor and the mouse will get married in the interest of promoting non-speciesism forever. Vive Jane.

> Heigh come diddlum lee.

Faux Graphic Panels 194 through 197:
Discontentment of Doorwin's Simians

On the Monday after the TCS's entertainment at the almost-wedding feast, all the Doorwin's Simians, including two new twelve-year old recruits, gathered around the orange dumpster. Huck's old man was walking the trail back toward the plant after his usual trek to the waterfall to console Chien Fou, Huck, and Lay Auto. He was never sure what he was consoling them for, but he tried anyhow. Huck's Dad saw the awaiting tow-head kids and took an extra slug of Maker's Mark.

"Did I ever tell you — "

"Mfff!" one of the more verbal Simians exclaimed, a thirteen-year-old blonde male normally fond of Huck's Dad's stories. The others assented, and the blonde took him by the hand. They led him to the huge rock he'd recently been using as target practice, and stopping in front of a thicket on the far side of the rock, they removed five camouflaged planters of foliage. A cave entrance lay bare.

"Mfff!" the faithful blonde Simian again exclaimed. Huck's Dad took a gulp of Maker's Mark.

"What's that smell?" He leaned toward the cave entrance.

The Simians shrugged.

Huck's Dad still had his gun. He took it out and counted the bullets, gave the pint bottle to the faithful Simian and intoned, "Follow me."

They lay aside their metaphorical clothes and followed.

∧∧∧∧∧*∧∧∧∧∧

Syntax error 101010-W: Pedagogy— Take A

America doesn't seem to be willing to force its schoolchildren to read, write, or work math problems. Kant can't help 'em. John Stuart Mill can't help 'em. Nietzsche's Overman can't help 'em. Even the $C\mathcal{A}$ — you remember him, way out in San Francisco — raises his electronic, e-mail hackles every time space for a word problem inserts itself in this tome. So he certainly isn't willing to help America's schoolchildren either.

But there is a channel yet open for educating American youngsters. Yes! Issue teachers convenient pint bottles of Maker's Mark; issue them pallets of Prozac, Ecstasy, marijuana, and cocaine. Let them distribute the same jauntily. Pied Pipers, they'd become. School attendance would soar.

Meanwhile, America could continue issuing work visas for Asians and Europeans to immigrate and handle all its heavy thinking, while Mexicans handle all its heavy work. What's left for Americans? Workspace provided:

∧∧∧∧∧*∧∧∧∧∧

Inside the cave, Huck's Dad and the Simians passed the first series of pornographic cave drawings.

"Better'n Lascaux," Huck's Dad commented, stopping to hitch his trousers. Studying one particularly livid depiction he tried to decode the male-female contortions and whispered to the Simians behind him: "Did I ever tell you about the time that three archeologists from the University hired me to help dig out Mammoth Cave? Filled to the brim with paintings and dead Injun skeletons, it was."

The Simians, even the faithful blonde, quietly pushed Huck's Dad forward until they reached rubble blocking the passageway. The smell of decay had been intensifying, and now facing the dusty rubble, all the Simians wanted a pull from the Maker's Mark to fight off the stench. Huck's Dad's eyes enlarged while following the bottle's progress around the group, and his hands shook. The blonde Simian, noticing his shaking, tugged his arm to reveal a virgin pint the Simian had secreted away in his oversized pants' pocket.

An older female Simian pulled out cones of incense and lit them, placing them on nearby rocks. A male Simian — the Simians seemed to have no definable hierarchy of leadership — pulled out a blunt and lit it off the girl's lighter. The Simians circled Huck's Dad and squatted on the cave's floor.

"Something's bad wrong," the girl who lit the incense started. "Did we ever tell you about the time we walked all the way to the end of this cave and dug into a room in the plant where we work?"

Huck's Dad shook his head. Another girl reached into the speaking girl's backpack and pulled out a book. She opened to one of the early pages. Seeing a book, Huck's Dad leaned forward warily, but once he spotted illustrations depicting the history of Doorwin's Simians, he grinned and opened the second pint of Maker's Mark.

/\/\/\/\/*/\/\/\/\/\

Syntax error 101010-X: Pedagogy — Take B

There is an alternative to drug and alcohol distribution, already making the rounds in America's schools: movies and comic books, mixed with sports. This solution has indeed made inroads to boost attendance and slow the dropout rate. Likely, substituting hard rock and rap for the comic books would bolster attendance even further. Go, Johnny, go! Run that ball! Twist them hips! Bap, bap, doo-bo-bips!

Meanwhile, America could continue to continue issuing extended work visas for Asians, Europeans, and Mexicans.

/\/\/\/\/*/\/\/\/\/\

"Wheelbarrow," Huck's Dad said, lifting up a finger.

The clearance began.

You might conjecture that this would lead to the discovery of Andrea's shredded husband and his rotting sidekick, the World's Tallest Detective. You might conjecture that this discovery would then free Andrea up for collecting insurance and remarrying someone with a modicum of sense. It didn't, for the dynamite and the falling rock had pulverized bones. All in all, the two bodies lay scattered in a form that only a forensic anthropologist would have recognized. There was such a woman at the nearby university, a Dr. Clarissa Circle, but Huck's Dad once had cornered her on the meat aisle of a supermarket, pushing a large chuck roast at her, describing the time he drove cattle in Texas three hundred miles during a hurricane. It was unlikely Dr. Circle would have helped with the excavation. Moreover, Andrea carried no insurance on her dead husband, and moreover than that, she'd promised herself she'd never marry again until the Commonwealth of Kentucky legalized same sex or at least inter-species marriages.

Still, with the assurances of Huck's Dad, whose expertise in coal-mining in eastern Kentucky prompted the Simians to shore up the cave's ceiling with two-by-fours and plywood, the entrance to the plant was restored within a fortnight, and any remains of the World's Tallest Detective and Andrea's husband were tossed into the waterfall, along with accompanying rubble. At the re-opening of the cave's passage, the

Simians gave Huck's Dad an honorary membership into Doorwin's Simians, which included a filched miniature monkey in honor of Doorwin himself.

Faux Graphic Panels 198 through 200:
Mary Lou's intervention with Dave

One night, it might have been a Wednesday, that statistical day when Americans feel most depressed, Mary Lou found herself in need of non-statistical cuddling and love. She searched Natalie's house for her partner of choice, finding him in the den sitting yoga style in front of the entertainment system, all of which was turned on. "All of which" included three TV screens, one showing a sitcom, one a video game, and one Fox News. There were six CD players, three of which were playing rap, two smarmy disco, and one flamenco. In a fit of inspiration, Mary Lou stepped between Dave and the global entertainment center, throwing her hips in a move that would have done any flamenco dancer proud.

Dave fingered his Sonic Bead bracelet.

Mary Lou had recently made a bold step by weaning herself from both Green Gong and the Starchilds. It had taken courage; it had taken will power. It had taken the *Upanishads*, the *New Testament*, *The Diamond Sutra*, Nietzsche's *Thus Spoke Zarathustra*, and four self-help books from the *NYTimes* bestseller list, written by authors of varying insight and competence. It had taken just saying, "No." How that word crick-cracked in Mary Lou's throat when she confronted Mr. and Mrs. Starchild as they offered a cozily warmed, gold-rimmed cup of warm Green Gong to fight the winter chill outside. Mary Lou had leaned forward, she had sniffed the aroma — and perhaps this olfactory imbibing awakened her as much as, say, *The Diamond Sutra*, for she caught the tiniest whiff of — could it be? — the tiniest whiff of petroleum. "No," she had said. "No."

Now, facing Dave, who had stared directly through her hips as they swayed first to Natalie's guitar and singing in a distant room, then shivered to the flamenco, then angularly tossed first to the disco and then to the rap, then jolted to the canned laughter on the sitcom, then shivered to the rockets exploding on the video game. Now facing Dave after all those gyrations, Mary Lou knew that an old-fashioned social work intervention was needed.

∧∧∧∧∧∧*∧∧∧∧∧∧

Syntax error 101010-Y: Brief thoughts on the origin of intervention

We ultra post-post-moderns tend to think that everything originated within our lifetimes or very shortly before. Didn't Gödel's grandson invent math in 1974? Wasn't he the one who proved that 2 + 2 equals 4? And gasoline, that came about during the Vietnam War, didn't it? Wasn't it compacted as napalm to help transport food to the starving peasants? Just so with interventions. Didn't Dolly Johnson, Ph.D., University of Tennessee, first come up with the concept on *Oprah?*
∧∧∧∧∧∧*∧∧∧∧∧∧

Mary Lou wasn't thinking of origins, she was thinking of practicality.

Should she yank off Dave's Sonic Beads and throw them in the fireplace? But there was no fireplace.

Should she open a bottle of fine wine and pass it under Dave's nose? But she'd drunk the bottle of rioja the night she'd bitten the nutcracker.

Should she kick and slap hell out of Dave until he came to his senses? But would Jesus do that?

Should she ram her tongue into Dave's mouth and grab his penis? But would Jesus do *that?*

She even thought about giving Dave a dose of Green Gong, though that would be substituting one addiction for another. But AA did that didn't they, by insisting on The Higher Power, as if it were some Gödelian or Pythagorean form floating just beyond the orbit of Mars.

The thought of Alcoholics Anonymous suggested: coffee. During one period, she and Dave had haunted Starbucks coffee shops, hunting them out like aficionados might haunt lighthouses along the Eastern coast, or say, covered bridges from state to state. Giving her hips a jaunty twist, Mary Lou ignored the blaring speakers and left for the kitchen.

When she returned twenty minutes later, Dave was still twisting the Sonic Beads. She placed a serving tray on the floor beside him, sat before him, and dipped two fingers into a cup of Columbian dark. Her be-wetted fingers then titillated his lips. "Tell me about Gödel." She batted her eyes and nudged his knees with her own. As movie actors and actresses — America's most real people — often declare, Mary Lou had slipped into something more comfortable while brewing the coffee. Now she sat beside Dave wearing a teddie red enough, as authors and poets — America's most un-real people — might metaphorically declare, to set the oldest, weakest bull in pasture to trot.

In the end, it took all her possible solutions to ease Dave from his obsession. She hit him, she snatched at the beads, she cajoled him, she wept, she laughed, she stuck her tongue down his throat, she tugged the nutcracker, she searched the kitchen cupboards and found a bottle of cognac hidden between cans of tuna and two boxes of pancake mix and poured the whole bottle into the Columbian Blend. Gödel, Gödel, Gödel, she gargled, gurgled, gobbled and giggled as she licked Dave's earlobes. At last, at last, at last, she was able to bring the intervention to an . . . ahem, climax.

But as she coaxed Dave into dropping his precious Sonic Beads into Natalie's food disposal and as they jointly listened to the grinding, bursting glass, she ran her fingers over the thin red teddie and humbly credited the Columbian Blend and Gödel for lighting the first fire.

"Let's go to bed," Dave said, surprising her, straightening her spine and perking her nipples. She could hear Natalie still playing in her makeshift garage studio just outside the kitchen. Mary Lou was certain that Natalie was playing a love song.

Of course, Natalie wasn't. She was playing a murder ballad called "Omie Wise."

> Come listen to my story,
> I'll tell you no lies,
> How John Henry murdered
> Little Omie Wise.

So it goes, by the banks of a flowing river, in a grim, grinding, grisly Gödelian world.

Joe Taylor

Faux Graphic Panels 201 through 202:
Willy and Natalie's Plan to intervene with Bad

In the days after Mary Lou's intervention, Dave's work output tripled. He installed a new computer interface that accelerated and magnified the accident prevention system threefold; he tinkered with the catalytic converter until each proto-car could get four, not three miles from a single KFC chicken thighbone. The blue boy, Huck, stood gazing over his shoulder and dutifully incorporated these changes into the original Lay Auto.

The original Lay Auto and Huck still made their daily trek to the waterfalls, and Chien Fou always trailed along. Noticing this, Huck's Dad convinced the Simians to go down daily to pet Chien Fou and polish Lay Auto's bonnet, telling them that even metal and stones have feelings.

"What about whiskey bottles then," one of the older girls asked.

She asked this because Huck's Dad had taken to target practicing on discarded bottles. He nodded at her and walked over to his target area and looked around. "You're right," he said. "I got to be respectful." That very day, he swept up the shards and began work on a collage of Maker's Mark pints that would some day cover the loading dock in a small town version of Picasso's *Guernica*.

Other than Huck's Dad and the Simians, no one seemed to notice that Lay Auto and the blue boy went missing for several hours a day, since they were all so busy overseeing an addition to the plant that would enable them to increase production and actually sell prototypes until a larger manufacturer picked the car up. This latter was the TCS's idea, for he was anxious to promote a green planet and lessen gasoline pollution. Speaking of the TCS, Natalie and Willy were planning their trip out to Texas to deliver a proto-car before tax time. Natalie was sure that the IRS hated the TCS for some darkly convoluted reason such as his fallout with the Nashville music establishment.

Now, while most of the workers and Pit Crew ignored Lay Auto and Huck, they did not ignore the change in Dave. His change left Bad's red hair and her angry disposition sticking out harshly.

Standing before the plant's trophy case, Willy and Natalie consulted with Mary Lou, who explained her whole sordid intervention with Dave. Neither Natalie nor Willy was willing to sleep with Bad — presuming that she would even consider either another male from Kentucky or a serene female folk-singer and her acoustic guitar as a sexual partner. Nor were Natalie and Willy willing to physically hit Bad to shock her — presuming that they could get past her third-degree karate black belt and not wind up in intensive care themselves.

Mary Lou sighed and studied the trophies. The tallest trophy was for the Dew-a-thon. Loop Y. Astro won. Loopy. Mr. Starchild, she realized. She was desperate enough that she considered Green Gong and the Starchilds until an idea came. She walked over to the office's newly installed paging system and paged Dave.

"This will work," she asserted.

Faux Graphic Panels 203 through 205: Dave's interview with Bad about Gödel, OR, how even math can effect crisis intervention

"She's out there! Go!" Natalie and Mary Lou each grabbed one of Dave's arms and pinched. Andrea and all the female Simians and the girl from Madame Nu Wa's carryout helped shove him out the loading dock's door. It was a female conspiracy to draw Bad from the dark side, that is, to get her to stop acting so male. Paradoxically, they were using a male to forward this goal, but even the youngest Simians were old enough not to be dismayed by paradoxes. Females always mature faster than males.

It was a chilly day, and Dave saw his breath condense in the air the moment the loading dock door slammed behind him. Then he saw Bad standing by the orange dumpster exotically inhaling a cigarette. As he approached, her breath exhaled duple smoke and condensation.

"I didn't know you smoked," she said to Dave when he stood beside her and lit up.

David didn't smoke, but Mary Lou had made him practice for this moment so that he wouldn't cough and give the ploy away. She and Natalie had even bought the same brand of cigarettes that Bad smoked, Camels, with the enigmatic humpy back on the pack. This enforced practicing had assured that Dave would never again light a cigarette once this therapy session was over. Call it a pre-crisis intervention intervention.

∧∧∧∧∧*∧∧∧∧∧
Syntax error 101010-Z: Pedagogy — Take C
Of Course! Force feed 'em drugs and whiskey and cigarettes! Make 'em cough and puke and pass out from dizziness! Tell 'em: "This is what Mommy and Daddy and your teachers do! You must grow up to be exactly like them! You must!"

A guaranteed cure for the education crisis.

Or maybe not. We force feed sports and idiot TV on 'em, and that's what Mommy and Daddy and their teachers do.

∧∧∧∧∧*∧∧∧∧∧

"I've been nervous," Dave replied to Bad's query about his smoking.

"Tell me about it. And that damned collage of whiskey bottles isn't helping." Bad pointed toward the loading dock, where Huck's Dad had started his Be-Considerate-to-Whiskey-Bottle-Shards-Because-They-Got-Feelings-Too artwork. So far, it stretched six feet.

Dave inhaled, deciding to get started quickly. "Gödel," he said.

Bad moved her gaze from the collage to Dave.

"Was he Satan or a saint? That's all I want to know." Dave exhaled, becoming dizzy from the smoke and swaying.

"Wittgenstein thought Gödel was just playing word games," Bad said, popping another Camel from her pack by slapping it on her wrist and snarling as if she were casting for a combo John Wayne-Rambo replacement. All the women crowding about the loading dock's windows shook their heads in dismay. "At least she isn't wearing steel-toed work boots," one of them whispered.

"The mess we don't know, we should pass over in silence," Dave said, mocking Wittgenstein's famous closing line.

"Exactly," Bad replied, lighting her cigarette. "Turing took Gödel's lead and proved that any computer program would always have inexplicable holes in it."

"Like that singular number that the Windows Platform couldn't solve, wasn't it a decade ago?"

"Exactly. Not exactly a decade ago, I don't know exactly when that happened, but that's exactly what I meant, what Turing meant." Bad sighed. "Turing killed himself. He ate a poisoned apple."

"Did you know there's a waterfall a hundred yards back there?" Dave pointed with his cigarette, something else that Mary Lou and Natalie made him practice.

"Nature isn't going to help. Nature's the problem," Bad replied. Then she brightened. "Do you want to walk there? Do you know the way? I've never been."

They took a stroll toward the waterfall. Lay Auto's accident avoidance system detected their approach from sixty yards away, so Huck, Lay Auto, Chien Fou and Huck's Dad all skedaddled, driving down a back trail onto the highway. Consequently the ledge by the falls smelled of whiskey and emotion recollected in tranquility, but since Bad's and Dave's sinuses were clogged with cigarette smoke, they judged the air pristine.

Dave sat first, and Bad followed, sitting surprisingly close to him.

"Do you know why Turing killed himself, after saving Great Britain's dumb ass by breaking Enigma, the German War Code?"

Dave shook his head. Bad offered him a cigarette, and he swayed, feeling even more lightheaded with the combination of the waterfall, the nicotine, and the tension seeping from Bad, whose entire forearm trembled as she offered the cigarette. Dave took it, just to stop her shaking hand.

"He was a faggot. He was queer. He was a homo. He was gay."

"There could be worse things," Dave said softly, ignoring the unlit cigarette.

"Yeah? Name one."

"You could be a mathematical genius who's shut off all the friends who love her."

Bad started to cry. When Dave put his arm around her, she didn't even karate chop him or throw him over the side of the waterfall for being male and touching her. What's more surprising is that she didn't even consider doing either. What's even more surprising is that Dave was being completely brotherly. Hormones, it seems, can misfire on occasion, just as do computer programs and closed mathematical systems.

A pair of eyes — steel gray, if the truth be known — watched the two consoling one another. These gray eyes watched through a pair of binoculars — bitch black, if the truth be known. Bitch black, coal black, dirty oil black, death black, heart-grinding black. There were seventeen cigarette butts lying by the equally black shoes of this watcher. And these shoes did sport a steel toe insert, to aid in street fighting and foiling assassination attempts. This gray-eyed watcher crushed an eighteenth butt into the ground then lit a nineteenth. This gray-eyed watcher snorted quietly as Bad turned to Dave and hugged him. Snorting quietly and committing myriad other oxymorons posed no problems to this woman. She worked for Homeland Security.

Faux Graphic Panels 206 through 207: Bad's intervention with Huck, Huck's reply

Now it was Bad's turn to make improvements on the proto-cars, and make them she did. Add one more mile per chicken bone. Add a self-correcting principle in the computer that allowed each proto-car to access every state's DOT files for updated road conditions, construction, and detours. She even inserted a slew of male memories into the machine, alongside the female ones she had duplicated from Lay Auto's original program. Balance, she thought. Yin-yang.

Huck, watching over her shoulder, shook his head, which Bad caught in an off reflection in her computer screen.

"What?" she asked.

"It won't help."

"What won't help?"

"Making those six computers hermaphrodites. There's still Gödel to face."

"Gödel, Gödel, Gödel! What's so worrisome about him?" Bad kept clicking in numbers, smiling at her screen as they appeared. The sound of her newly polished and sculpted nails against the keyboard amazed her. It was like she'd grown ten new appendages. Mary Lou had done them two nights before, over a shared bottle of Chablis.

"It's him and Turing together. And Plato's Cave, and Zeno's Paradox."

The keyboard stopped clicking. Bad turned to face Huck, who was shimmering bluely, per usual. "Honey, you just have to let it go. You just need to work with the axioms you're given, you know."

"That's what Mary Lou told me."

Bad's initial reaction was surprise, but then Mary Lou had been plenty wise enough two nights ago when they were drinking wine and Mary Lou was painting her nails. In fact, Mary Lou had set Bad up with a blind date, a young woman who had just opened a psychology practice in Lexington. They were meeting with Mary Lou and Dave to listen to Natalie at Como's tomorrow evening.

Huck sighed. As he did, his blue hue deepened to a violet, then to a purple. "That's the problem, isn't it? The axioms we're given, I mean. It's all just a crapshoot, just chance, or hormones, or computer chips and input. If these axioms, why not those? And then, with whatever axioms or axons you're given, the problems surface. You'd think — "

"You would," Bad agreed, her fingernails slowing. She felt a headache coming on. She opened a Diet Coke, offering one to Huck, who refused. No one had ever seen the blue boy eat or drink.

"Mary Lou," Huck said, "told me that the philosopher Nietzsche thought that the problem of free will was a bogus question. Does that make sense to you?"

Bad sipped her soda, internally hearing Kate's Chung's Chinese singsong as they'd made love on a snowy afternoon. A tear seeped from one eye, then the other. Spring's around the corner, Bad thought, bravely trying to cheer herself. Is it? She thought. Is it really? When she looked for the blue boy, Huck, he was no longer there.

Faux Graphic Panels 208 through 209:
The double date

It took only one look into the psychologist's green eyes for Bad to tumble. The psychologist already was sitting in a booth at Como's when Bad, Mary Lou, and Dave arrived. Though Dave hadn't forgotten Gödel completely, he had forgotten the ridiculous bead bracelet he'd been wearing for months. He had eyes only for Mary Lou, which Bad, uncharacteristically, found sweet. Just the word "sweet" itself typically made Bad cringe when it concerned anything other than confections, and frankly it didn't do much even then, for she hated candy. But the moment she sat in the booth in Como's, across from those green psychological eyes, she knew exactly how Dave felt. Sweet.

Not one hour into those green eyes, Bad listened as Natalie began her set. Bad had never particularly thought herself a fan of acoustic music; she preferred the mathematical intricacies of Bach or Mozart on a pianoforte with orchestra. Still, she always tried to be polite when Natalie played. Being polite came hard to Bad. But tonight, with the green eyes, a bottle of Chianti, and Como's Super Around the World Pizza with four types of cheeses, even Natalie's rendition of the folk song standby "House Carpenter" started Bad's bones and gristle moving. And Willy was up there, too, plunking on a banjo, "claw hammer style," Mary Lou had called it. Love can work wonders, Bad thought. If points can be earned to lighten karma, I should be earning bushels of them, she thought. Were these thoughts characteristic? Is it characteristic that a camel pass through the eye of a needle? Is it characteristic that a mouse escape a mousetrap?

So Bad leaned toward the green eyes while Dave and Mary Lou were cooing privately, goofily sharing one piece of pizza and saliva like pre-teens under the influence of a barrage of hormones. "Free will," Bad queried. "What do you make of it, as a psychologist, I mean."

The green eyes did their bong-bong trick, tugging Bad even closer, hook, line, and sinker as the fisher folk, those eternal progenies of the twelve apostles, say. "As a psychologist, I stand in the Skinnerian camp. We're a bundle – a 'repertoire' as B. F. Skinner claimed – of acquired responses. But as a human, I think free will's a bogus question anyway. We are what we are. And we'll be what we are whether we have an immaculately clear crystal ball called free will imbedded in our skulls, or whether we have a murky coil of responses – Skinner's repertoire – creeping through the axons and neurons of our bodies and our brains. We're just who we are."

"Go with the axons and the axioms you're given, in other words."

The psychologist, originally from Cincinnati, smiled; then she breathed in Bad's breath. Bad had recently, as in three days back, given up cigarettes, so her breathing was often stentorian. As chance and the three Weird Sisters would have it, Bad gave a long exhale of Chianti and garlic just as the psychologist was breathing inwards. To the psychologist, that exhalation smelled entrancing. It smelled bold, feminine, feline, *haute cuisine*. She pinched Bad's cheek and took a quick nibble at her lips.

On stage, Willy plunked, Natalie sang:

"What hills, what hills are those my love, those hills so dark and low? / Those are the hills of hell, my love, where you and I must go."

∧∧∧∧∧*∧∧∧∧∧
Syntax error 101010-Z-a: Hell and history

"Love is hell," Sherman pronounced while courting the lasses around West Point. He later changed his tune to "War is hell," while bringing the South to its knees and ending that tragedy known as The American Civil War. Sherman should be commended for straight talk, even though The Nuremburg War Trials Council, had it existed then, might have wanted to do some straight talking of its own with him. But, taking the long look at things, there's plenty of hell to go around, love often as not serving as a cleverly disguised germ incubating that disease.
∧∧∧∧∧*∧∧∧∧∧

As Natalie finished singing "House Carpenter" and Willy finished plunking his banjo, Bad and the psychologist finished a single piece of pizza, munching close enough that each felt the other's satisfying, warm, moist garlic breath.

"What hills, what hills are those my love, those hills so dark and low? / Those are the hills of hell, my love, where you and I must go."

Faux Graphic Panels 210 through 211:
Green Gong bonkers

"You're what? With whom?" Mrs. Starchild fell into a recliner, knocking over a bottle of Green Gong. Loopy rushed to her side, though it must be noted that he first scooped up the Gong bottle and righted it to avoid further spillage.

Mrs. Starchild fought him off to sit upright and glare at her grandniece, the psychologist. "How could you and sweet Mary Lou do this to us? And especially how could you do it with that redheaded so-called friend of hers, that home-breaker, that jezebel who has such an appropriate name? That throwback woman should stick with numbers and computers. Everyone would be happier. What can you possibly see in her?"

The grandniece was stunned. "I thought you two, of all people, would be happy. I'm twenty-seven years old, I'm a psychologist who's been denying a crucial part of my psychic makeup, and I've finally faced it."

"It's not the lesbian part we mind," Loopy interjected. He finished off the Green Gong bottle that had that toppled.

"What about Bill?" Mrs. Starchild asked. Her voice was even, the type of even that holds menace.

Bill was the foreman of the Winchester plant who was on the verge of agreeing to bend the rules and supply the Starchilds with Mountain Dew in a tanker, at a nearly wholesale price. He and the grandniece had been dating for nearly a year. She had yet to have an orgasm with the man, though she figured he'd topped three hundred of his own several weeks back. She stared at her great aunt. "That's it, isn't it? It's about the damned Mountain Dew and your damned Green Gong. You're addicts! And you two call yourselves counselors."

The grandniece walked out the door and got into her sensible blue Toyota and drove her sensible, newly discovered self away, leaving the

Starchilds posed, *tableau vivant*, by the recliner in a modified Pieta. That position didn't last long. Mrs. Starchild made a quick call to Madame Nu Wa.

Who had just the person for them to contact, a friend who'd recently been hired by Homeland Security.

Faux Graphic Panels 212 through 215: The week before the wedding

Bad laughed when she finally heard from Andrea that Gabriel and the real estate agent named Tiger Leigh were getting married and planning to move into a three-story Victorian house on High Street in Lexington. Her laugh wasn't mean and filled with karate chops; it was filled with Buddha compassion. And when she heard the same about Willy and Natalie, minus the Victorian house bit, she cooed. And when she heard ditto about Mary Lou and Dave, she broke into tears, whether of happiness or sadness or frustration, she wasn't sure.

One thing she was sure of though, was the gift she was buying Mary Lou and Dave: a framed photo of Kurt Gödel in his super thick-lensed glasses that inspected the world in every detail — with a blue superimposition of the Buddha and his hooded eyes that shunned the world in every detail, gazing over Gödel's shoulder.

For a while it seemed that Jane Austen might step into the 21st century, for there were rumors of a triple wedding. But neither Tiger nor Gabriel could stomach the thought of the Simians — who would surely be invited to the other two weddings — running amuck in Lexington's hallowed Episcopal Church and its austere enclosed garden, much less Huck's Dad stacked drunkenly against that garden's brick wall, so the triple wedding possibility fizzled. Mary Lou and Dave, and Natalie and Willy had no such qualms, so the Episcopal Church and its gardens were booked two weekends in a row in early April, not even one full month before Derby Day and the running for the roses, the stumbling for the mint juleps.

Imagine those gardens with an apple tree, an oak, a plane tree, and a weeping willow. Imagine roaming from tree to tree, leaning on each burly trunk, imbibing vegetable wisdom. Imagine a mint julep with shaved ice in a silver cup chilling your right palm as you roamed. Even without a graphic novel, that picture would make any willow weep copious Southern Belle tears over the passing of time, the onset of mortality. The Buddha himself, in such a situation, might lift his mint julep and belt out a sad Stephen Foster song. . . . Well, maybe not; the guy did carry some class. Need I clarify that I'm referring to the Buddha, not Stephen Foster?

The weddings once more put off the trip to Texas, but the TCS was so delighted that he didn't care. In fact, he planned on flying in for the double wedding and even offered to sing . . . not "Ave Maria," he told Mary Lou, and not "Your Cheatin' Heart" either. "I'll think of somethin'," he drawled in his best Texas style. But being a sport, the TCS reconsidered and finally emailed that indeed he would sing "Ave Maria." Why not, he thought as he took a toke of some primo weed and stared at his computer. He and every other singer of his era had done a cover for "Danny Boy," that king of sappy songs. "Ave Maria," though just as sappy and just as overdone, at least offered the swank of being in Latin. Upon hearing the news that the TCS would be singing, the Episcopal priest, in a moment of sectarian amplitude, allowed to Mary Lou that the Popish hymn would be acceptable.

∧∧∧∧∧*∧∧∧∧∧
Syntax error 101010-Z-b: Feminist literature:
Jane, thou much maligned spirit! I speak of Jane of the Austen clan who ended each novel with a marriage. And just what could be wrong with inserting five or six pages of happiness into life's woe, woe, woe? Jane, with crow-like perspective could see the bleak chapters surrounding those few pages, fore and aft. My vote? Elect Jane queen! Elect Jane pope! White smoke, white smoke! Vive la Jane!
∧∧∧∧∧*∧∧∧∧∧

There was an odd incident in the week preceding the wedding. A private plane, laden with homemade explosives, crashed into an abandoned warehouse three-quarters of a mile from the Lay Auto plant. Police conjectured it was anything from a weird suicide to an even weirder attempt at collecting insurance. Maybe the pilot was supposed to bail out before impact, who knew? What no one did notice — with the exception of the seven, eight, or nine happy crows that still perched on the fence outside the plant — was that from the air the abandoned warehouse greatly resembled the Lay Auto plant.

Other than the private plane incident, matters played so gay and loose that for the entire week before the double wedding the proto-plant may as well have shut down. The Simians had made friends with several of the younger Chinese group from Madame Nu Wa's, and on Wednesday they led them into their newly refurbished cave during an extended lunch period. In a burst of mania, the Simians had planted roses around the great rock marking the cave's entrance, and on the cave's inside they had smoked enough pot in blunts and burned enough incense that it no longer smelled of dead bodies and expended explosives. One of them had found a ring in the rubble around the previously collapsed walls — it was Andrea's husband's wedding ring, though of course none of them recognized it — and they had nailed this artifact from what they presumed to be the Pleistocene Era to a support beam and used it as a rallying point for their rituals. Whenever they smoked or ran their fingers along graphic novels in ecstasy before this wedding ring they imagined stooped, grunting brotherly creatures tearing flesh and howling to the moon as a dinosaur sent tremors through the earth from three miles away. Had Andrea ever learned of this ring, she would have confirmed that their Simian fantasies weren't far off: just toss in a titty bar and cheap beer and they would have been on target insofar as her deceased husband and his male friends were concerned. As she lived in ignorance of the ring's nearby charred existence, however, she imagined him now stomping galoshes in Alaska while nuzzling a six-pack of Budweiser in a titty bar with bearskins covering its walls. He'd always claimed he was going to Alaska where men were men and where petroleum flowed like — of course he didn't say "like honey"; he'd said something most vulgar and puerile.

While Doorwin's Simians had taken to the Chinese, Huck's Dad had never completely trusted that slant-eyed crew, especially one dumpling girl who stuck out from her friends because of her weight. "She's got a problem locked under that yellow skin, else why would she eat so much noodles and pork?" / "Well, what about you and whiskey, then," the older Simian girl who'd inspired Huck's Dad to respect Maker's Mark bottles and start the loading dock collage asked. / "That's what I mean," Huck's Dad had replied. " 'At's exactly what I mean."

Huck's Dad was right about the dumpling girl, for while the Simians and their newly found Chinese comrades were smoking blunts and eating rice with chopsticks and conjuring cave men from graphic novels, the dumpling girl was carrying her double serving of noodles and pork to wander the cave until she reached the entrance that led into the plant. Ignoring the happy hoots and yelps echoing from some distance back in the cave, she climbed makeshift steps of compacted dirt and slid open a panel of wall to make sure; then she settled on the floor inside the plant to eat more noodles and pork, smiling at her discovery.

Faux Graphic Panels 216 through 218:
An almost happy ending: the marriages;
the tossing of the bridal bouquets;
the running for the roses

While there would be plenty of friends at the double wedding, there was a dearth of parents, something that would have saddened Queen Jane. Mary Lou's parents had been killed by terrorists in some impoverished African kingdom when they were trying to deliver medical supplies for the World Sight Foundation. For twelve years, Natalie's mom and dad had lived incommunicado in Colorado on an old hippie commune, where the youngest person, a sixty-four-year-old woman, was made to do all the worldly drudgery like writing checks and depositing money earned from the silvery trinkets and raspberry tarts the commune sold to tourists and locals. This woman was jealous of Natalie's mom and consequently threw most of her mail away, including the three letters that Natalie had written about the wedding. This woman was not only the commune's de facto banker, but also its sole member who knew how to use a cell phone and email, though she guarded such accesses to the outer world wildly, insisting they were for emergencies only. (The entire commune did watch TV, however, and she had become addicted to the young, swashbuckling male hips appearing perennially on *American Idol*. With every new show she voted fanatically for her favorite pair of hips and biceps. In fact, her voting patterns were encroaching on the commune's savings.) So, never hearing from her hippie parents, Natalie had resigned herself to forgo their presence at her wedding. She figured that maybe Bad or the TCS or even Huck's Dad would have to give her away. Willy's father and mother were similarly incommunicado, for they had split up when Willy dropped out of high school, both of them judging his action as reflecting poorly upon their parenting skills. They'd remarried, one living in California, the other in upstate New York. They typically ignored Willy's letters until their respective spouses tossed them into the trash with bulk mail circulars. Dave's parents, however, did keep in touch, even though they were ethereal academics. His father taught German and his mother taught math, being the first female to get a math Ph.D. from her university. They arrived at the wedding in somber matching gray suits.

Because of Dave's German heritage, sauerkraut and sausages loaded the wedding table. Mary Lou wanted cruciform veggies: three types of broccoli, one with ginger sauce and almonds, one with the little trees encrusted in Parmesan and cracker crumbles, and the last dipped raw in a honey-coconut-peanut butter mix. Cauliflower also received a triad representation: as a cold, spicy pickled appetizer; a Velveeta-soaked casserole; and a deep-fried hand-munchie. Even Brussels sprouts were given their due, appearing with cider vinegar and dill. Besides veggies, there were bagels for Dave's New York cousin. There were seven-grain wheat breads, corn breads, rye breads, and sourdough breads, the last for the TCS, who'd become addicted to that bread after a concert in San Francisco. Since it was still chilly out, there was a variant of Keeneland's burgoo stew. There was red-eye gravy in consideration of Huck's Dad, who said his grandmother had let him sop buttermilk biscuits in it every morning. Hearing how that particular gravy was rendered, no one, for once, had any doubt but that he was telling the truth. There was beer-steamed shrimp. A college friend of Mary Lou's was coming from Louisiana, and she'd recommended a turducken, so that three-bird monstrosity shared the middle of the table alongside barbecued ribs, roast beef, and salt-cured country ham. The Simians requested cheddar-flavored popcorn. Two silver bowls of the same resided at each end of the lengthy table. There were wines, champagnes, beers, hot ciders, Cokes, and scotch enough to wash it all down. There was no Green Gong, for the Starchilds refused to attend, being in a snit over their grandniece and Bad. Lastly, for Huck's Dad there were three fifths of Maker's Mark, though four Simians were assigned to guard each fifth and parcel as parsimoniously as they could.

When the TCS sang "Ave Maria" everyone teared-up, even the tall Simian girl, who was standing next to Huck's Dad and Huck.

After that song was finished and the ceremony proper was about to begin, the Simians began tossing popcorn and bagels at each other in anger because one of the gang had slipped up with the Maker's Mark and Huck's Dad stood as petrified as the trunk of the ponderous oak tree. Fearing a repeat of Thanksgiving, Willy broke up the fight, took one look at Huck's Dad and offered a solution. Since all the man had to do was hand over the rings, if three or four Simians could hide in the azaleas surrounding the oak, hold him up, and push his hand forward at the appropriate time, they could duck-tape both rings in his palm. This is what they did; the oak tree and its surrounding azaleas never betrayed the secret. Even the Episcopal priest was fooled.

However, during the double kisses ending the ceremony, Huck's Dad sobered up enough to start a story about the time he drove to New York City during a thunderstorm with three women. One of the Simians had the presence of mind to pull the tape from his right hand and slip it over his lips.

One week before, Andrea had caught the bouquet at Tiger and Gabriel's wedding. Everyone was eyeing the TCS, who was known to like tall women. Of course there was the problem of her husband's status, which remained unknown. At this double wedding, though, Bad and the psychologist caught the double bouquets. Natalie's roses had bounced off Bad's forehead and landed in her hand. The psychologist was more aggressive, since Kentucky's legislature was once more considering same-sex marriages: she leaped into the air with the grace of a basketball player to snatch the bouquet Mary Lou tossed. Bad and the psychologist intertwined their bouquets and touched foreheads, to the coos of the Simians.

When Huck's Dad blinked and recovered from his second stupor to raise his Maker's Mark mixed with champagne in a toast, everyone groaned when he said, "Did I ever tell you about the time that I was going to be a preacher?" He laughed and added, "That's a joke. Here's to the brides, here's to the grooms." He raised his glass and drank, then once more fell against the oak tree, this third fall promising some finality for the day.

At wedding's end, five limousines carried the guests and the couples off to varied destinations. Huck's Dad and one Simian lay passed out under the azaleas in the courtyard and were found the next morning by the sexton. All in all, the double weddings and the week's proceeding festivities were a roaring success that would have tickled Queen Jane Austen, straight through her whalebone corset. Even the woman perched atop a roof three buildings away gave out a sniffle as she focused her binoculars on the license numbers of the limousines.

Faux Graphic Panels 219 through 222:
Alison Taber, Maria Gompers,
and Homeland Security plan a surprise

The disappearance of Ralph and Louise Johnson late in the previous summer had sent shivers through Homeland Security. It was agent Maria Gompers who insisted upon dragging Tibet's Pond, and it was she who was subsequently promoted to oversee all of Kentucky's Homeland Security after the three bodies were discovered. Kentucky, as did each of the fifty states in the Union, suspected that it was number one on every terrorist's list, and Maria, an ex-stripper from her college days, fed into this mindset. One of the first people Maria hired upon her promotion was Alison Taber, a dear friend whose underworld connections would prove invaluable. In Alison's three-month tenure since her hire, she had worked patriotic wonders. She'd flooded the basement of a Victorian house on High Street, pre-empting a devastating strike from a terrorist cell located therein. She'd scrambled the phones of a real estate agency that was renting and even selling property to suspected terrorists. She'd introduced cane syrup and field mice into a suspect law office that had been undermining American offshore oil production by supporting a vehicle reportedly able to run on table scraps. Within two weeks, the office's paper files were shreds. Hi-tech or lo-tech, Alison aimed to make her boss Maria a star in the world of counter-terrorism.

One of Alison's dearest connections, in turn, was Madame Nu Wa. And one of Madame Nu Wa's dearest connections was a dumpling girl addicted to noodles and pork. Alison was already familiar with the Nicholasville plant because of Gabriel Gatestrait's legal ties, and because a nonagenarian couple named Starchild had reported that homosexual and even lesbian activities were promoted there. Alison, in her new position as junior investigator for Homeland Security, was clean and American, as pure as a Ford Mustang or Chevy Corvette. She'd even shared love offerings with a Baptist deacon under a black walnut tree.

So it was a sign from heaven when the dumpling girl offered information about a cave leading into the Nicholasville plant. If only, Alison lamented, the girl had come forward a week before, Alison could have planned a wedding gift beyond compare for the lawyer and his un-American friends. But gift horses should never be looked in the mouth. And, of course, never chew your dumplings till they're between your teeth.

ʌʌʌʌʌ*ʌʌʌʌʌ

Syntax error 101010-Z-c: A reflection upon Trojan horses

Some gift horses *should* be second-guessed. If for instance, the Trojans had looked their gift horse in the mouth, Troy might still be in the olive oil market. If Jesus had probed Judas Iscariot's teeth for cavities, gingivitis, and fish bones before accepting that brotherly kiss, Jesus could have quadrupled his soothing parable output. If the Mohawk or Blackfoot tribes had taken just one string of those beads and slapped it between two rocks to determine its worth, Manhattan still might sport teepees — or at least those tribes might be war-whooping prices down in the stock market's pit. And if the plains Indians had checked out the grime under the privates' and corporals' delivering fingernails and then dropped those smallpox-infected blankets into boiling water, they might now be tending buffalo herds and officiating at public parks. The moral? O do look those gift horses in their mouths. Don't settle for a new leviathan Department of Education or Office of Homeland Security promising to right all wrongs. Check their dentifrices! Do they possess bicuspids capable of gnawing truth or only incisors that will shred tax dollars and the occasional limp dumpling?
ʌʌʌʌʌ*ʌʌʌʌʌ

Maria Gompers concurred with Alison about the Nicholasville plant. How could any group wanting to manufacture cars whose top speed was sixty-seven bode well for America? How would that possibly fit in with Madame Nu Wa's uncle's plan for a new, elevated Route 66? But Maria didn't want any Watergate bungling, so she insisted that Alison be discreet. "Screech is my middle name," Alison replied, hearing what she wanted to hear. Maria, similarly, heard what she wanted to hear.

The first thing Alison did was buy a case of Maker's Mark, for she'd espied Huck's Dad and knew he was a wild card that needed controlling. The next thing she did was prepare shrink-wrapped packets of pornographic graphic novels, X-stasy, and marijuana blunts, for she wanted the Simians out of the way, too. Derby Day was approaching, and Alison counted on distributing her gifts well before, to insure that day's reigning Kentuycky confusion would push matters along.

Her plan continued: she personally convinced four Iraqi graduate students who frequented Girly Deelites that not only was the Nicholasville Lay Auto plant a threat to the Mid-eastern oil market, but that the Green Gong manufactured there blasphemed the Prophet Muhammad by rivaling and indeed threatening to replace far eastern meditation, prayer wheels, and chants, which of course in themselves rivaled, blasphemed, and threatened to replace the Mid-eastern Prophet Muhammad. "Blasphemy squared," she told the avid group of young males, who split their time betwixt staring at her cleavage and listening to her Paris lips. "And," she continued, "Green Gong uses the same petroleum that most Holy Muhammad once trod over with his most holy toes, uses it to promote an infidel religion disguised as therapy." Alison had done her homework: after mentioning that New Age babble known as therapy, she told the four grad students about the blaspheming Fourfold Delights, the unholy Fivefold Truth of Gong, and the wickedly satanic Eightfold path of misery. She saved the best fold for last, reminding them of the Twelvefold virgins they each would obtain.

"Did any of you know Acmar Jihal?" None of them had. She smiled with relief. She hadn't known Mr. Jihal either, but she'd read the file about his botched terrorist attempt against the Nicholasville plant. Alison figured it just as well these students didn't know Jihal, for a main tenant of hers was that incompetence was contagious. "Acmar attended the university here," she said. "He died a martyr's death last Fall." She painted a picture of olives, dates, and goat cheese carried on a silver platter to Acmar — and to any of his martyr friends — by multitudinous blonde virgins rubbing silken fingertips and honey-coated breasts over each martyr as he reclined under a palm tree beside a babbling brook.

Alison had worn her blondest wig. The four young men were panting by the time she finished. She promised that a teenaged sister, also blonde, would email them soon with details of stores that sold bulk fertilizer and other interesting items necessary to further the explosive glory of Allah.

"Can she not call me instead?" the youngest male asked.

"Can she not *visit* me instead?" the oldest male asked, cutting to the core of matters.

She could do either, Alison assured them, though in truth this sister didn't exist. Hey, if you were Alison's mother, would you give her a sister?

Faux Graphic Panel 223:
Maundy Thursday, Or,
two days before Derby Day in KY

Alison's loving gifts had been distributed on a Thursday, a Maundy Thursday, if there ever was one. The Simians were all missing from work after lunch that day, having holed up in the tunnel with the graphic pornography and the marijuana blunts, which they had taken to smoking along with Green Gong. Madame Nu Wa, in on the conspiracy, summarily summoned the Chinese for a math quiz about her uncle's proposed new cross-country highway. None of them could resist the challenge, so they too were absent after lunch.

"We might as well close the plant. We could drive the new proto-car out to Texas tonight," Willy said.

"Are you crazy? Saturday is Derby Day! You've been in Florida too long. We have to go home early tonight and polish the silver and aerate the mint growing near Natalie's back porch for the juleps. Let's close all right, and let's close tomorrow, too. But no one's driving to Texas *this* weekend. That can wait."

So the plant was closed. Locked tight, the now eight proto-cars parked inside the loading dock.

That night at homes, apartment buildings, bars, and hospital rooms across the Commonwealth of Kentucky, abundant prayers were offered for the horse of choice: some prayers proffered on knees, some on backsides while engaged in tantric sex, some whilst staring into a glass of Kentucky's finest bourbon, some whilst inhaling Kentucky's finest burley, and some from a meditative pose on King crapper.

Faux Graphic Panels 224 through 227:
Good Friday, Or
the day before Derby Day in KY

The plant, like every other business in Kentucky, had a Derby pot. Mary Lou had taken Loopy's trophy out of the case and filled it with numbers for the horses. After these numbers were drawn she'd filled it with five-dollar bills from the bets. She and Dave drove this toward Natalie's on Friday mid-morning.

Dave had been acting strange since their marriage, and Mary Lou constantly inspected his wrist for signs of rubbing from a new set of Sonic Beads. What she didn't know was that he kept a new set hidden on a loop inside his waistband. The bosomy high priestess had predicted this might even be more effective, being closer to a source of life, as she said with hooded gray eyes. It had yet to prove so, hence, Dave's edginess. It had nothing to do with the beads; it had everything to do with the beads. It had nothing to do with not taking a honeymoon; it had everything to do with not taking a honeymoon. It had nothing to do with Gödel; it had everything to do with Gödel. It was the best of times, it was the worst of times, etc. I swear to Pythagoras, if you've read one novel about humans, you've read them all. Where's the Green Gong? Where's the Maker's Mark? Where's Squire Gabriel's stash? Where's the graphic graphic novel? Pass me something before I go frantic.

"Let's stop at the Starchilds' house. I want to make a peace offering," Mary Lou said once they got into her car. Mary Lou's very car posed one more problem atop the other problems, for Dave's truck had been in the shop since they were married two weeks back, stranded by some ineluctable part problem that even the Sonic Beads couldn't solve. Still, Mary Lou and Dave made the best of sitting low to the highway in the economy car and drove to the Starchilds with no stops, though the Sonic Beads itched mightily against Dave's bare hip when they passed stores, especially an antique shop, which nearly sent him into a curiosity swoon, for he'd never cared for antiques. Watching the store's sign diminish in the side view mirror, he pawed the beads near his groin and fretted over what wondrous oldie-goldie he might be missing. A slide rule used by Einstein? Babbage's original calculating machine? The core of Turing's poisoned apple, still showing that great man's teeth marks? Gödel's thick goggles?

When Dave and Mary Lou arrived at the Starchilds' house, their reception was icy enough to chill any silver mint julep cup. But when Mary Lou showed Loopy the trophy with his name on it and rubbed her hip against his, and when Dave mentioned to Binky that they'd closed the plant down for the day in anticipation of celebrating the Derby tomorrow, both Loopy and Binky turned quite cordial, even offering Green Gong, which Dave took, though Mary Lou kindly refused. Still the Starchilds remained cordial. In fact, their grins widened.

∿∿∿∿∿*∿∿∿∿∿

Syntax error 101010-Z-d: A smile is a smile is a smile, Or, Did Gertrude get it wrong?

Does your boss, who's previously considered you dirt on the carpet, suddenly smile and pat your lint-ridden shoulder? Does your boyfriend, who's previously shown more interest in Formula One cars dizzily circling an extended oval, suddenly set his beer can down and musically call your name, managing to overcome the racetrack's roar? Does your wife, who's previously spent spans of time meditating upon rows of cosmetics and toenail polish suddenly gaze at you with moon eyes and speak entire sentences?

Beware! Even a resurrected Kurt Gödel and his favorite-most improvable axiom could not disengage you from the "tee-tiny favor" about to be foisted on you.

∿∿∿∿∿*∿∿∿∿∿

"I'd long forgotten about that trophy. Do you think I could have it — once you've announced the Derby pot, of course."

"Do you mean that the plant is entirely empty? That no one is there?"

The Starchilds gathered about Mary Lou and Dave and doled their most jaunty smiles. Their eyes even twinkled like, well, stars, like childs.

Meanwhile, back at what will have to pass for a ranch, the Simians were cavorting in the tunnel, playing music at entirely too many decibels for any human ear with more than 24 years logged in to withstand. Filling the tunnel with a marijuana haze, mixing X-stasy with Green Gong, and eyeing one another over the pornographic graphic novels, they had been partying for twenty straight hours. And Huck's Dad, who discovered a mysterious cache of Maker's Mark bottles beside the orange dumpster, was lying passed out *in* that same dumpster, Willy having had it moved into the woods not far from the water falls, replacing it with a solid green one. (It seemed the sanitation drivers kept inordinately banging the orange dumpster, its color angering them.)

Meanwhile-meanwhile, back at what will have to pass for a mountain pass, the four graduate students whom Alison had converted into terrorists had amassed their half ton of fertilizer explosives and were jauntily driving toward Nicholasville. Layla, the same sultry blonde virgin who'd appeared to Acmar months before, happened to be haunting the highway at the eight-mile approach to the plant, and she seeped into the truck's cab as it drove by her favorite crab apple tree, which was in full bloom. Crabapple perfume filled the cab's air, and there was nearly an accident as she twirled her blonde curls and spread her legs to settle on the gearshift knob and look each young man in his newly converted jihadist eyes.

"For the love of Allah," she intoned, easing down on the knob.

"For the love of Allah," they responded, panting and passing around a second fifth of vodka and a single Diet Coke.

Meanwhile-meanwhile-meanwhile, back at the sheriff's office, a.k.a. Homeland Security, Alison Taber was caressing the Lay Auto file to tenderly place it on a weighing machine: 15.3 ounces. She prided herself on closing cases before they reached a pound in paperwork, for she held an abiding belief in tree conservation, although she kept this liberal peccadillo mum around Homeland Security. Trees were so tall, so lovely, so phallic — who could ever want to cut one down, debark it, and saw it into planks? Alison, mentally hearing a huge saw ripping a lovely tree, placed her pinkly painted fingernail atop the Lay Auto file, sending the scale's indicator to five and a half pounds.

Leaving the Starchilds' house, Mary Lou and Dave arrived at Natalie's. Natalie had one last set to play at Como's, so she and Willy were gone. Aloysius the Second burbled and turned when Dave and Mary Lou walked in the house with the trophy. Simultaneously, the red eye on the kitchen ceiling clicked. Dave was too busy rubbing his new pair of Sonic Beads, and Mary Lou was too busy carrying the bulky trophy to notice. They sat the trophy on the kitchen table and walked out back, where Bad and the psychological grandniece were sitting on lawn chairs by the grill, drinking Francis Coppola claret.

Extremely out of character, Bad had two extra glasses awaiting company. She poured the claret and offered a glass each to Mary Lou and Dave. Two hours later when Willy and Natalie showed up, the ritual was repeated. Bad had even grilled pork ribs in anticipation of a late night celebration.

Statewide that night, abundant prayers were offered for the horse of choice: some proffered on knees (as previously mentioned), some proffered on backsides while engaged in tantric sex (as previously mentioned), and some proffered on King crapper (as, also, previously mentioned). In Natalie's household, three couples slept soundly, dreaming of thumping hooves hastening toward victory. Did each couple perform some tantric sex ritual in support of its collective horse?

Does moonshine glow? Does Gödel make me gag?

Faux Graphic Panels 228 through 229:
Derby Day Itself, Or
Holy Saturday comes to KY

The first Saturday of May, and every KY heart thirrupped with the coming of dawn's rosy hooves. Silver had been polished, bourbons chilled, mint plants aerated and watered one last time before their harvest. Ice-cube makers had been working overtime for three previous days, as if preparing for the approaching sacred and sweaty work of rolling back the stone blocking the tomb and conversing with an angel.

In Natalie's house, Bad woke first. Upon seeing the lovely grandniece next to her, she swooned back to sleep. The grandniece herself felt the tugging of febrile Mother Earth and sighed. In the next room, Dave moaned, feeling an itch under his Jockey shorts, where the Sonic Beads were pressed. Mary Lou felt Dave's movement and offered a mantra for restless, wandering souls. And in the room down from theirs, Willy, ever the oddball, dreamed of walking into a Chinese clothing store and encountering a lanky, sallow-faced Chinese father throwing bones at his daughter whilst she sewed a sleeve with red thread. Unraveling *that* dream would be akin to refuting Gödel's proof. Natalie, still feeling a hostess's obligation after all these months, awoke and went into the kitchen. As she filled the coffee pot and as it percolated, Aloysius the Second followed her every move, as did the ceiling's secret infrared monitor.

Meanwhile, back at the ranch, the jihadist graduate students awoke in the cave where Alison had directed them to go. Four Simian girls lay on their laps. Nearby sat two bottles of Strawberry wine and a plate of Velveeta cheese. One by one, the graduate students put a hand to their temples and groaned. One by one, the Simian girls curled more tightly next to each student. A marijuana haze hung within two feet of the cave's floor, suffused into an eerie blue by some distant light.

"Paradise?" the oldest student asked. "Did we blow up the infidel plant?"

The three others shrugged. The Simian girl lying in the oldest student's lap reached for the bottle of wine and put it to his lips. As he sipped, a roar came overhead, and powdery dust dropped from the cave's roof to mingle with the marijuana smoke. The rest of the Simians, still gathered by the Sacred Altar of the Wedding Ring, awoke, variously remembering the four foreign males who, like the Magi, had bought gifts of vodka and a new CD player the previous night.

"What was that?" One Simian asked, swaying as he sat.

In the orange dumpster by the stream, Huck's Dad similarly queried, "What the hell was that? It reminds me of the time I built Boulder Dam and had to dynamite twenty-five boulders in a row." His voice echoed hollowly in the orange dumpster, so he opened another pint.

Inside the plant, Loopy had just time enough to turn to Binky and say, "Wha — ?"

And down by the waterfall, Lay Auto and Huck heard the roar and accepted the inevitable. After all, amidst an infinite array of Gödelian arithmetic systems, an infinite array of improvable axioms will present themselves. It only stands to reason that some will be undesirable.

All that remained of the Nicholasville plant was the loading dock with its Maker's Mark collage.

Faux Graphic Panels 230 through 231:
Jane Austen could never . . .

Four of the Simians were sisters, one year apart; that is, one was eighteen, one was seventeen, one was sixteen, and one was fifteen. Once the dust in the cave settled, these sisters each reached for a bottle of strawberry wine and took a sip. The four strangers who'd walked in last night had so fascinated these sisters that they in turn had immediately culled the strangers off from the rest of the Simians, who were busily listening to the CD player the strangers bought in and blowing the marijuana that had appeared from nearly nowhere, it seemed, along with a bundle of pornographic graphic novels. Not to mention the gift of vodka and Xstasy.

It was the penises that fascinated the sisters. Each one was so brown, so squat, and so tender, and each one tasted of figs and dates from the Middle East. No wonder that three major religions had arisen in that area, the oldest sister whispered to her siblings, who giggled and nodded. "I have a little sister, whose breasts are small," the second oldest sibling announced as she rubbed her own sizeable nipples over the rough brown cheek of her especial stranger.

"But she will grow like us," the third sister said, grinding her hips into the brown hips of her especial stranger, who gasped at the sight of blonde hair swaying in his eyes. *Layla?* he wondered.

"And I will be sixteen in just four months," the youngest sister said, tickling her brown stranger's toes with her own and nibbling at his small moustache. "A Gatlinburg, Tennessee, wedding for all four of us. Good enough for Juliet and Romeo, good enough for us."

Though Jane Austen would never write it like that, she surely would have meant it like that. And the youngest sister's prediction will surely come to pass, for when the Pit Crew return to the plant on Monday, when they call the police, and when the police find the remains of Mr. and Mrs. Starchild inside the plant, along with the scattered fragments of the Starchild's van outside — when all this occurs, I say, the youngest sister will be in Lexington, in the arms of her thick, brown lover. And she will be two days — forty-eight adolescent hours! — closer to her sixteenth birthday. And her three sisters will likewise be in the arms of their thick, brown lovers. Here it must be noted that the four sisters, in salamander-like fashion and through some genetic mutation, had learned the secret of regenerating their hymens, so the four of them will be able to eternally please the four Arabic graduate students, who will return to their studies with a vengeance, forgetting they'd ever met a woman named — well, what was her name? — at that titty bar — well, what was it called? Who cared? For all four were majoring in geology and would never ever encounter Kurt Gödel in their studies, no matter how assiduous those studies might be. And if they ever should, those renewable hymens will surely render that discovery utterly passé.

And the four sisters? With so much merit and true love, and no want of fortune or friends, the happiness of the married sisters must appear as secure as earthly happiness can be.

Now . . . even Jane Austen couldn't have written that any better.

Faux Graphic Panel 232 through 233:
What might have passed for Easter Monday,
but what turned into Blue Monday

That the Derby pot had been won by one of the Chinese seemed un-American to Dave. It seemed promising of a global future to Mary Lou. Natalie wrote a song about it; Willy plucked his banjo and sang along. Bad and the grandniece pondered Jungian Synchronicity in that the Chinese girl's name and the winning horse's name sounded alike, if you said them quickly enough. After dropping off the grandniece at the clinic where she worked, the five of them drove — in Dave's truck, which finally had been repaired — to the Nicholasville plant, where Huck had promised to polish Lay Auto and the eight other proto-cars over the weekend.

Dave's cherry red truck pulled short at the parking lot entrance. A collective "My God," exhaled from all five mouths, with varying degrees of belief attached. For of course, the plant was leveled. They drove around the foundation to the loading dock, which was still standing, its Maker's Mark bottles embedded in stucco for as close to eternity as any human project will remain embedded.

Singing reverberated from the path. They peered down to spy the orange dumpster and ran. Inside, Huck's Dad sat surrounded by four cases of Maker's Mark pints, warbling "Camptown Races."

Seeing the five he said, "Did I ever tell you about the time I was onstage with Elvis Presley?"

"Do you have any idea— do you have any idea what happened to the plant?" Willy shouted.

Huck's Dad grabbed his ears as the echo bounced around the metal interior, which was also painted orange, by the bye.

"Did *Southern Living* stop to take photos? I'd hate to have missed that."

Willy and Dave reached in to haul out Huck's Dad, noting that the blue recliner which had been missing from the office sat inside the dumpster. They pulled him out and turned him around. With a stagger he reached for the pint in his pants pocket.

"I dreamed I was a butterfly. Then I awoke to dream I was me."

They realized none of them could have said it better, even had they studied at the petite feet of Queen Jane Austen.

Faux Graphic Panels 234 through 235: Disappearance of Huck and Lay Auto

"Where's your son?" Mary Lou yelled at Huck's Dad, who still staggered, naturally enough.

"I'm not my son's keeper. Anyway, that's just a joke. I ain't got no son. The little feller wanted me to pretend to be his daddy." Huck's Dad straightened his shoulders and licked his lips. "Can't blame him for that. I'm a damned fine catch."

"But where is he?" Mary Lou looked frantically at the rubble.

"Check down by the waterfall. He and that car go there to talk to one another."

"Talk?" Dave and Bad asked.

"If butterflies can dream they're me, and I can dream I'm butterflies, then why can't cars talk? I ever tell you about the time a ventriloquist — "

The Pit Crew ran to the waterfall. From the crook of a wild crabapple tree hung a pair of binoculars with a brass tag embossed "Homeland Security — we watch so that you may be free." On the ground underneath were a broken stiletto heel, cigarette butts, and a half-empty box of matches.

"Look at this!" exclaimed Bad, who'd drawn aside to execute a karate kata on seeing Alison Perrier's broken stiletto heel. Bad pointed to a piece of paper — actually it was parchment exhumed from who knows where. On it was written, with a Victorian flourish, these words:

Dear Moms and Dads:

We chased the creepy woman away, but not in time. It was fated, just as is our inability to . . . this lack of words almost makes us believe in You-Know-Whom, the guy with the gargling, gurgling name and the thick eyeball lenses. Anyway, thanks for everything. We hope you each find what you want. Kick the bracelet addiction,

Dave. Go back to Mary Lou, Frodo, and math. Ms. Mary Lou, our dearest Mom, who gave us the Buddha and Our Lady of Guadalupe, remember: the right chant lies just around the corner. Bad, you need to have sense enough to stay with the nice psychobobble lady. Have you ever thought of being a role model for young women in the field of math? Maybe one of your protégés will find an alternative to You-Know-Whom. Or refute him. Or come to peace with him. We can't. We hate him. Willy, our dearest Dad, maybe the chicken bone solution will find its time in America if you keep at it. Name it after us: the Huckmobile. Natalie, sing him some songs and he will.

With affection and regret, we are headed West, where humped buffalo but nary a single Gödel roams,

Huck and Lay

"Where's Chien Fou?" Mary Lou yelled, looking helplessly down at the water splashing fifty feet below.

Epilogue, Or,
How I came to this manuscript

Last summer in the exact middle of May, a blue-eyed, freckle-faced boy seemingly no more than sweet sixteen strolled unannounced past my secretary, accompanied by a brown mutt of a dog. Accustomed to offbeat authors, I tossed the pooch a beef treat and considered tossing the kid a Double Bubble. But the kid gawked forward to hand me a slick legal document declaring power of attorney for the author whose "novel" I'd been long-distance editing for over a year, prepping it as an auction block bestseller.

The pooch chomped as I scanned the power of attorney. I reappraised the kid, whose skin quivered blue and extra-terrestrial, like something one of my more loony sci-fi authors would write, say cobalt ray emanation deep-space teleported from Bela-Glucose IV. Blue Boy opened a black attaché case and hefted a weighty manuscript. He stood wearing cut-offs, for Peter's sake, in San Francisco. How'd he make it past all the gays preying the streets, doorsteps, and alleys? Did the mutt protect him? The dog showed ample canines, wanting another treat. I'm not Hindu, what's a beef treat to me? Wait. I have nothing against Hindus. In fact I wish Bollywood would give a closer look at the novels in my stable. And I have nothing against gays: selling another Broke Back Mountain would suit me fine. The blue kid not from Bela-Glucose IV spoke:

"That's the final draft. There's the matter of distributing royalties: the contacts are on the draft and a CD. There's also the matter of a pen name."

"Not L.A.?"

Blue boy inhaled. "Definitely not L.A."

"So what's *your* name?" I waved off my secretary who took a break from E-bay to notice a client.

"Huck," the boy said, staring at his shoes.

From his gosh and golly attitude I expected Buster Browns or Penny Loafers. Not far off: the kid was wearing Ked Pro's, with glowing cherry red lights embedded in the heels. One cherry winked.

"Well, Huck, how about 'Huck' for a pen name?"

"No way. That's given us enough trouble already. We need a common name: Smith, Brown, Cox."

"And a common first name also, yes?"

"We were thinking maybe some quack author already published would lead bad people off track."

Bad people. They run rife throughout this bombshell manuscript, which really isn't a novel. No, it's a thinly disguised exposé of corporate and international greed, of bullheadedness and intrigue combating all genuine attempts to revamp the automotive industry into an ecological and green profession. Long live BP.

"We were—"

"Well," I huffed, "it so happens that for the past five years I've been plagued with untold reams from an author living in god-bedraggled Kentucky. Can they even spell in that state? The last book he sent centered on Coaches Adolph Rupp and Paul Bear Bryant being gay, so there are people willing to look him up for a long and excellent noose talk if he's been so foolish as to shop that little ditty in the land of horses and basketball. He even proposed turning it into a graphic novel, making Bryant and Rupp vampires or urban zombies. Anyway, this guy fits the common name requirement in spades. So, how about Joe for a first name?"

Blue Boy's face lit. "Neat. Wish I'd gotten that name instead of what I got."

"What's wrong with 'Huck'?"

"Huh."

I figured the kid would mention Mark Twain, but: "Rhymes with too many dirty words. That's what's wrong with it."

"I see. Well, Huck, this third-rate writer's named Joe Taylor. How would that do for a *nom de plume*?"

"Perfect." Blue Boy didn't bat an eye at my snooty French.

I took the CD and the manuscript from him. He still refused a comfy leather chair — maybe I should reassess that leather in case Bollywood ever does stop by. The kid shifted with nervous, buzzing, electronic kid energy.

"Did the sex scenes get added?" I asked.

"We figured you'd ask." His blush beamed ephemeral: spirit-baby pink over Bela-Glucose blue. "We put in two extra ones. I guess — *we* guess it'll be okay if you change them some."

Two extra sex scenes? Cum on. Pun intended. I knew I'd need to add scenes and lubricate affairs. I opened the manuscript, pondering just where I might insert them when . . .

"Here, what's this?" The previous messy title was *Let There Be Lite: How Detroit's International Cabal Zapped this Century's First True Automotive Innovation.* It now read an even messier, *Let There Be Lite: How I Came To Know and Hate Gödel's Incompleteness Proof.*

"It's got to stay," Huck of the too many dirty words said.

A deal breaker. I sat back, consoling myself that anything with the word *God* in it would sell to the Christians. And I could shift that negative *Hate* to a positive *Love.* The book might even wind up cross-listed in self-help lists.

"That's okay," the blue boy named Huck sighed out, as if he'd read my mind.

I blurted a last shot: "Huck was a happy-go-lucky kid in Mark Twain, you know."

"That was Tom Sawyer, who was a conniving idiot. Huck was sad and headed out west."

"Well, you're here. As west as you can get."

"Not yet." Blue Boy tossed Pooch a fluorescent green Wilson tennis ball and started out, but then turned at the door. "Not . . . yet."

And that's where the sadness comes in. . . .

Epilogue to an Epilogue

On May 28 at noon a registered letter will be received by Natalie and Willy Ellender-Turner. It will direct them to Lexington's airport on the 29th, to pick up Chien Fou and a cashier's check for 70 thousand dollars, made out from a California Agent. There will also be directions to leave a daily pint of Maker's Mark whiskey in a brown bag by the orange dumpster near the remains of the Nicholasville plant. This brown-bag-gift is to be given in perpetuity or until the previous day's bottle isn't picked up. "Forget the two-pint a day regimen, that was going to kill him," the note will say. "And toss in a Chinese take-out meal. He'll at least get vegetables."

On May 30th, once receipt of canine and check have been confirmed, an experimental automobile will break through barriers and plunge into San Francisco Bay, hopefully not killing any sea lions. That afternoon, divers, led by the flashing cherry lights of a Ked Pro Tennis shoe trapped against a windshield, will find the automobile, its pontoons water-logged, its circuits shorted and extinct from the incursion of salt water. Other than the single glowing shoe they will also find brown cut-offs, Fruit-of-the-Loom briefs, and a T-shirt that reads in cryptic golden script, "West, where nary a Gödel roams."

Mark Twain and Huck Finn, though neither had heard of Kurt F. Gödel, could hardly have written it better.

The author, in an abnormally happy moment.

Joe Taylor was mysteriously born in Cincinnati to be transported immediately to Corbin, Kentucky. He then lived in Lexington and Bardstown before moving to Florida, where he obtained a Ph.D., with much help and understanding from that University's faculty. Then, in Atlanta, he was a reader for Peachtree Press. In Alabama, he was a judge for the first Fred Bonnie Memorial Award and its wonderful winner, Lisa Borders' *Cloud Cuckoo Land.* He taught at St. Leo College and now teaches at the University of West Alabama, where he has served as editor and publisher of Livingston Press for nearly twenty years. He lives well outside the hubbub with his wife Tricia. He has a previously published novel, *Oldcat & Ms. Puss: A Book of Days for You and Me,* three published story collections, and several edited anthologies of stories.